Praise for the b
by Charles Sal

"Salzberg is a true talent, and his Henry Swann is a classic—complex, hilarious, and completely charming."
—Hank Phillippi Ryan, award winning author

"Charles Salzberg's *Devil in the Hole* is a fine piece of crime writing and a hell of a fun read."
—Reed Farrel Coleman, three-time
Shamus Award-winning author

"I always love it when I come across a new private detective to admire and worship, someone who is brave where I'm weak, someone who gets his hands dirty while I keep mine clean. Henry Swann is such a detective and he tells a great story. For fans of hard-boiled mysteries or just plain old good fiction, I'm sure you'll love *Swann Dives In.*"
—Jonathan Ames, author of *Wake Up, Sir!*
and the creator of *Bored to Death.*

"Salzberg's a hell of a writer. He delivers thrills, insight and plenty of laughs. Swann is a very cool take on the classic PI."
—Andrew Klavan, author of *True Crime*

"In this smartly constructed crime novel, Salzberg uses multiple viewpoints to portray an unlikely killer who methodically slaughters his family...an intriguing collage of impressions and personal perspectives for the reader to ponder."
—*Publishers Weekly*

"Salzberg does an ingenious job of weaving together the various voices—each distinct in its own right—and giving us the story as told by the people who experienced it. Brilliant and captivating storytelling."
—Erica Ruth Neubauer, *Crimespree Magazine*

"Henry Swann is in the great tradition of American mystery heroes: world-weary, philosophical, tough, and competent. This novel is totally entertaining."
— Laurence Klavan, Edgar Award-winning author of *The Cutting Room* and *The Shooting Script*

"*Swann Dives In* takes you in all kinds of unexpected directions, not only giving the reader a fresh view of the crime novel but a fresh view of the nature of crime itself."
— Lauren Weisberger, author of *The Devil Wears Prada*

"Salzberg's anti-hero is a soulful investigator and one of the most paradoxically endearing characters I've come across."
— Joy Behar, co-host of *The View*

"Swann's got the smarts and hard-boiled cynicism of Sam Spade, but he's also got a wicked sense of humor that keeps things cool even when the action gets hot."
— Brian Kilmeade, author of *New York Times* bestseller *The Games Do Count*

"Salzberg defies expectations left and right in this subtly subversive, genre-twisting page turner. *Swann's Last Song* is where literature meets entertainment"
— Mark Goldblatt, author of *Africa Speaks*

"...a novel which few readers will want to put down, turning pages mostly, I think, to find out how in the world the author pulls it off. The buildup becomes more and more absorbing because Salzberg has a lot to say about human nature that is thought-provokingly wise and penetrating."
— Duff Brenna, *South Carolina Review*

"*Devil in the Hole* is one of the best books that I have read this year and I most highly recommend it."
— Robin Thomas, *New Mystery Review*

SWANN'S WAY OUT

ALSO BY CHARLES SALZBERG

Henry Swann Mystery Series
Swann's Last Song
Swann Dives In
Swann's Lake of Despair
Swann's Way Out

Stand Alone
Devil in the Hole

Novella
Triple Shot (Twist of Fate)

CHARLES SALZBERG

SWANN'S WAY OUT

A Henry Swann Mystery

DOWN&OUT
BOOKS

Down & Out Books
3959 Van Dyke Rd, Ste. 265
Lutz, FL 33558
www.DownAndOutBooks.com

The characters and events in this book are fictitious. Any similarity to real persons, living or dead, is coincidental and not intended by the author.

Cover design by JT Lindroos

ISBN: 1-943402-54-X
ISBN-13: 978-1-943402-54-0

PART 1
NEW YORK

"It is better for you not to know
this than to know it."
—Aeschylus, *Prometheus Bound*

"Quick...ain't no time for fooling
around and moaning."
—Mark Twain,
The Adventures of Huckleberry Finn

1
Raising the Stakes

"What am I going to do with the rest of my life?" I asked no one in particular.

I don't know why it occurred to me at that very moment to ask directions. It wasn't as if I expected anyone in the room to answer my question, much less provide me with any kind of useful road map to my future. And looking around, would I actually want any of these assholes to give me life instruction? The obvious, to paraphrase Conan Doyle, need not be stated.

"Is that a rhetorical question?" Goldblatt asked. He glared at the cards in his hand, as if staring at them hard enough would miraculously change the crap he was no doubt holding into a winning hand.

"I thought this was a card game, not group therapy," growled Klavan as he pushed several multi-colored chips to the center of the table, where the growing pile now represented close to fifty bucks, a large pot for the relative chump change stakes we were betting. "I'm raising ten bucks. Any of you losers got the *cojones* to see me?"

"Too rich for my blood," squeaked Stan Katz, whose voice sounded much like chalk scraping across a blackboard. I'd met him for the first time an hour or so earlier when Goldblatt introduced him to the game. "This is Stan," Goldblatt said. "He does my taxes, so he's good with numbers." Evidently, that was all the recommendation Stan needed to join what had been for the last few months a semi-regular, once a month poker game. The idea was Goldblatt's. He felt it would be a good bonding experience. I like poker, though I am certainly no fan of bond-

1

ing experiences, so I acquiesced in large part because it passed the time and kept me from feeling too sorry for myself, a result of evenings left with nothing to do. I'd pretty much given up hanging out at dive bars so what did I have left? Goldblatt even begrudgingly agreed to include Klavan, not one of his favorite people in the world.

"I know he's a friend of yours, though I have no idea why, so you can ask him if he wants to play," Goldblatt had said. "But tell him I'm not putting up with any of his condescending bullshit."

So I invited Klavan and he jumped at the opportunity to redistribute Goldblatt's—and everyone else's—wealth.

"I'm in," said a much too enthusiastic Doug Garr, a friend from my college days at Columbia. We'd reconnected a year or so earlier when I bumped into him on Broadway just as he was about to disappear down into the subway. He was actually a working journalist, which meant he was able to eke out a living by writing for magazines, newspapers and writing and ghostwriting nonfiction books. He informed me he was on his way to the gym to play squash, making me feel guilty for totally neglecting exercise for the past half-dozen years.

"What about you, O'Mara?" Klavan asked, peeking over the cards he held at eye level. "In or out?"

T.J. O'Mara, another old acquaintance of mine, was a former cop turned local prosecutor who was now looking to change careers again. I first met him when he was a beat cop and he caught me repossessing a car. When I explained what I was doing, he looked the other way and we've been friends ever since. The last time we'd had lunch, he told me he was considering "the writing game," as he called it. "I've got stories up the wazoo just waiting to be told," he said.

"I'm sure you do," I agreed.

"And how difficult can it be to write them up?" he asked.

"Not difficult at all," I assured him, trying hard to suppress a smile. "I'm sure any moron can do it."

"Yeah, and from what I've been reading, a lot of them are," he said. "I figure I'll take a few classes, you know, just to get the form and all that shit, then sit down, write up a few stories, get myself an agent. And there you have it."

If it were that easy we'd all be best-selling authors, but who was I to burst his bubble?

"So, T.J., you in or out?" Klavan persisted.

"I think I'll sit this one out," said T.J., tossing his cards face down on the table. Goldblatt made a slight move to check them out but I slapped his hand.

"Hey..."

"Next time you try something like that, or even think about it, you'll lose a finger. Maybe more," I warned.

"What was it you said you did for a living?" Kenny Glassman asked me. Glassman was a friend of Klavan's. He owned a small bookstore in lower Manhattan. The bookstore was this close to going under, but family money was keeping it afloat, Klavan had explained to me earlier. "He's a good guy in a bad business, but he'll come out okay. His folks just bought the building, so he's existing rent-free, which is the only way to make it in the book game, unless you're buying and selling rare books, like me."

"Swann's a private detective," Goldblatt said. "We're partners," he added quickly, puffing up his ample chest, as if no one had slipped him the memo that private detecting was not exactly at the top of anyone's list of preferred occupations, mine included.

"You in or out?" growled Klavan, peering at the rest of the players over his heavy, black-framed eyeglasses, which were balanced precariously near the end of his nose. I thought he was bluffing, but I couldn't be sure. He was used to bidding on rare books, so he knew how to project a poker face. Still, his being so anxious was probably meant to make us believe he had a winning hand, but it was doing the opposite for me. When people try too hard, and when they try not hard enough, they're lying. The truth, I've found if there is one, lies somewhere in the middle.

"I'm thinking," said Goldblatt, shuffling his cards back and forth, hoping, I guessed, they'd miraculously morph into the straight I figured he was pulling for.

"I'm not a private detective," I protested, pushing the appropriate number of chips toward the center of the table. I wasn't about to let Klavan or anyone else steal that pot without a fight.

"Then what are you?" asked Kenny, whose thick, nasal, heavily-accented voice left little mystery as to which borough he hailed from.

"Not one of those guys who peeps through windows and rummages through garbage, are you?" kidded Garr.

I ignored him, though those were things that were not beneath me, so long as I was being paid for doing them.

"Therein, Kenny, lies the problem," I said.

"Fucking identity crisis," said Klavan. "Can we just leave it at that and finish the damn hand before we make any attempt to help Swann figure his way out of the morass that is his sad, pathetic life."

This insulting commentary was from someone closest to being my best friend, although I would never say that to Goldblatt, whom I was sure believed he held that unenviable position.

"Okay, I'm in," announced Goldblatt, pushing an indeterminate number of blue chips into the growing pile of reds and whites. "Hey, where's the dip?"

"There is no dip," replied an exasperated Klavan, in whose apartment we were playing, his living room, to be precise, which also doubled as his library. It gave the game a comfortable, cozy feel, amongst all those books.

"Where there are chips there should be dip," said Goldblatt. "It's one of the immutable laws of life."

Kenny, not knowing any better, had generously brought a few bags of chips, along with the two six-packs of beer he'd offered to provide.

"You want fuckin' dip, go the fuck out and get it," snapped Klavan.

"Easy, Ross," I said. "Goldblatt, forget the damn dip. We're here to play cards, not feed our faces."

"Okay, but I have to tell ya, every game I've ever been in there's been some kind of edibles. Usually provided by the host," he added, never missing an opportunity to needle Klavan.

Klavan shot him a look that was at least as lethal as an AK-47.

"We can call out for pizza," Kenny offered, obviously trying to bring peace and tranquility to the land. Good luck with that.

"I could go for some pizza," said Doug. "I know a great place in the neighborhood." He checked his watch. "And I don't think it's too late for them to deliver."

"Could we please just finish this goddamn hand," said Klavan, whose face was turning a bright shade of red. Now, I was sure he was bluffing.

"You boys are pretty serious about your poker, aren't you?" said T.J. who, with a big smirk on his face, was balancing back and forth in his chair. He was out, so what did he care?

Me, I was enjoying myself, too. Maybe because I was having

a pretty good night for a change. The buy-in was fifty bucks, the stakes relatively low—two bucks maximum, until the last round, when you could go as high as ten. That's where we were now. Being ahead for the night, I figured with a high flush in hand it was worth it to see Klavan's cards.

"I'll raise it another five," I said, not wanting to scare him out of the game.

Goldblatt looked me in the eye with an accusing squint. "You've got some hand there, don't you, Swannie?"

"You can pay another five bucks to see it," I said, ignoring the fact that I hated being called Swannie and he knew it. But in poker, anything goes, trash talk, psychological warfare, any kind of distraction, so I let it slide.

"I'll let you and Klavan duke it out," Goldblatt said.

"Kenny?" Klavan said, nodding in his direction.

Kenny shook his head and folded his cards.

"Looks like it's just you and me, Ross."

He eyed me, then the pot, then back to me.

"It's only five bucks," I taunted.

"I'm hungry," he said, folding his hand and laying it on the table. "Garr, call that place you know. But no friggin' anchovies. They're an insult to the world of fish."

The pizza arrived and, as the big winner for the night, I uncharacteristically sprung for it, though Klavan, still grumbling about playing with "amateurs" added a generous tip. We ate in the kitchen, at a large wood-top table, because Ross didn't want any flying cheese or sauce to land on his precious books. And with Goldblatt on board, that was a very plausible outcome.

We finished the pizza in record time, washed it down with

imported beer, then returned to the table for another hour or so of poker.

By the time the evening ended, just short of midnight, I was up about a hundred and fifty bucks, well beyond the price of the pizza. This made the third game in a row I'd come up a winner and I was sure Goldblatt, who lost every week, was about ready to call for a federal investigation.

As Klavan dutifully emptied the rooms of the detritus of beer bottles, pizza boxes and paper plates, and Goldblatt studied the pizza stains on his shirt as if he was trying to decipher some arcane code, Stan Katz pulled me aside.

"I understand you're in the business of finding people," he said, his squeaky voice whispered so low I had a little trouble hearing him.

"I guess."

"That's what Goldblatt told me."

"Then it must be true."

"I'd like to speak to you about something."

"Sure thing."

"Not here, though." He handed me his card. "Can you call me tomorrow? And if you don't mind, I'd appreciate it if you didn't say anything to Goldblatt about this."

I took the card, slipped it into the pocket of my T-shirt. "My lips are sealed."

"Thank you. And for the record, you're a pretty good poker player."

"No offense, Stan, but I'm only as good as my competition is bad. And believe me," I said, "it doesn't get much worse."

He smiled and backed away, his index finger pressed to his lips.

I mimicked his gesture, and backed into the living room, where Goldblatt and Garr were putting on their jackets. It was mid-spring and though the days had warmed up a bit, the nights were still chilly. I had worn a sweater, figuring the brisk walk home would keep me warm enough. Not to mention the wad of ones and fives swelling the size of my wallet.

2
There's a Sucker Born Every Minute and There Are Sixty Minutes in Every Hour

Stan's office was in one of those fancy mid-town glass buildings. Not only was I required to show I.D. but also pose for what turned out to be a grainy, out of focus photograph that was then transferred to a sticky label. The irony was that the photo, which was dark and muddy, made me look just like the imaginary terrorist they were ostensibly trying to deny admittance. What could be so important in this decidedly non-descript skyscraper that such security was necessary? Was there a secret floor filled with CIA operatives? A branch of the Federal Reserve where ingots of gold bullion were stored? A top secret government operation aimed at world domination?

Stan shared a twenty-third floor office suite with a dentist in one wing and a small boutique law firm in the other. The one in the middle was Stan's. I knew that because it had his name stenciled on the door.

"I'm here to see Stan Katz," I announced to the receptionist, a middle-aged woman who was busily engaged in doing a cross-word puzzle.

"Your name, please?" she asked, her pencil filling squares with small, precise letters.

"Henry Swann, with two Ns."

She reached for an appointment book and searched for my name. "Here we go. If you take a seat, I'll let him know you're here, Mr. Swann with two Ns."

Before I could settle my ass comfortably into the plush

cream-colored couch, Stan popped his head out of his office and spotted me.

"Henry. Thanks so much for coming. Let's go into my office."

Unlike the night before when he was dressed casually in jeans, this morning Stan was all business, duded up in a grey, pinstriped suit, white shirt and red necktie.

"Pretty impressive," I said and I meant it. I always admire men who can wear a suit and look comfortable in it. On the rare occasion when I try it, it only reinforces the notion that I'm a fraud.

"Oh, this," he said, looking down with unhidden enthusiasm at his attire. "I just wear it for work. For some reason people seem to trust a man in a suit."

"That's a mistake," I said, as I moved toward the window so I could get a better look at the view. "Some of the biggest crooks I've come across shopped at Brooks Brothers. And the red tie, nice touch."

"Trump always wears one."

"That would be reason enough," I said, as I peered out over an unobstructed view of the Hudson. It was a clear day so I could see all the way into Jersey and, looking downtown, I could even make out a small piece of the Statue of Liberty.

"Can I get you something?"

"I'm good," I said, backing away from the window.

"You're sure?"

"I'm fine."

"Please, have a seat." He gestured toward a cream-colored leather couch against the wall opposite his desk. I was impressed. It was not the only expensive leather item in the office. There was also an Eames chair, which I happened to know cost a few grand. Stan did all right for himself and he wasn't shy about showing it. If I asked he'd probably tell me it was all part of the image. After all, no one wants a pauper watching their money, do they? I did have to wonder what he was doing in a penny ante poker game when he could easily have been a high roller in some Atlantic City or Connecticut casino.

Once I'd made myself comfortable on the couch, Stan took a seat opposite me in the matching cream-colored leather chair.

"That was fun last night, wasn't it?" he said, as he fiddled with the knot of his tie.

"Stan, you don't need to small-talk me. It's a waste of your time but more important, it's wasting mine. You didn't ask me here to rehash last night's hands."

"I know. It's just this is difficult for me. A little embarrassing, actually. I'm not even sure I should be talking to you about it."

"You want me to tell you this is confidential?"

He nodded. "Yes, that would make this a lot easier."

"Then it's all confidential. Now, what's going on?"

"I want you to find somebody, which is something you do, isn't it?"

"It is."

"I guess I should start at the beginning."

"That would be nice." I steeled myself to hear another sad story of betrayal and loss. It's what I specialize in. Happy, contented people have nothing to do with me. I am a human can of Raid. It is the people on the edge of desperation who seek me out, who need my help, who crave my attention. They are drawn to me and I to them. They are my people and I am theirs. I am a magnet and they are shards of free-floating metal. Under most circumstances they avoid me like I am a carrier of some contagious, life-threatening disease. But when there is trouble, I am their man. I am a human life-saver, the person

11

who will, they hope, let them grab onto me and keep them afloat. It is a heavy responsibility and if I thought too much about it, it would be too heavy. So I don't.

"You see, a year or so ago, I met a woman at a party," Stan said, nervously playing with his tie. "We kind of hit it off. We got together a few times, you know, like after work, and we got to know each other. She was smart and beautiful and..."

Oh, God, could I stand to hear another sordid tale of infidelity? Of hearts broken? Promises un-kept? Betrayal? Not really. So I put him on fast-forward. "You're a married man, aren't you?"

"How did you know?"

"The ring on your finger is a dead giveaway."

He reached over with his right hand and twisted the ring, as if trying to twist it off. But it was too late.

"Yes. I am. And I love my wife very much. Please don't get the wrong idea, Henry."

"This other woman..."

He became more agitated, twisting his tie into knots. "She's not the *other* woman like you mean. Her name is Sarah Byrne. And yes, I was attracted to her. She's a beautiful woman. But nothing happened. I swear. It couldn't. Not only am I married, but I have two kids. So I don't want you to get the wrong idea. This isn't really about her. About Sarah, I mean. It's about this man she introduced me to. A friend of hers. His name is Rusty Jacobs. It was meant to be a business connection. Rusty and I hit it off. He was a former lawyer who'd became a sports agent. At least that's what he told me. I love sports, so we had that in common. He told me all kinds of amazing stories, but he wasn't happy dealing with demanding athletes and duplicitous owners, not to mention his fellow agents. He wanted to get into another line of work. He was intrigued by what I do, which in case you didn't know is money management. Do you know how that works?"

"If you mean knowing how much money is in my wallet at any particular time, yes. Anything beyond that, not so much."

"People entrust their money to me and I invest it for them. Depending on the client, I'm either very cautious, making conservative investments, or if someone is out for a higher return, I put them in somewhat riskier ventures. But I always invest their money as if it's mine. They're people to me, Henry. I'm friends with all my clients. I know their families. I feel a moral obligation to them. Their family's future is in my hands. They trust me. I take my responsibility very seriously. I would never do anything to break that trust."

I didn't have the heart to tell him the last people in the world I would trust would be my family, so I kept my mouth shut. It felt good.

"I know what you're thinking, Henry" he said.

"I doubt that, Stan, because most of the time I don't even know what I'm thinking."

"Bernie Madoff, AIG, derivatives, Ponzi schemes. That's what you're thinking. You think I'm a crook, right?"

"It crossed my mind."

"That's not me, Henry. I am scrupulously honest."

"When someone tells me that, Stan, I have this reflex where I immediately check my wallet to make sure what little money I have is still there."

"I can understand that. We don't have the best reputation right now. But in this case, it's true. I'm an honest man. And you can probably add naïve and too trusting to the package." He took a deep breath. "It's why I asked to meet with you, why I need your help. I need you to find Rusty Jacobs. I invited him to join my firm about three months ago then he disappeared a week ago. When I couldn't find him I went through the books. I found there's some money missing."

"How much money?"

He took another breath. "A lot."

"Give me a figure."

"A million. Maybe more. I haven't done the final calculations yet. The thing of it is, Henry, it's not *my* money. It's my clients' money. And I would replace it if I could. But I can't. I just don't have that kind of money. That's why I need you. I need you to find him and the money. I can hold things off for a week maybe even two or three, but after that the shit is going to hit the fan. I'll be ruined. So will many of my clients, my friends. And I'm the one who'll go to jail because I'm the one responsible. I really need you to help me, Henry. Will you do it?"

I could smell the stench of desperation like the stink of garlic off Goldblatt after an Italian meal.

"I don't work for free Stan. Not even for people I know."

"I didn't expect a freebie, Henry. I'm not exactly broke. I've got savings, but I just don't have a spare million lying around. What's your rate?"

Ah, the moment of truth, so to speak, although this particular truth has a sliding scale. "A grand a day," I lied. "Week's minimum. Anything less than that isn't worth my time."

"I gotta tell you, Henry, that's pretty steep."

I shrugged and held firm while trying to maintain a straight face. "You get what you pay for. Besides, Goldblatt has to get his cut. We're partners."

Katz shook his head vigorously. "No, no, no. Goldblatt can't know anything about this."

"Why's that?"

"Because I can't let it get out that people's money isn't safe with me. If that ever happened, I'd be flipping Big Macs across the street."

"Like I said, Stan, he's my partner."

"I don't care if you split your fee with him, I just don't want you to tell him where it came from. Why not think of it as a freelance job? And what if I sweeten the pot a little."

"How's that?:

"I'd be willing to add a five percent finder's fee, if you get all my money back. That might give you a little more time to ponder the direction of your future."

My future. Oh, yes. That. Did I really want this to be my future? Sitting around listening to sad tales of woe, then trying to fix things for other people? Trying to put other people's lives in order while mine dangled over the edge of an abyss? I was pushing fifty, had very little in the bank—make that practically nothing—was partnered with a man who required a bib when he ate and was forever hustling for a buck—okay, the latter was true of me, too. And the other side of my coin? Alone. Floating in space like those astronauts. Totally alone. Untethered. If I died in my sleep how many days or possibly weeks would it take for someone to find me? And then who would it likely be who found me? Goldblatt? The next door neighbor, alerted by the stench of death seeping out from the crack under my apartment door? That's the future I saw for myself unless I made some changes. And the only way to make those changes was to have money. Money provides options, few of which I had right now.

I waited a moment so it would look like I was considering Stan's offer. I wasn't, of course. Truth is, I would have taken the job for half the amount and no finder's fee. And, in fact, I had no qualms about keeping it quiet from Goldblatt. I was certain he conducted business on the side and didn't split it with me. I didn't expect him to. I knew he'd scream bloody murder about this, though, because he'd insist the only reason I got the job was because he brought Stan into the game last night. But this was business, which has its own set of rules, and in most cases that meant no rules at all.

"Okay. I'll do it. But I'll want the seven grand up front and I'll need to know everything you know about Rusty Jacobs and that means everything. And about you and this woman, Sarah Byrnes."

So, he told me. And it wasn't much. He kind of knew where Jacobs lived, "somewhere on the Upper West Side." Kind of knew where he went to school, "one of those Ivy League schools, maybe it was Dartmouth or Penn. At least that's what he led me to believe. He grew up in the suburbs, on Long Island, or maybe it was Westchester." Married? Katz said he was divorced. Kids? Katz didn't think so.

I listened to all this with my head buried deeper and deeper into my hands, although I occasionally awoke from my stupor to jot down a note or two.

Finally, I could take it no longer.

"Stop!"

"That's all you need?"

"Stan, you've given me nothing. Zilch. Zero. Nada."

"I'm sorry. I've given you everything I have."

"You hired the guy. Didn't you have to get information like his home address, his social security number, things like that?"

"I didn't so much hire him as bring him on as a partner, Henry. He didn't draw a salary, so there was no need to get that kind of information till the end of the year. And as for a mailing address, all he gave me was a P.O. Box. He said it was because of the divorce. He didn't want his ex-wife knowing where he was living."

"Yes. And that's nothing. He might have been this he might have done that. Jesus, Stan, when you took him on didn't it cross your mind to get a resume, references, anything?"

He looked embarrassed. He should have been. Men do stupid things when women are involved. Wait. Let me amend that. They do stupid things all the time, but especially when women are involved.

"I guess his only reference was Sarah," he said.

"And that was good enough?"

He bowed his head. "At the time, yes."

"Okay. What do you know about her? And how can I find her? And please don't tell me you don't know."

"Oh, I do know that. We haven't been in touch in a while, but I definitely know how to find her."

He pulled out his cellphone, found what he was looking for, grabbed an index card from his desk, scribbled down some information, and handed it to me.

"Sarah Byrnes. And that's her number."

"Home or work?"

"Both, I guess. She works from home."

"What does she do?"

"She's a recruiter."

"For the army?"

He smiled. "An executive recruiter. Large companies hire her to find the proper candidates for corporate positions. She's very successful. I think that's probably how she met Rusty, but you'd have to ask her."

"I assume you've spoken to her about this."

"Actually no, I haven't."

"Why the hell not?"

"I told you. I didn't want this—" he stumbled for the right word "—matter to get out. I haven't been in touch with her in a few weeks. Truth is, I was kind of embarrassed. But I'm sure she doesn't have anything to do with this."

Alarm bells started to ring in my head. His money disappears, Rusty Jacobs disappears. Sarah Byrnes disappears. Freud maintained there are no coincidences. Freud was a genius, ergo he knew what he was talking about.

"Why would you think that?"

"She just doesn't seem to be that kind of person. I don't even think she knew Rusty all that well. Besides, I didn't want to tell her about it because I didn't want her to feel responsible."

"She *is* responsible, you idiot. She introduced you to him."

"She was trying to do him and me a favor."

"Some favor. One that cost you a million bucks, your reputation and probably your business, not to mention the very real possibility of jail time."

He turned pale at the mention of jail. "I'm an idiot, Henry. An absolute idiot. But can you help me?"

"I don't know, Stan. Someone who's smart enough to fleece you out of a million bucks is smart enough to cover his trail. The best con men always have excellent exit strategies. They don't stick around waiting to get caught. You wouldn't happen to have a photograph of either of them, would you?"

He thought a moment. His eyes lit up. "Yes. Yes, I do. I have one of Sarah and me at a reception. It's on my phone."

"Good. E-mail it to me. What about Jacobs?"

"No. But maybe we can get one of those sketch artists, you know, and we can come up with something."

I laughed. Amateurs. Can't live with 'em, can't live without 'em.

"I don't think that's a viable option at this point, Stan."

"I know. I know. I'm just grasping at straws. But as you can tell, I'm desperate. I don't know what I'll do if you can't find him...and my money."

"You'll do what everyone else does who's gotten robbed. You'll call the police and let them take care of it. They've got resources I don't have, Stan. And there's the FBI. You could save yourself a whole lot of dough if you skipped me and went to them. I'm not one to look a gift horse in the mouth, not that I run into that many, but in this case that's what I suggest you do."

"I told you why I can't do that. I don't want this advertised all over the goddamn world. Haven't you seen *The Wolf of Wall Street?* No. I don't want that. I want you to find him, Henry. Here, I'll even give you a check for the first week. That's seven grand, right?"

Before I could say anything, he pulled out his checkbook and began writing. At that point, I didn't have the option of saying no. Well, maybe I had it, but I certainly wasn't going to use it. Not when I saw that check for seven grand with my name on it.

3
A Meating of the Minds

"What was all that about the other night?" Goldblatt asked, as we entered E.J.'s Diner a few minutes before noon. It was our weekly meeting—his idea—lunch every Friday, and we were at what passed as an upscale diner Goldblatt discovered after what I assumed was a good deal of painstaking culinary research. But only after I protested I was tired of eating in greasy spoon joints of the kind he favored. E.J.'s was his idea of a compromise. He was especially fond of the daily specials which included, according to him, "exotic" dishes like pulled pork sandwiches and shrimp po' boys. When I pointed out those dishes weren't particularly exotic, he countered with, "They are for a diner." He was right.

I wasn't crazy about the idea of a weekly meeting, which seemed to me was just an excuse to expense a meal, but Goldblatt insisted. "If we're going to have a business we have to run it like a business."

"If we really ran it like a business then we'd have an actual office," I pointed out.

Eleven forty-five was a little early for lunch, but there was a method to Goldblatt's seeming madness—there usually is. "We get a good booth, with a little privacy, so we can discuss our business."

I refrained from pointing out we hadn't actually had any business to discuss for some time now.

As soon as we sat in a roomy both near the back of the restaurant, Goldblatt's eyes lit up when he saw the daily special menu insert. "Yessss," he shouted, pumping his fist in the air triumphantly, as if he'd scored the winning Super Bowl touch-down. "It's my lucky day. They've got the pulled pork sandwich with sweet potato fries. And chocolate mud cake!"

"You're just living la Vida Loca, aren't you?"

The waiter appeared, took our order, and it didn't take long before Goldblatt came back to the question I'd neatly managed to sidestep earlier.

"So, having a mid-life crisis, are we?"

"What do you mean?"

"That question you asked the boys the other night about what you were going to do with the rest of your life."

"That was just to throw you guys off, so I could steal the pot."

"Bullshit. You meant it. You're questioning your existence, aren't you?"

"I know exactly why I'm here."

"Why's that?"

"To make your life a living hell."

He threw back his head and laughed. "You're doing a bang-up job of it, Swann."

"I consider it some of my best work."

"I don't care what you question so long as it's not our rela-tionship."

"Is that what we've got?"

"It sure is, pal."

"Why would I question one of the best relationships I've ever had? But do you think I want to do this kind of work the rest of my life?"

"Face it, Swann, it's what you're good at. It's what defines you."

"I hope not. It bears absolutely no resemblance to what I

wanted my life to be, where I wanted to go, what I wanted to be."

"I'm not even going to ask you what the hell that was. You think you're unique? How many people end up living the life they imagined they would? How many people do you think are happy with their lives?"

"If you're going to measure that by using me as an example, damn few. Maybe no one."

"That's my point. You make the best of what you've got, or don't have. That's how you get by. And you keep busy, doing what you do best, so at the end of the day you can feel like you've accomplished something. Like you made a difference."

"You been spending your afternoons watching Dr. Phil?"

"Common sense, my friend," he tapped the side of his head, "common sense."

Our order arrived. Goldblatt's face broke into a wide grin and I had to smile, too. I don't know why. Maybe because I envied Goldblatt because he still had something that could excite him. The man lived to eat, but at least he lived for something. What about me? What joy did I get out of life?

Goldblatt paused a moment to shove some food in his mouth and I thought, *damn, maybe sometimes he does make sense. Maybe just a little. But sometimes just a little is enough.*

He wiped a few spots of barbecue sauce from his chin with his napkin, snapping me back to reality. "A couple years ago," he said, "I got this gift from a chick I was seeing. It was a T-shirt that said, 'What if the hokey-pokey *is* what it's all about?' That, my friend, is life in a nutshell. It's all hokey-pokey. You know, you put your right foot in, you take your right foot out..."

I was afraid he was going to get up and demonstrate it right in the middle of the restaurant, but then he'd have to take a pause in his favorite activity. Eating.

"Okay, end of amateur shrink hour," he said. "Let's get down to real business."

The talk of business inevitably led to talk of the lack of business with Goldblatt lamenting he was in the midst of a puzzling dry spell. Obviously, I wasn't going to mention Stan, despite the fact he was Goldblatt's friend. A promise is a promise, after all.

"I got nothin'," he admitted, as he bit off a big chunk of his pulled pork sandwich. I averted my eyes as a dollop of barbecue sauce sprung from between the two halves of the bun and dribbled down the napkin he'd been wise enough to tuck into his shirt.

"Me, neither," I lied. Sometimes lies come frighteningly easy to me, but I tell myself it's only because it's a necessary tool of the trade. The trick is to convince myself that any lie I tell is for the greater good, which let's face it, means good for me. This is not something I am proud of. The consequences of this kind of thinking are dangerous. I know that. And still, I cannot help myself. What's good for Swann is not always what's good for anyone else. And yet, what's good for Swann is always what's good for Swann and that's the way it is and that's the way it's going to be until it isn't that way any longer.

"I feel like I'm letting us down," Goldblatt said. "It's my job to be the rainmaker and it's dry as the Sahara out there."

"Something'll come up," I said, in a rare attempt at trying to lift someone's spirits other than my own.

"Yeah, it always does. But I gotta get myself out there because opportunity does not come a knockin'."

He took another bite, chewed it for a moment then said, "Hey, I think I know what I can do."

"What's that?"

"We go on Facebook and put out the word."

I buried my head in my hands. "Please. Not that."

"What's wrong with Facebook? That's the way everyone communicates nowadays. We gotta get in step with the times, Swann. You might not believe this, but I've got over three-hundred friends."

"That beats me by two hundred and ninety-nine."

"You're not on Facebook, are you? 'Cause if you are, then I gotta friend you."

"No, I am not on Facebook nor will I ever be on Facebook."

"This is the twenty-first century, my friend. If you aren't on Facebook or what's that other thing? Oh, yeah, Twitter, then you're nowhere. Yeah, Twitter. I can put the word out there, too. You know, I tweet it. I can't do all that stuff myself yet, but I got a guy who does all that social media stuff for me. He's a former client. Had a few problems with the IRS, but I took care of that."

"Leave me out of this, okay?"

"So you don't care where we get our clients."

"Bingo."

"You're right. All your energy should be going into following through with our cases. As soon as I get to a computer, I'll take care of everything."

"Which brings me to a question that's been gnawing at me for a while," I said.

"What's that?"

"You don't have an office and I have no idea where you actually reside."

"That surprises me because as someone who makes a living finding people you'd think you'd have figured out where I live."

"First off I would have to give a damn."

"Obviously, from the way you phrased your question, you do."

"Idle curiosity. When you say you're going to go to your computer, exactly where would this computer be?"

"First of all, I didn't say *my* computer, I said *a* computer. And to answer that question, there are computers all over. Libraries. Internet cafes. Hotel business centers."

"Are you telling me you don't have your own computer?"

"I didn't say that. I have a network of computers all over the city. And"—he pulled his phone out of his pants pocket—"I've got this. A smartphone. I'm never out of touch."

"I'll try not to take that as a threat."

"Take it any way you like. In the meantime, I think we ought to brainstorm as to how to drum up some business. Times are tough, Swann, the unemployment rate is still hovering around seven, eight percent, which means it's a perfect time for us to take advantage of the situation. I think maybe advertising might be the way to go."

"*The New York Times? The New Yorker?*"

"Not quite our demographics, but I appreciate that you're aiming high. The best way is always word of mouth. I think we have to network more."

"And how would you go about that?"

He took another huge bite of his sandwich, this time releasing another torrent of barbecue sauce, which this time landed on the table not him. To make up for what was lost, he squirted more barbecue sauce onto his sandwich then took the last bite.

"Parties. We need to be invited to more parties. That's where all the best connections are made."

"When was the last time you were invited to a party?"

"Good question. And the answer is, all the time. I just don't *go* very often."

"Why's that?"

"Because I don't like to play the game."

"What game is that?"

"You know, the small talk game. Whaddya do for a living, what's your latest project, yadda, yadda, yadda. Meaningless crap."

"So you're shy about your accomplishments?"

He shook his head. "I just don't see the point. I refuse to be summed up by a list of my credits."

"That's very deep, Goldblatt."

He wiped his face with his napkin. "I'm a lot deeper than you think, Swann."

"Not me. I'm more shallow than you or anyone else could possibly imagine."

"See, that's why we're the perfect team. Neither one of us labors under any false illusions of who or what we are. We are what we are and that's all that we are. And we get the job done. Hey, that's pretty good. Maybe we oughta think about putting that on our business cards."

"We don't have business cards."

"Right. That's also on my list."

"You have a list?"

"Lots of 'em. Trouble is, I keep losing them."

"This conversation is giving me a headache." I looked up and noticed the restaurant had begun to get crowded. Mostly with young mothers with infant children. I checked my watch. It was almost one. "I think there are some people who could use the table."

"I'm in no rush. We're paying customers. We can take as long as we need. I might even have dessert. The desserts here are *incredable,* as the French say."

The last thing in the world I wanted to do was watch Goldblatt stuff himself while lecturing me on how to fix my life. Besides, I wanted to get started on Stan's case. But I couldn't tell that to Goldblatt. So what I'd have to do was lie to him. Again, it would be for the greater good. In this case, the greater good was getting me the hell out of there.

"If you're having dessert you're having it alone. And while you're indulging yourself, I'm going to get out here and try to drum up some business for us."

"How are you going to do that?"

"You think you're the only one with connections."

"I never said that." He leaned forward. "You know, Swann, I'm beginning to get a lump in my throat."

"Pulled pork?"

"Nope. You. I think you're finally accepting the two of us as a team, and I applaud your initiative. You go. I'll just finish up here and then I'm going to beat the bushes for clients, and between us we'll come up with something. And you know what? I don't want you to have a heart attack or anything, but this lunch is on me. Not Goldblatt and Swann. Me. That's right. I'm digging into my pocket and treating you to lunch. Whaddya think of that?"

"I'm deeply touched," I said, as I pushed away from the table. "But right now I've got some things to take care of."

"What things?"

"I've got a news flash for you, Goldblatt. Although we are business partners..." I could hardly get that out without choking a little, "I do have a life of my own. I'll see you next Friday."

He glanced at the menu the waiter had just tossed on the table. "Not if I see you first."

Goldblatt laughed at his joke and you know what, I almost did, too.

4

You Oughta Be In Pictures

Some people like challenges. I am not one of them. I like things nice and easy. The less I have to do to earn my money, the better. Fortunately, the Internet has made my life much easier. I Googled Rusty Jacobs first, but nothing came up. Odd, that someone could stay completely off the Internet grid, but not impossible. Part of the explanation might have been that either Rusty Jacobs was not his real name, or that Rusty was a nickname and without his actual first name there was no way of finding him amongst all the other Jacobs.

Sarah Byrnes was another story. I not only found images fitting the description Stan gave me, but I also learned she belonged to a couple of professional organizations. She even had a website that advertised her services as an executive head-hunter. I clicked on the Contact tab and sent her an e-mail, explaining I was an employer looking for an office manager for my private investigation agency. I was betting she wouldn't take the time to check me out, but even if she did, she'd find I was listed with the Better Business Bureau and that, surprisingly, there were no complaints filed against me. The kinds of clients I worked with either wouldn't even know there was such a thing as the BBB, or if they did wouldn't know how to contact them.

I still had much of the day in front of me, so I decided to drop in on Klavan, figuring he was good for at least an hour or two of interesting banter, killing time before it killed me, so to speak. I liked bouncing my cases off him because he'd often come up with a good idea or two. And even if he didn't, his new assistant, Angie, made a great cup of joe.

When I arrived at Klavan's I found him in a very familiar position: sitting in his over-sized, well-worn brown leather chair, his feet propped on a matching ottoman, reading a book.

"Am I interrupting something important?" I asked, as I plopped down on the couch across from him, swinging my legs up onto his coffee table.

"Mary hates it when people put their feet up on her coffee table."

"How do you feel about it?"

"Frankly, Scarlet, I don't give a damn."

"That's what I thought. Where's Mary?"

"Out."

"Then I'll just keep 'em where they are. What are you reading?"

"I wish I could tell you. Truth is, I'm having a hell of a time getting through this book, so a visit from you is a damn good reason to put it down."

"Why bother finishing it if you don't like it?"

"Compulsion. I keep thinking, make that hoping, it's going to get better and if I quit too soon I'll have missed something. I hate missing anything."

"How often does that happen?"

"Not very."

"Nothing kills pleasure more than compulsion," I pronounced, having plenty of experience to draw from.

"You're right. Once again you've managed to change the course of my life, Swann. So, what's new in the wonderful, whacky world of Henry Swann and his partner, Goldblatt?"

"You remember Stan, the one from the poker game the other night?"

"Mr. Personality?"

"That's the one. He's hired me to do a job for him."

"He's a friend of Goldblatt's and he actually has a job?"

"He does."

"What kind of job?"

"He's in money."

"So what's his problem?"

"It's supposed to be hush-hush."

"My lips are sealed."

"Someone who used to work with him walked away with a shitload of money that wasn't his."

"I hate when that happens. I have to hear this."

So I told him.

"So what's the dude's name who ankled with the dough?"

"Rusty Jacobs."

Klavan scratched the back of his neck. "For some reason that name rings a bell. Seems like I've heard it before or read about him. Somewhere. Recently, in fact. Did you do a search on him?"

"Nothing came up. Found the chick, though, the one who put him onto Stan, and e-mailed her. Hoping to hear back soon."

"Rusty Jacobs. Rusty Jacobs. I know I've heard that name before or seen it somewhere. Wait! I just read about him in the trades."

"The trades? What trades are you talking about?"

"*Variety.*"

"What the hell are you doing reading *Variety*?"

"In case you haven't noticed, Swann, I'm your quintessential Renaissance man. There is nothing that gets by me."

"And that's precisely why I hang out with you. What did you read about him, and why didn't the name come up in my Google search?"

"It was just in the last day or two, which could explain why your search didn't bring him up. Can't remember exactly what the story was, but it won't be difficult to find it."

He jumped up from his chair, which in Klavan's case was a series of slow, methodical movements, and headed into his office, where he sat down on at the computer as I stood over him.

He tapped a few keys and the online edition of *Variety* appeared on the screen. He typed "Rusty Jacobs" into the search box and almost immediately a story popped up.

"Here it is. Evidently, he just signed on as co-producer on some slice-and-dice film. Just what we need, another vampire meets werewolf meets zombie flick." He looked up at me. "Tell me, Swann, you're a man of the world, what do chicks see in vampires?"

"I guess they think they're sexy."

"Yeah, but why?"

"Something about the biting and sucking, sleeping all day and going out all night, I suppose."

He shook his head. "This is why I'll never understand women."

"It's only one of the reasons *we* don't understand women. But I guess it's okay, because they can't figure us out either. They think we're a lot more complicated than we are, which if you play it right, can work to our advantage."

"And the zombie thing?"

"I'm guessing it's a deep-seated Freudian complex. Fear of death, drawn to death kind of stuff."

"We are a very complicated, fucked up species, Swann." He looked back to the screen. "There's more. He's in some kind of other film as a sole producer, but they don't say what it is. According to him, it's on the 'back burner,' which probably means it'll never get done. I'll send you the link."

"So Jacobs is in the movie business."

"Swann, let me clue you in on something. Most of the items in the trades are planted by press agents or Hollywood wannabes. It's all about the hype. You say something often enough and with enough authority behind it and it takes on the veneer of truth. 'The Big Lie' is no lie at all."

"How the hell do you know so much about the movie business?"

"I was in it for a while."

"You're kidding."

"Hand to God."

"Why don't I know this?"

"It wasn't exactly my finest hour, hence not something I brag about, especially when there's so much else that makes me such a fascinating man."

"You weren't an actor, were you?"

"With this face? You gotta be kidding. I wrote a screenplay. Even had it produced. What I like to think of as a dark, suspense thriller. I got stars in my eyes and moved out there for about six months, six months of my life I'll never get back. Worst experience of my life. It's a horrible place, Swann. Imagine the worst and then multiply it by a hundred. No, a thousand. It's the kind of place where they pay you a shitload of money until you get used to it. People there not only lie behind your back but to your face. And the stupidity? You cannot imagine. That town chews you up and spits you out, then grinds its heel into your face, just to make sure you get the point. But you know something? I wouldn't trade the experience for anything, because it's a constant reminder to appreciate what I've got."

"What was the name of the flick?"

"I don't even want to say. That's how bad it was. It didn't

start out that way, but by the time they finished with it and me...well, best not get me started. They shot it in three weeks, on the fly. I made them take my name off of it. I could tell you stories."

"Like what?"

"Don't you have work to do?"

"You know me, I'll do anything to avoid work. That's why I'm here in the first place."

"Okay, you asked for it. So, they buy the script from me and then I get a call, a conference call, mind you, with one of the producers and the creative head of the production company. 'We don't like the ending,' they say. I say, 'Why not?' 'It just doesn't work for us,' they say. 'Okay,' I say. "Got any ideas?'

"'Well,' says the head of creative, 'I saw this movie the other night and I think the ending would work great for this movie.'

"'Wait a minute,' I say. 'You want me to steal the fucking ending from another movie and use it on mine?'

"'It's not really stealing,' he says. 'Think of it as creative borrowing. We do it all the time.'

"Then he told me the ending and, Swann, I swear, hand to God, it was the worst, most clichéd ending you could imagine. And what's worse it didn't even fit my movie."

"So what'd you do?"

"I told them no fucking way."

"And what'd they say?"

"They said, in effect, take a hike, pal."

"But you didn't."

"Nope. I sold out, because I needed the money and I figured a screen credit even on a shitty film was better than no screen credit, and at the time I thought that's what I wanted to do with my life, be in the movie business."

"So you used their ending?'

"Not quite. I came up with my own incredibly clichéd ending, but at least it wasn't stealing and it wasn't quite as bad as the one they wanted me to use."

"And they made it?"

"Yeah, but it was a piece of shit. They lied about the budget, it was much less than they said it was going to be, and they shot it so quickly some of the scenes didn't even match. Let me tell you something, I like money as much as the next guy, maybe even more, but not that much. I got the hell out of there as fast as I could. When I saw what it looked like, that's when I made them take my name off it. The rare book business, as rough and tumble as it might be, is a lot easier on the soul. It doesn't surprise me that your man winds up trying to make a flick. If he's a crook, he's found the right place to work."

"Now I've got to find him."

"You know what they say, 'Follow the money.'"

My phone spoke to me, alerting me that an e-mail had come in.

"It's her, the chick who put Jacobs and Stan together," I told Klavan. "She's wants to get together for a drink tonight. She's even picked the time and the place."

I wrote back, accepting her offer. Then I let Klavan regale me with more of his Hollywood tales.

5
Dressed So Fine

Sarah Byrnes suggested a hip bar down in SoHo, the kind of place that hires an expensive publicist and winds up on *Page Six* in the *New York Post* a couple times a week.

In honor of the occasion, I changed into a clean black Gap T-shirt, jeans and the only sport jacket I owned. An uptown tailor I once did a job for by finding his runaway wife advised shunning the single-vented style. "You put your hands in your pants pockets, your ass sticks out like a neon sign," he warned. So this was a double-vented and black, which meant it hid stains remarkably well, which substantially cut down on my dry-cleaning costs.

The jacket had seen better days. There were a few creases in it where they weren't supposed to be, but I took care of that by heating a frying pan and then moving it slowly over the offending areas until it appeared to make a slight difference. Along with gravity, that would do the trick.

Even though we'd never met I had no trouble spotting Byrnes when she sashayed into the bar. She was wearing a short, black, low-cut cocktail dress, four-inch heels and carried an expensive looking designer purse. I could see how Stan had been taken in by her. I could see how anyone might be.

She scanned the room a few moments before her gaze finally settled on me, sitting at a table in the corner, my back to the wall. I didn't get up, but flashed a half-smile to let her know she was on the right track. I stood when she got within a few feet because I've been told it's the gentlemanly thing to do. I am not a gentleman, but sometimes I pretend I am. It seems to make people, especially women, happy.

"Mr. Swann," she said, offering her hand. "It's a pleasure to meet you."

"I wouldn't jump to conclusions, Ms. Byrnes." I looked her up and down. "Nice threads. I'd like to think you dressed up for the occasion, for which I would be very honored, but I suspect I'm just the first stop of the evening."

"I should lie and say this is all for you, but the truth is I've got an art opening to attend after we've completed our business. I hope you're not too offended."

"Not much offends me."

She smiled and shook her head, her long blonde hair sliding over one eye as she pulled up a chair and in one graceful motion glided into it.

I motioned to the pretty, hip, young, skimpily clad waitress that we were ready to order.

As she headed in our direction, Byrnes leaned toward me, close enough so I could smell her expensive perfume. The only reason I knew it was expensive is because I've sampled more than my share of the cheap variety and this was much subtler and therefore far more effective in making the point.

"Have anything you like, Mr. Swann. It's a business expense."

"My two favorite words in the English language."

I was feeling adventurous so I ordered a designer beer, one of the three on the menu I'd never heard of with cutesy names like "Death Rides a Pale Horse Blonde Ale" or "Queen of the Night Pale Ale." She ordered a Cosmopolitan which seemed to suit her fine.

I was tempted to string her along a little, but there was something about her that made me uncomfortable. Maybe it was the way she looked at me, or to be more precise, through me.

"You're here under false pretenses, Ms. Byrnes."

"Really? Now I'm intrigued. Oh, and please call me Sarah. At least until you break my heart."

"I doubt we'll get that far. I'm looking for a friend of yours. Rusty Jacobs."

Not a flinch. Not a flutter. Not the slightest change of expression. She was good. If I'd expected this to be easy I would have been disappointed. But when women are involved, I've learned nothing is ever easy. Especially the so-called easy ones, the ones who like to make you think what you see is what you get. It never is. In the end, that's what makes them exciting. That's what makes us coming back for more. That's also, in the end, what breaks our hearts.

"Why would that be?" she asked, raising her glass to her lips.

"I've been hired to find him."

"Is he lost?" she asked nonchalantly, setting her glass down gently on the table.

"I don't know. Is he?"

"You're the one looking for him. Who is it who wants to find him?"

"I think you know why I'm looking for him and I think you probably know who hired me."

She shrugged. "I'm a smart woman, Mr. Swann, but I'm no mind reader. I suspect you're very good at what you do and so you're only going to tell me what you want me to know."

"And vice versa."

"It's as if you can read my mind."

"I don't think there's even a remote chance that's going to happen."

This was going to be work. But it was also going to be fun.

Because, the thing is, I was getting to like her. It wasn't because she was a knockout, which she was. And it wasn't because she probably knew lots of hip places like the one we were in, which I'm sure she did. It was because she was cool and in control. I like that. At least for a while. Until it gets in the way, which it inevitably does. But until it does it's fun.

"Cards on the table, Sarah. Your friend, Rusty Jacobs, took my friend, Stan Katz, for a nice piece of change. Stan hired me to find Jacobs and get it back. I'm starting with you because you're the one who introduced them, the one that got the ball rolling."

She shook her head, her thick, blonde hair moving ever so gently from side to side, like in one of those TV shampoo ads. "I have nothing to do with any of this."

"Maybe you're in on it, maybe you aren't. That doesn't concern me. I'm not a cop. I'm not looking to do anything to anyone. All I want is to get the dough back to its rightful owner. That means finding Jacobs because that's where the dough is. I think you can set me on the right track."

She sipped her drink. I knew she was considering just how much she could get away with telling me. Or not telling me.

"I really haven't seen or heard from him in some time," she finally said.

"When was the last time?"

She thought for a moment. "A few weeks ago, I guess. Maybe a bit longer. I'm so busy I tend to lose track of time. I really don't know all that much about him." She stared into my eyes. "Honestly. He's not a close friend or anything like that. I met him at a party."

"What kind of party?"

"A business thing."

"What kind of business?"

"Oh, just one of those networking parties. People in the arts things. He latched onto me and I found him interesting. He's a charming guy. He knows how to talk to women."

"Yeah, well, when I find him maybe he'll give me some lessons. In the meantime, I'm stuck with what I've got. Interesting how?"

"He's a smart guy, knows a lot of things, but he's not the kind of guy who lays it on too thick, if you know what I mean. He's got a little bit of that boyish bad boy quality women tend to fall for. Charisma."

"I don't meet many guys like that."

"Me, neither. That's why I let him take me out for dinner."

"And where'd that lead?"

"Are you getting ready to insult me, Mr. Swann?"

"I guess it depends on how thin-skinned you are and what you consider an insult. Did you sleep with him?"

"You really think I'm going to answer a question like that?"

"I don't know you well enough to know if you will or won't, that's why I asked."

"It's really none of your business." She paused a moment. "But for the record, no, I did not sleep with him." She smiled. "Then."

"Why not?"

She laughed. Throaty. Sexy. The kind of laugh that's an invitation for something other than a drink, something that takes place in a far less public place.

"You think I'm going to answer that question?"

"You never know what people are going to answer until you ask. So where's Jacobs now?"

"I have no idea."

"I don't believe that."

"Believe what you like. I don't really care one way or the other."

"Are you going to help me out or not?"

"Why should I?"

"Because I'm a great guy and maybe someday I can do a favor for you."

"I can't imagine what that favor might be, but there's something about you that makes a girl want to lend a hand."

I wasn't exactly the boyish type but maybe there was something bad about me, but in all the wrong ways.

"Well, that's a first," I said.

"Don't fight it, Swann. Maybe it's that hang-dog look and, well, you've got kind eyes."

"I don't know what that means but I'm going to make it work to my advantage."

She smiled. "I have an idea how you might find him. There's this party I was invited to and there's a good chance he might be there. And if he's not there's a chance someone who is might know how to find him."

"What kind of party?"

"A book party being thrown for an old friend of mine by another old friend of mine who happens to be a big-time film producer. That's what Rusty was always talking about—getting into the movies. He got to know Nina through me. She's the one throwing the party. If he's in town he'll be there. He'd see it as a pond full of fish waiting to be caught."

"Are you going to take me with you?"

She eyed me up and down. "If I did, I'd have to clean you up a little."

"Many have tried, few have succeeded."

"This Goodwill jacket you're wearing won't do. You own a suit? A tie?"

"Is this a wedding or a wake?"

"First impressions are very important, Swann."

"So I've been told. It's probably why I am who I am and where I am. I'm a project, right?"

"A big one."

"A work in progress is more the way I like to think of it."

"I presume you have footwear other than sneakers."

"I believe, way in the back of my closet I might be able to dig something out."

"Well, start digging. The party is tomorrow night."

6
How the Other Half Lives

I am not a party animal. When I was in my early-twenties, after sleepwalking through my college years without attending one frat party or social event that didn't take place in a bar, I misguidedly took a few piano lessons in hopes of becoming proficient enough to pound out one or two boogie-woogie numbers. The aim was to become if not the life of the party—I never did have quite the personality for that—at least the center of attention for a few precious moments. It didn't work. Not that the idea itself was flawed, but with very little musical talent other than being able to turn on the radio and shove in a few tapes, one or two numbers weren't enough to do the trick. The flaw in the plan was simple: lack of follow-through. When someone yelled out, "How about something by James Brown or the Beatles?" I was undone. The thought of being unmasked as a poseur was more than enough to keep me away from any piano that might be sitting around and, eventually, from the black and whites forever.

But this was business, so I treated it accordingly. I opted for a pair of black jeans that might pass as slacks from a distance, a black silk shirt, and a steel grey sport jacket that somehow made it through my closet unwrinkled. I even donned a pair of decent lace-up shoes, shunning my customary Chucks. Granted the shoes were brown, and they laced up to the ankle, making them more like boots, but who, I convinced myself, would be looking at my feet?

As I was about to walk out the door to meet Sarah, my cell vibrated in my pocket. It was Goldblatt.

"What's up?" I asked, juggling the phone from one hand to another as I slipped my free arm into my jacket. "I'm kind of busy."

"With what?"

"It's personal."

"This'll only take a minute. I'm sure you can put a hold on your personal life for that long."

I checked my watch. I was a little ahead of schedule but if I let Goldblatt get started I wouldn't be for long. Goldblatt likes to talk. You ask him the time he tells you how to make a watch. And yes, he really does know how a watch is made. I know this because he once gave me a five-minute lecture on the art of watchmaking.

"You're on the clock. One minute."

"Why the hell are you in such a hurry?"

"Because I am. Now what's up?"

"I got us a case."

"What kind of case?"

"What've I got, forty seconds left?"

"Thirty-five and counting."

"You expect me to tell you what the case is in half a minute?"

"Not really."

"Then we'll meet tomorrow."

"I'm not available," I said.

"What the fuck? We partners or not?"

"Associates, not partners."

"Associates. Partners. Call it whatever the hell you want. This is business, Swann." He paused a moment, I thought to take a breath, but I was mistaken. I heard him chewing. He was taking a quick food break.

"This doesn't have anything to do with that crap about finding yourself, does it?"

If only I could take back that moment in time when I uttered those words because now they threatened to haunt me forever. "At this moment I know exactly where I am and where I have to be in a few minutes. I'll call you in the morning and if I've got some time during the day we'll meet up."

There was an unusual, ominous silence. Goldblatt wasn't stupid. He probably suspected I had something on the side, something I was hiding from him.

"What time?"

"Ten o'clock."

"Okay. I'll be waiting. Don't disappoint me. And none of this on the clock bullshit. This is business and it'll take whatever it'll take."

Sarah told me to meet her in front of the swanky Park Avenue co-op where the party was being held. She was fifteen minutes late. But she more than made up for it when she appeared wearing a sexy, tight black cocktail dress, a black, sequined jacket, and black achingly high-heeled stiletto heels. And then there was her hair. Oh, that hair. Dirty blonde with streaked golden highlights. She'd obviously dropped big bucks at some fancy hair salon since I'd seen her the day before.

"You look terrific," I said.

"Thanks, but that's more than I can say for you. Is this the best you could do?"

"This is as good as it gets. This," I said, rubbing the material of silk shirt between two fingers, "didn't come from a thrift shop."

She shook her head disapprovingly. "I mean, those shoes. What Dumpster did you rescue them from?"

"Flattery will get you nowhere."

"Well, we might as well go in," she muttered as she led our way into the lobby. She gave the name of the folks throwing the party to the concierge and then we took the elevator up to their penthouse apartment.

When I stepped inside it was as if I had entered a world I'd never known existed: the world of the rich and famous, the movers and shakers of the entertainment industry, a world of people who made things happen.

It wasn't only the way I was dressed that set me apart. There's something about the way the rich and powerful hold themselves that makes them different from the rest of us. No matter how hard I tried to fake it, I would just be another loser, someone more likely to be passing around trays of pigs in a blanket and smoked salmon topped with fish eggs than an invited guest. This was a different species from a planet where people like me were hired to take out their trash.

And yet being on the outside gives me an advantage. I see people for who they really are not who they pretend to be. And in so many ways they are no different from the rest of us. They lie and cheat and steal, only when they do it's on a grander scale. They create fantasies and crush dreams. They feed on the hopes, the greed and the desires of the rest of us. In so many ways they are no different from or better than the small-time crooks who knock over a 7-Eleven, write bad checks, or rob a bank.

"What's next?" I whispered into Sarah's ear as she led me into the fray, heading toward a bar set up in a corner of the large foyer.

"Easy. We get ourselves a drink."

"After that?"

"You'll wait here while I'll look for someone who knows Rusty because," she said, swiveling her head so quick her hair hardly moved, "I can tell you this. He's not here."

"How can you be so sure?"

"The Rusty Jacobs I know would be out in the open, networking. Besides, if he did what you say he did, do you really think he'd be stupid enough to stick around and risk the chance of being seen?"

"Then why the hell are we here in the first place?"

She smiled, then gave me a quick kiss on the cheek, so quick and so superficial I hardly felt anything but the breeze she made as her face passed mine. "I needed an escort, darling. A girl like me can't come to a place like this alone. You can understand that, can't you?"

I couldn't and yet somehow I did.

"But I didn't lie. We'll find something about him here. And then both of us will be happy. Now let me do my thing."

She turned her attention toward the bar area. "Oh, there's someone over there you ought to meet," she cooed.

She grabbed my hand and we headed toward the bar. Once we arrived she edged herself in front of an elderly, white-haired gentleman wearing the most expensive looking designer suit I'd ever seen. I knew it was expensive because it hugged his pear-shaped body like a second skin.

"Joel, it's so good to see you again," Sarah purred, leaning forward slightly so her breasts were directly in his line of sight.

There was a blank look on his face, like he was having trouble placing her. That didn't stop Sarah. She smiled coyly and said nothing, waiting for him to catch up. Finally, there was a glimmer of recognition on his face. Either he remembered meeting her before or was hoping he had.

"It's Sarah Byrnes. We met a few months ago at the Redford screening. Please don't tell me I made no impression on you, darling."

"Oh, yes. Sarah. How could I forget?" He leaned over and kissed her on the cheek, his shoulder brushing against her breast. She didn't bat an eye. Not even when he put his arm around her shoulder. "How are you?"

"I'm fine, Joel," removing his arm in one smooth motion. "I'd like you to meet my good friend, Henry Swann," she said, tugging at my sleeve. "Henry, this is Joel Reynolds. Henry's in the movie business, too."

The lie came out of her mouth so effortlessly for a split second I wondered if it were true and no one had ever told me.

"Nice to meet you." Joel bowed slightly. "Should I know you?"

I turned to Sarah. She smiled, cocked her head to the left and folded her arms across her chest. She was done. I was on my own.

"It depends on who and what you know, Joel."

"What part of the business are you in?"

"A little of this, a little of that."

"Oh?" He looked baffled. "What are you involved in at the moment?"

"Trying to raise dough for an independent film."

Out of the corner of my eye I could see Sarah's smile widen. She was enjoying this. But as I got rolling, so was I.

"That's exciting. What's the budget you're looking at, if I might ask?"

"We're not looking to break the bank, Joel. Somewhere in the neighborhood of twenty, thirty mil, depending on the cast and where we shoot it. No car crashes. No explosions. I'm not targeting the kiddie market here."

"What kind of flick is it?" he asked, leaning in close enough to me that I couldn't help but pick up the aroma of whiskey on his breath.

"I'd call it an upscale literary spy thriller."

There was a blank look on his face, as he rattled the ice in his nearly empty glass. He wanted to get out of there in the worst way and I couldn't blame him because I did, too.

"I'm afraid I'm not sure what that means."

"Okay, how about this? What if T.S. Eliot was a spy for the Nazis and Ezra Pound was a double agent for the Americans?"

The expression on his face got even blanker, which only spurred me on.

"It's based on an absolutely true story. We uncovered some secret government documents through the Freedom of Information Act. We also have a source in MI5. It's a mind-blower, Joel. Can you imagine the crossover audience? We get the poetry lovers, the espionage lovers and the World War II lovers. And Nazis! Well, you know as well as I do that Nazis on film is like minting money. We're even throwing in a little romance. You know all about those passionate poets, right? Interested?"

"Uh. Actually, I'm a little over-extended at the moment. But I wish you luck, Mr. Swann, because it sounds to me like you might have something there."

"We like to think so, Joel. Otherwise it'd be a colossal waste of my time, wouldn't it?"

Finally, Sarah broke in. "Are you still doing business with Rusty Jacobs, Joel?"

A look of disgust crossed his face. "You know, we were never actually doing any business, Sarah. He's a little too, well, I don't want to malign the guy, but he was a little too…unstable for me."

"What do you mean?" I asked.

"Too hungry. You're that hungry, you're bound to be unreliable. You've got to want it but not show you want it." He looked to Sarah, and winked. "You know what I mean, don't you, Sarah?"

"Whatever you say, Joel."

Joel checked his watch. A Rolex and it sure didn't look like a knock-off to me. "You'll excuse me, Sarah, and, uh, Henry. I've got to be someplace in half an hour and I haven't worked the room yet."

"You wouldn't happen to have a card with you, would you, Joel?" I asked, not because I actually wanted it but because I wasn't quite finished with him yet.

He hesitated, then reached into his pocket, removed his wallet and handed me his card.

"Thanks," I said. "I'd return the favor except that my new ones aren't in yet."

"That's okay," he said, as he began to back slowly away.

As soon as he vanished into the crowd, Sarah punched me on the arm. Not too hard, just hard enough to make an impression.

"What was that all about?"

"What?"

"Ezra Pound and T.S. Eliot spies? You've got to be kidding."

"Not bad, huh? I just opened my mouth and that's what came out."

"Absolutely awful."

"I think he bought it."

"Of course he bought it. But what if he goes and tells someone about your idea, because he will, you know? Even if he hasn't got the foggiest idea who the heck you were talking about."

"And it winds up being a film? I'd probably kick myself."

I felt a hand grip my shoulder, squeezing hard into my flesh. Before I could turn around to see who it was, I heard a familiar growl, "Swann, what the hell are you doing here? A little out of your element, aren't you?"

I spun around to see who had my in a death grip. "Klavan."

"The one and only. We've got to stop meeting like this, pal."

"A friend of yours?" Sarah asked seductively.

"Afraid so. Ross Klavan, meet Sarah Byrnes."

"Pleased to make your acquaintance, Ms. Byrnes," Klavan said in his hypnotically smooth as maple syrup radio voice. He took her hand, bowed slightly and kissed it.

"Likewise, I'm sure," she purred. "I think I'll let you boys chat while I do a little detective work."

"But we were just getting to know each other," said Klavan.

"Familiarity breeds contempt," I said.

"You boys have fun. I'll be back soon."

Klavan's gaze was glued to Sarah's ass as she disappeared into the crowd.

"Who's the broad, Swann? She's far too classy for the likes of you."

"A source."

"You can do better than that."

"I could if I wanted to, but it's the truth."

"For what?"

"The Stan thing."

"What's she got to do with that and why are you here amongst the riff-raff and detritus of the film and literary world?"

"Seems Jacobs is trying to break into the film scene. She thought there might be someone here who knows where he is. What are you doing here?"

"Unlike you, I was actually invited, and I never pass up a chance for free booze, decent food, and a chance to hang out with people who have more money than I do."

Out of the corner of my eye I saw Sarah slowly snaking her way back to us through party-goers. From the grin on her face I could tell she'd been successful.

"See that chick over there," she asked, gesturing toward a corner of the room where three or four men were surrounding a very curvy, sexy looking blonde in a slinky silver dress so low-cut that it didn't seem to have a top to it.

"Yeah."

"That's who you want to talk to."

"Who is she?"

"A nobody."

"A pretty good looking nobody, if you ask me," said Klavan.

I turned to him with an annoyed look. "Aren't you happily married?"

"That doesn't mean I can't enjoy the scenery."

"It's *because* she's a nobody and wants to be a *somebody* that you want to talk to her," said Sarah. "She knows Jacobs. She met him a few days ago. Seems he promised her the moon, not that she's smart enough to find it without a telescope and a celestial map. Her name's Madison, at least that's the name she's using tonight. She's an actress. Surprised? Come on, I'll clear the field and introduce you. By the way, I happened to mention you were a writer/producer and you were casting your new film. I didn't tell her what it is, so please come up with something halfway plausible if she asks, not that ridiculous poet spy thriller thing."

"Huh?" said Klavan.

"I'll fill you in later."

"Mind if I tag along?" asked Klavan, a big grin plastered over across his kisser.

"Only if you promise keep your mellifluous mouth shut."

"You're asking the near impossible, Swann, but I'll give it a shot."

When we got closer I could see Madison's name wasn't the only thing phony about her. Tits and nose for starters. And when she opened her mouth I could tell she'd also thrown good money after bad for elocution lessons, because no one but a rabbi pronounces every syllable in "pleased to make your acquaintance."

Byrnes and Klavan did their best to elbow away the crowd around her until it was just the four of us. Sarah made the introductions, thankfully leaving the drooling Klavan out of the equation.

"I understand you're in the fil-um bus-a-ness," she said, cradling a drink in her two hands.

"My reputation precedes me."

"Actually, I never heard of you until Ms. Byrnes here—"

"Please, it's Sarah."

"Sarah told me all about you. I mean, I've probably heard of you," she said, trying to recover some credibility—mine and hers, "but I don't think I ever actually met you before."

"My loss, Madison. Is that your first name or last?"

"First. My last name is Eberle, but I'm considering changing it."

"Now why would you do that?"

"Well, it sounds kind of...kind of harsh. Don't you think?"

"Maybe something more melodic, alliterative."

"I'm not quite sure what you mean," she said.

Sarah poked me in the ribs, but it was too late. Once I get started, it's hard to stop.

"Maybe something like Madison Mulholland. You know, like the Drive."

Her eyes lit up. "You mean like Mulholland Drive!"

"That's the one."

"Madison Mulholland..." She rolled it over in her mind. I could practically see the wheels turning, and not too quick. "You know, it does have a ring to it. And the initials. M.M. Like Marilyn Monroe."

"An apt comparison," said Klavan.

I turned and hissed in his ear, "You might want to put your eyes back in their sockets." I doubt Madison heard me. She was too busy mulling over her new stage name.

"Sarah says you're an acquaintance of Rusty Jacobs," she said.

"I am, though I haven't seen him in years. What about you?"

"I met him a few days ago."

"Where was that?"

"Oh, I'd rather not say."

"State secret?"

"Huh?"

"Nothing. Did he pitch you a part in his next flick?"

She leaned into me and whispered, "How good a friend of yours is he?"

I leaned closer to her and whispered, "He owes me some dough. I'm looking for him so I can collect."

"You know, that doesn't surprise me in the least."

"How's that?"

"Well..." She slowly licked her top lip with her tongue. "To tell you the truth, I think he's a bit of a bullshitter."

"That sounds like Rusty."

"He tried to hit on me."

"Who wouldn't?" said Klavan. I smiled when Sarah elbowed him in the ribs.

"Hey!" said Klavan.

"You should see her left-hook," I said. I turned back to Madison.

"What my rude friend here means is that it doesn't surprise us. You're a very attractive woman."

"I know," she said without the slightest hint of humility. "But he was feeding me this incredible bullshit hustle, as if I was stupid or something."

"That was a mistake," I said.

"It sure was."

"What line was he feeding you?" asked Klavan, "if you don't mind my asking."

"Oh, you know, the one about getting me into his movie. It's kind of like the oldest line in the book, don't you think?"

"Do you think he's actually got a movie?" I asked.

"Not if you ask me, and I'm a pretty good judge of character. He's definitely the player type."

"I hate that type," said Klavan.

"You wouldn't happen to know where he is or maybe how I can find him?" I asked.

"Not exactly, but I might have an idea."

"What's that?"

"If I were looking for him which I am *definitely not,* I would go out to L.A. That's where he said he was headed because that's where he said all the action is. But you know, guys like that are always saying things like that."

"How come you're not out there, because you definitely look like you belong where the action is?" said Klavan, who was starting to get on my nerves. He was breaking my rhythm, so I shot him a look as I stepped not so gently on his toe. He got the message.

"So, Madison, did he happen to say where he was likely to land once he was out there?"

"As a matter of fact he did, but you know, it might just have been more bullshit."

"Yeah, probably so. But where would that be?"

"He said when he's in Los Angeles he only stays at The Beverly Hills Hotel. But you know, he was probably just trying to impress me, like he's some kind of big shot or something."

"I wouldn't be surprised," I said, but I knew if Stan was willing to foot the bill, it wouldn't be long before I would be Hollywood bound.

7
Easy-Peasy

I cannot say precisely how, but in some manner unbe-knownst to me, because my mind was, shall we say, a bit be-fogged by drink by the time we left the party, a somewhat besotted me wound up at Sarah Byrnes's apartment that night. She lived in Brooklyn of all places, a borough I had not seen much of since my skip tracing days. A borough that has changed so much in the past ten years, they would not allow the likes of me over there if it weren't in the dead of night. In the past I associated Williamsburg with the Hassidic Jews who resided there, as well as low-life types trying to skip out on their monthly payments on items they did not even need; not hipsters and up-and-coming artists who were already migrating deeper into Brooklyn as a result of the ever-rising rents—I like to call it the Manhattanization of the outer boroughs. But alas, the world changes and with it Brooklyn.

I did the cowardly and decidedly ungentlemanly but very Swann-like thing and sneaked out of Sarah's funky, chic, expensively-furnished spacious loft just after the break of dawn. Feeling a pang of guilt, something I am usually able to suppress, I did rouse her gently to thank her and let her know I was skipping town. It did not seem to matter much, as she simply muttered, "okay," and with a wave of her hand then rolled over and went back to sleep. Had I cared even slightly, my feelings would have been hurt. But it has been a long time since I've had any feelings to be hurt and even longer since I'd cared.

I did not forget my promise to connect with Goldblatt in the morning. He prefers face-to-face meetings, probably because he suspects I'm only half-listening when we're on the phone. That would be a generous estimate because I doubt he has more than a third of my attention most of the time. I informed him I'd give him half an hour. "But no diners," I said, placing my foot squarely on the floor.

He negotiated us up to forty-five minutes—"I need at least fifteen of those minutes to clear my throat," he said, quickly adding, "What's wrong with meeting over a little something to eat?"

"Because it means having to watch you eat. So, if you want to see me you'll meet me at the Citigroup Center atrium."

"That's the one with a Barnes and Noble, right?"

"Correct."

"And I think they got a Starbucks connected to the book-store, am I right?"

"Also correct."

"So let's meet there. A compromise."

"That's your idea of a compromise?"

"Yeah. It's in a bookstore and it's got something to drink and eat. You like books, right?"

I was not going to win this argument, so I agreed to meet him there at eleven o'clock.

Before leaving my place I called Stan and told him if I were to continue the search for Jacobs I had to go to L.A.

"He's there?" he said with more than a hint of excitement in his voice.

"He *might* be there."

"How do you know? How did you find out? Did you speak to Sarah?"

"It's not important how I know, Stan. Let's just say I have a pretty good idea he's out there, trying to break into the movies. But he might not be there long. People like him, and believe me,

I've seen my fair share, don't stay in one place for too long. There's always someone on their tail, so they have to keep moving. So I'll have to act fast."

"The movies?" I could sense him mulling it over in his mind. "Come to think of it, that kind of makes sense. He was always talking about movies. I think maybe he was an actor when he was younger. And there was this screenplay he said he once wrote, but couldn't sell. Yes, Henry, I think you're probably on the right track. I'm so glad I hired you."

"It's going to add considerably to your bill."

"Yes. Yes. I understand. It's fine. Totally fine."

"Don't start counting the money yet, Stan. Finding him is the easy part. Getting your money back, that's the hard part."

"How long do you think it'll take?"

"I have no idea. Calm down. This is just the beginning. It's a lead. Nothing more. There are no guarantees."

"I understand. I really do. But I've got a good feeling about this, Henry, and about you."

I pulled the phone away from my ear, held it to my side, and hung my head. Expectations have always been hard on me. I heard a faint voice coming from the phone: "Henry, are you still there?"

I brought the phone back up to my ear. "Yeah, I'm still here. It's not gonna be cheap, Stan. We're talking a couple grand, at least. And that's just for the flight and the hotel. I'm sure there'll be other incidentals."

"Oh, don't worry about that. I've got plenty of frequent flyer points, so I'll buy the ticket for you on my miles. And you're going first class, my friend. Remember, we're talking about a million dollars here. Your expenses will be less than a week's interest on that amount. Just tell me when you want to go and I'll take care of everything."

"Today's Wednesday. I've got a few things to take care of in town, so let's say Saturday. And, Stan, while you're at it, how about making a reservation for me at The Beverly Hills Hotel? That's where I think he might be staying."

He whistled. "The Beverly Hills, huh? Top of the line. But if you find him, it'll be worth it. I'll get right on it. Four days? You don't think you'll need more than that, do you?"

I didn't know how long I'd need but I saw no reason to tell him that. Even though it was mid-April, there was still a lingering winter chill in the air, so the warm weather would be a nice change. "If I can't find him in four days, he can't be found," I bragged, even though I knew that was an outright lie. But what did I care? I was getting a first class, all-expenses paid trip to L.A. I hadn't been there in almost a dozen years and the last time I was there, it hadn't turned out so swell. But this was a new decade, a new me, so maybe things would be different.

Now the tough part. I had to explain all this to Goldblatt. He was sure to notice my disappearance from New York for four or five days—his leash wasn't all that short but that was a long time for me to be unavailable without an explanation. I could tell him the truth, but then I'd have to break Stan's confidence and, even worse, split the dough with him. I'd have to think of something good, something he'd buy. My "associate" was a lot of things but stupid wasn't one of them.

Goldblatt was already seated at a small, round table near the window in the Barnes & Noble Starbucks. He was hunched over, staring intently at a laptop computer. There were two cups of coffee in front of him, but surprisingly no food.

"I've never seen you in front of a computer before," I said as I sat down opposite him.

"You think I practiced law all those years without using a computer?"

"I meant I didn't think you actually owned one."

"It's a new one. Got it on Amazon-dot-com. You can't believe the deals they offer. You ought to get yourself one, Swann. I can have it linked up with mine. That way we're always connected. They call it a network."

"I don't want to be connected to you. In fact, that's my worst nightmare. Besides, what makes you think I don't already own a computer?"

"Because you're a twentieth-century guy in a twenty-first-century world. I'm amazed you got yourself that smart phone."

I sat down and reached for the coffee. "Thanks for this. Wait, something's wrong with this picture," I said.

"What do you mean?"

"There's no food on the table."

"I'm trying to watch my weight."

"Give me a break."

"Really. I am." He patted his gut. "It's for the ladies."

"The ladies?"

"Yeah. There's just a little too much of me to love. I figure I could stand to lose ten, fifteen pounds."

"I'd say it's more like twenty-five. But I applaud your efforts and wish you luck…with the ladies, I mean."

"I'm going to take that as if you mean it, Swann, not as one of your usual caustic put-downs which, by the way, reflect how unhappy you are about yourself and your own sad, pathetic life."

"Did you just swallow a psychology book?"

"Funny man."

I leaned over and tilted the screen toward me. "What are you looking at?

"Art."

On the screen were a series of paintings, mostly abstracts.

Some of which I actually recognized from an art history class I took in college.

"Yeah, art. Which brings me to why I asked you to meet me. We've got us another case. It's a juicy one, but it's a little..." He paused a moment, his eyes directed toward the ceiling. "A little unconventional."

"What's that supposed to mean?"

"It means it's a little outside your normal range of expertise."

"What do you know about my range of expertise?"

"You know. Antiquities. Rare books. Photography. Litera-ture. I like to think of you, of us really, as Renaissance men." He pulled out a notebook and pen and started scribbling some-thing down.

"What are you writing?"

"Notes. For our brochure."

"We have a brochure?"

"Not yet, but we will. Renaissance men. I like that. We're an agency with a broad range of expertise." He stopped writing and closed the computer. "Now it's time to broaden your hori-zons a little."

"I think they're broad enough, thank you."

"You have to grow, Swann. If you stand still you fall behind. This is not your usual kind of case."

"Which is?"

"Finding people."

I sunk my head into my hands. What could this possibly mean? I looked back up to see Goldblatt was smiling.

"I can't wait to find out what you've got in mind, but remember, I'm under no obligation to take on a case just because you brought it in."

"I know that. You're not working *for* me, you're working

with me. We're partners. We have to come to a consensus on every case we take on. But this is one you're gonna love. See, I've got this friend, well actually he's not a friend, he's a former client." He paused.

I knew what he was doing. He was trying to word it in the most favorable light so I wouldn't shoot it down. "And?"

"He's got a problem."

"We've all got problems. Right now mine is sitting across from me."

"Yeah, well, he's got this problem and I told him I thought I could help him out."

"You have your pronouns mixed up, don't you?"

"Huh?"

"By *I* you actually meant *me*, didn't you?"

"Yeah. It's the kind of thing you could take a care of like this." He snapped his fingers. "Easy as pie."

"I've got news for you, Goldblatt, the easier something appears to be, the harder it is."

Goldblatt shrugged. "Well, I can't argue with you there, my friend, because you make a lot of sense. But there are two reasons we should get involved in this particular case. First, we stand to make a bundle. Second, this is a good person to have owe us a favor."

I picked up my source of caffeine. "All right," I said, "you've got me slightly intrigued. But do me two favors. One, don't say *we* when you really mean *me*, and two, don't bullshit me. I don't want a replay of that Long Beach fiasco a while back. I want to know exactly what I'm getting into, how I'm getting into it and why I'm getting into it. In other words, I want the whole story, not just the convenient parts you want me to know."

"I can do that. Easy-peasy. So, here's the deal. I got this friend—"

"You already said that. Get to the point." I tapped the face of my watch. "Tick-tock, tick-tock."

"So there's this guy who kind of ripped him off."

I dropped my head, "Oh, Jesus, please tell me you're not hiring me out to be a collection agency or, even worse, muscle to get back dough. You know I don't do that kind of shit."

He shook his head. "Hold your horses, will you? If it was muscle I wanted, I sure as hell wouldn't come to you. It's a little bit more complicated than that."

"I'm sure it is."

"Here's the deal. My friend, Tom Seligson, is an art collector, not an official art collector, you understand, kind of an amateur art collector. Mostly high-end stuff."

"What's that mean?"

"It means he's got a lot of dough, so he can afford the good stuff, and he's got pretty good taste, but it's not like he hires experts to go out and buy art for him or anything like that. He gets a tip on something, he buys it if he likes it. He visits galleries, sees something he likes, he buys it. Anyway, he meets this guy, name's Glenn Raucher, who says he's an art dealer. Tom winds up buying this painting from him. It's some big-shot name painter and he pays a nice chunk of dough for it, but it's supposedly under market value because it's a private transaction and Tom's saving the middle-man fee."

"How much?"

"We're talking telephone numbers here."

"You've got friends with that kind of dough to throw around?"

"You think I hang around with punks, homeless people and guys like you all the time?"

He had me there.

"So he's got the painting hanging in his living room, right? Like right alongside a Picasso and a Matisse drawing and what's the guy's name who used to spill the paint on the canvas?"

"Pollock."

"Yeah. He's got one of those. Anyway, this one's some modern artist named Rothstein or Rotterdam—"

"Rothko?"

"Yeah, yeah, that's the guy. Anyway, it's hanging there and he's really proud of it and he's showing it off to all his friends, and then one day he gets a call from some dealer he doesn't know who wants to come by and sell him some more art. Tom invites him over to see his collection. He takes one look at the Rothko and says, 'Hey, I don't think this is the real deal.'"

"Your friend bought a fake?"

"Maybe yes, maybe no. But he's starting to have doubts, right? So he goes back to Raucher and he says, 'Hey, someone I know, another dealer, took a look at the painting and says it's not a real Rothko, that it's a fake,' and he wants his money back. So Raucher says, 'No way.' Caveat emptor, and all that shit. So, my guy, Seligson, starts to smell a rat and says, 'If you don't give me my money back, I'm gonna spread it all over the city that you're a thief and that you sell forged art. You'll never make another sale. If you still won't give me my money back, I'm going to the cops. And if they don't do anything, I'll see you in court.' So Raucher says, 'Okay, okay, I'll give you your money back even though I know it's the real thing. Bring me the painting and then I'll give you your dough, only I'm going to take out fifty grand for all the trouble you're causing me.' So Tom, who wants to avoid the embarrassment of having bought a phony, which would make him look like a real jerk, a sucker, a mark for every two-bit art hustler in the city, brings him the painting and Raucher gives him a check, minus the fifty grand."

"Let me guess. The check bounces."

"Nope. The check is good."

"So what's the problem? Seems to me this is a pretty valuable lesson for only fifty grand, which he can obviously afford. Your friend learns he ought to do due diligence before parting with that kind of dough."

"If that were the end of it, you'd probably be right. But it isn't. One day Tom's visiting a gallery and he runs into Raucher and there's a guy with him Tom recognizes. It's the same guy who told him his painting was a fake."

"So Raucher and the guy know each other. So what?"

"So what is that Tom starts asking around, does a little research, and it turns out these two guys are partners. Tom starts to put two and two together and keeps coming up with five. He figures Raucher and the other guy are in it together. They sell a real painting. They create doubt about its authenticity. The pigeon panics and sells it back, minus fifty grand, maybe more, maybe less, depending on the pigeon. It's like the perfect rip-off. They're not doing anything illegal, so what can the mark do? He can't go to the cops because there's no crime. If it's a fake, he's covered, and if it's real, well, that's what they told him it was. So what's he gonna do?'

"What is he going to do?"

"He's gonna come to me and we come up with a plan. And that's where you come in."

"I don't like the sound of this, Goldblatt. First off, how come he didn't go to another expert before he asked for his dough back?"

"He was embarrassed. He didn't want to take the chance it was a fake and that he'd be a laughing stock. Word spreads quick in that community. It was worth the fifty grand bath to hold onto his reputation."

"I don't know what it is you want me to do."

"He wants me to go to Raucher as an art collector and buy the same painting at that steep discount, maybe even drive a better bargain. Then, when the other guy shows up and plants the seed of doubt, he wants me to ignore it and keep the painting. That way, he gets the painting back at a great price, because he buys it again under market value. But the truth is, he doesn't really care about the dough. He just hates the fact he's been taken. He wants revenge. And for this he's willing to pay me a nice little commission for pulling it off."

"Sounds perfect."

"It does, doesn't it?" Goldblatt puffed up his ample chest.

"Good luck with it."

"Hold on. That's where you come in, partner."

"Why the hell do you need me? You just explained how you were going to pull it off."

"Look at me, Swann. Do I look like an art collector? Is there any world we know and live in where I could pass as an art collector, much less a wealthy one?"

I looked at him. He was right. He didn't even look good enough to be a garbage collector much less a collector of fine art.

I shook my head. "I don't want any part of this."

"Why not?"

"Because it sounds like trouble."

"Trouble how?"

"First of all, you'd have to pass me off as an art collector, and I know nothing about that business."

"Klavan's wife is an artist, isn't she? She can give you a crash course."

"And don't you think he's going to ask to see my collection or check me out, like my credit rating, for instance."

"You have a credit rating?"

"That's the point."

"Don't worry, I can take care of all that."

"How are you going to take care of anything? You can hardly take care of yourself."

"I'm insulted."

"Live with it."

"I know people who know how to do things with computers."

"Hackers?"

"I didn't say that."

"But that's what we're talking about."

"What do you care how it gets done so long as it gets done?"

"I don't care if it gets done at all because I don't want to have anything to do with it."

"Come on. We're partners, remember?"

"What if these guys are connected?"

"What do you mean?"

I bent my nose to the side. "You know, wise guys."

"Nah. This is just a rinky-dink two-man operation. Besides, I know connected guys and believe me, these guys aren't connected. They're just two schnooks who came up with what they think is a fool-proof way to con other schnooks out of money."

"How can you be so sure?"

"I feel it."

"You feel it?"

"That's right. There's no muscle involved, all guile." He tapped the side of his head. "Much too subtle for the mob."

"How do you know what's too subtle for the mob? How do you know anything about the mob?"

"I know what I know, Swann. Let's just leave it at that. This could be a nice payday for us and it's not like it would be the first time you passed yourself off as someone or something you aren't."

"True that," I admitted and suddenly it occurred to me that this might be just the leverage I needed to cut Goldblatt out of the Stan deal. And frankly, even if I acquiesced to this wacky plan who knew if it would even get off the ground? So why not say yes, then let the chips fall where they would.

"I'll think about it."

"How long do you think you'll need to think about it?"

"As long as it takes."

"Yeah, well, how long do you think that'll be? I need to give Tom an answer."

"You'll know by tomorrow."

He smiled. "I can live with that." He looked at his watch. "It's almost noon. How about some lunch?"

"I'm afraid I'm going to have to pass on that tempting offer."

"I'm buying."

"As much as I love to hear the sound of those two words, I'll still pass." The time seemed right to drop the bomb. "By the way, I'm going to be out of town for a few days."

"Yeah?" he said absently, as he began to pack up his computer. He stopped and looked up. "Where you going?"

"Out of town."

"Where?"

"None of your business."

"That's pretty nasty."

"I have a private life."

"I didn't say you didn't. So, where are you going?"

I could sit there and argue with him all day but in the end

he'd probably wear me down. "California."

"Where in California?"

"I don't have to answer to you just because we work together."

"You can't say the word partners, can you?"

"I can say it. I choose not to." I started to get up.

"Where in California?"

"L.A."

"What's in L.A.?"

"Palm trees. Movie stars."

"Yeah, but that's not why you're going there."

"Personal business."

"You're not going to tell me, are you?"

"You're not going to let this go unless I do."

"You know me so well."

"Do you want me to break a confidence?"

"What are you some kind of priest? Because I know you're not a lawyer."

"It has to do with your friend, Stan."

"What about him?"

"He hired me to do a job for him."

"What kind of job?"

"That I cannot tell you."

"Why not?"

"Because he asked me not to and I feel like enough of a shit by even telling you he hired me."

Goldblatt was silent a moment, staring past me. Finally he said, "He's paying you for this job?"

"He is."

"How much?"

"It's mostly a percentage thing," I lied.

"And you weren't going to tell me about this?"

"He specifically asked me not to."

Goldblatt cocked his head and gave me what he was trying to make a puppy dog look, but instead it just came out Goofy not Benjie.

"But we're partners."

"He asked me, Goldblatt. What was I gonna do?"

"Okay, I see your moral dilemma."

"Thank you."

"I didn't say I approved of it. I said I saw it. But when it was all over, you were going to tell me about it or at least split the fee with me, weren't you?"

"Of course I was," I lied. "What kind of asshole do you think I am?"

He gave me the fish-eye. "Okay, I get it. You can't tell me what the job is. Now. But I'll be expecting a check when it's over. It'll be our usual split because you know, in a way, I got this job for you."

"How's that?"

"If it hadn't been for me putting together the poker game, and if it hadn't been for me inviting Stan, then this never would have happened. So it's perfectly legit I get my split. And in that case, go to L.A. with my blessings."

"You don't know how much that means to me."

I knew he did not get my sarcasm when he replied, "That's okay," and waved his arm. "But now, about this Seligson thing, you're gonna have to do it because you owe me."

How could I possibly argue with that irrefutable logic?

PART 2
HOLLYWOOD

"Show things really as they are."
—Lord Byron, *Don Juan*

"T'aint worth de trouble."
—Zora Neale Hurston,
Their Eyes Were Watching God

8

But What I Really Want To Do Is Direct

Sunglasses.

Check.

Polo shirt.

Check.

Red convertible.

Check.

I had everything I needed to find Rusty Jacobs.

The last time I was in L.A., over a decade ago, I needed a *Thomas Guide* to get around town. Now, due to the march of time and technological progress, GPS made that unnecessary. As a result, it took me less than forty-five minutes before I pulled up in front of The Beverly Hills Hotel, where an impeccably dressed, annoyingly efficient parking valet wrestled my rental car from me and pointed me in the direction of the hotel lobby.

After checking in, I asked if Rusty Jacobs registered at the hotel. Yes, I was informed, he was. Between this and my sudden change of luck at the poker table, perhaps the stars were suddenly realigning for me and now, nearing the age of fifty, dare I believe my life was poised to take a turn for the better? Not that I was counting on it, of course. Life has a better curve ball than Clayton Kershaw.

"You wouldn't happen to know if he's in his room, would you?" I asked.

Without bothering to look up, the officious looking desk clerk, said, "I believe I saw him leave the hotel a few hours ago, sir. Would you like to leave a message?"

"No," I checked the nametag on his lapel, "Ralph. I want to

surprise him. Maybe I'll catch him before he gets back to his room. You wouldn't happen to know if he has a favorite spot he likes to hang out at the hotel?"

"In the afternoon you'll most likely find him out by the pool. In the evening, before dinner, you might look for him at the bar."

I pulled out my wallet and extracted a couple twenties, "I'd really get a kick out of seeing the look on his face when he sees me, assuming he recognizes me after all these years, so I'd really appreciate it if you'd keep this between the two of us." I slid the bills toward him. He cocked his head slightly to my right then my left. He covered the bills with his hand, slid them toward him until they miraculously disappeared under the counter.

"I understand," he whispered.

It was nearly three o'clock, L.A. time, so I figured I'd take a little nap, then hit the bar around six-thirty in hopes of finding Jacobs there. If not, the next day I'd try the coffee shop and then the pool in hopes of bumping into him. Eventually he'd surface.

Around five-thirty, after showering, I headed downstairs to the bar, where I found a strategically placed table, ordered a beer and waited. A half hour and two beers later, a slim fellow, about six feet tall, with short, curly, close-cropped red-hair appeared at the bar. He was wearing black trousers, and a blue, yellow and red Hawaiian shirt. When the bartender greeted him as Mr. Jacobs, I knew I had my man. I waited a few minutes to be sure he was alone and then I got up and grabbed an open stool next to him. I wasn't even settled in before he turned to me and asked cheerily, "Hey, pal, whatcha drinking?"

"Nothing yet."

"When you decide what you want it's on me."

"Do I know you?"

"No, but you will."

"And that'll be a good thing?"

"The best."

"Fine by me. What do you suggest?"

"How's about white wine?"

"Not my usual drink, but I'll drink what the natives are drinking," I said.

He extended his hand. "I'm Rusty Jacobs."

"Henry Swann," I said, meeting him halfway.

"Great name, Henry Swann. That real?"

"As real as it gets."

"Well, pleased to meet you, Henry Swann. Just blow into town?"

"Good guess."

"Not really a guess. You got that East Coast pallor, man. New York City, am I right?"

"You got me."

"Me, too. Everyone here's from someplace else, you know."

"I do now. So what do you do for a living, Mr. Jacobs?"

"Everyone calls me Rusty, so you might as well do the same. As for what I do, a lot of things, actually. I'm a man for all seasons and all reasons. Right now, if you guessed I'm in the movie business, you'd be right on the..." He touched his nose with his finger.

"I don't think I've ever actually met anyone in the movie business before."

"Then it's your lucky day, pal. Most people don't, unless they live out here where you can throw a rock and hit a wanna-be actor, producer, director, or screenwriter."

"Which one are you?"

"I'm a hybrid. A triple slash. Writer/producer/director. What about you, my friend? What are you doing in Hollywood? What kind of wannabe are you?"

"It's a long time since I've been a wannabe anything. Actually, it's a question I've been grappling with lately."

"Ah, the old what do I wannabe when I grow up question. I hear you, man. But you've got to be here for a reason. No one just comes here to come here."

"Because there is no *here* here."

"Huh?"

I didn't expect him to get the reference, but it would have been nice.

"You're right. I am here for a reason."

"What would that reason be, if you don't mind my asking?"

"I'm looking for someone."

"Is that what you do for a living? Look for people?"

"It is."

"And people pay you for that?"

"Most of the time."

"You mean like you're a private eye?"

"Not exactly."

"Well, you've piqued my interest, Henry Swann. So, who is it you're looking for, and why are you looking for him...or her, if you don't mind my asking?"

"I don't mind at all, Rusty. Because the funny thing is, I'm looking for you. And it seems like I found you."

His back straightened like someone had shoved a ramrod up his ass. The genial pasted-on smile disappeared from his face. "You're shitting me." He forced a smile. "Yeah, you're pulling my leg."

"Nah. I don't have much of a sense of humor, Rusty. Especially after a five-and-a-half-hour flight from New York."

He started to back off the stool, but before he could get far I put my hand on his shoulder and pressed down to restrain him.

"So why are you looking for me?"

"I think that might qualify as a rhetorical question."

"You mean like I already know the answer?"

"Exactly."

He paused a moment as the color drained from his face and his body tensed. "You're not the law, are you?"

"No, Rusty, I'm not the law. Far from it."

His body relaxed slightly. I could feel his shoulder collapse beneath my hand. "And you don't look like you're here to break both my arms and legs."

"Even if I could manage something like that it's not my style. So relax."

"How's about another drink?"

"You trying to get me drunk, Rusty?"

"No, no, I wouldn't do that."

"Relax. I'm hungry. Let's get something to eat and talk this over."

"You like Mexican? I know a place. I'll get my car, you get yours, and we'll meet out front and you can follow me."

"Nice try. You can take your car, if you like, but I'll be sitting right beside you."

"Yeah, yeah. That's what I meant. There's a place called El Coyote, on Beverly. It's where Sharon Tate had dinner the night before that Manson thing."

"Sounds appropriate."

We took my car and as soon as we ordered I got down to business.

"You know why I'm here, don't you, Rusty?"

"Yeah, you're looking for me," he said, as he methodically licked the salt from the rim of his margarita.

"And you know why I'm looking for you."

"That, to be honest, I'm not so sure about."

"A guy disappears with a million bucks and he doesn't figure someone's eventually going to come looking for him?"

"I don't know what you're talking about," he said, nervously reaching for a chip, then twirling it around a bowl of guacamole.

"You're not going to sit here and deny knowing Stan Katz."

"Sure I know Stan. I've worked with him. Why would I tell you I didn't know him?"

"I don't know. Why would you tell me you didn't steal a million bucks from him?"

"Because I didn't steal a million bucks from him, that's why."

Our order arrived. Enchiladas. Chicken for me, beef for him.

Rusty stared at his food then looked up at me. "Is that what he told you?"

"Yeah, that's what he told me."

"That's crazy. He knows that's not the truth."

"So you don't have his money?"

Rusty looked back down and I knew what was going to come out of his mouth next would not be the truth.

"Look," he said, "what we have here is a misunderstanding. First of all, let's get this straight, strictly speaking it wasn't even his money."

"Whose money was it?"

"Technically, it's the company's money."

"And who's the company?"

"Well, we were the company."

"You and Stan?"

"We're getting into very murky territory here."

"How's that?"

He carved up his enchilada into remarkably even slices,

picked one up with his knife and fork, put it in his mouth, washed it down with a slug of margarita, then carefully dabbed his chin with his napkin. Jesus, it was like watching the anti-Goldblatt eat and in its own way just as disgusting.

"It was Stan's company but I was working for him, no, make that working with him. Kind of."

"What does 'kind of' mean?"

"I was an independent contractor. We were working together. In tandem."

"Explain that."

"I would suggest investments for him and then if we made those investments and the investments paid off, I would get a percentage of the profit, a commission. As far as it being his money, well, let me explain it this way. You put your money in a bank, right?"

"When I have money, which isn't all that often, I might put it in a bank, though if I did, it wouldn't stay there all that long."

"And when you put the money in the bank, whose money is it, the bank's or yours?"

"I'm beginning to see where you're going with this..."

"Right. It's on loan to the bank. The bank uses your money to make investments and the bank pays you interest on your money. But the money is still yours and you can withdraw it any time you like. Hence, it's your money. But it's also the bank's money, while they have it. See how complicated it is? The money Stan was holding was on loan to him, he'd be the first to tell you that. It's his responsibility to take that money and make it grow. I am part of that responsibility. I help make it grow. That's what I'm doing with the million bucks. I didn't steal it. I simply moved it across country to give it a chance to grow in more fertile soil, so to speak."

"So your story is that Stan gave you the million bucks to invest in 'fertile soil.'"

Rusty picked up another section of the enchilada with his fork, dipped it gently in a bowl of salsa, and ate it.

"Well, I'm not sure 'gave' is the proper word."

"You're not sure *gave* is the proper word because he didn't give it to you. In other words, you didn't have his permission. The truth is you *took* a million bucks. Without telling him. So *took* is the operative word here, not *gave*."

"Took?" he rolled the word over in his head. "I'm not sure that's the proper word either."

"Stole. How's that for the proper word?"

"I *know* that's not the proper word."

"I'm not going to sit here all night looking for the proper word, Rusty. All I want is Stan's money back. You have his money, right?"

"Well, it's complicated."

"I don't like the sound of that, Rusty. I hear the word complicated, I hear the word problem. I hear the word problem, I hear the word work, and that means it becomes very personal. I like things to be nice and easy. I don't like it out here. I'm a New York City kind of guy. L.A. gives me the heebie-jeebies. I'm only here to bring back Stan's million bucks. That's what I call simple. I don't want to hear the word complicated. I don't care about explanations. I just want the money. Understand? I don't want to hear about it being buried in 'fertile' Hollywood soil. And if that's where it is buried, I want you to unbury it, give it to me and I'll bring it back to New York and hand it over to Stan. If you do that there will be no consequences for you. You can continue following your bliss out here to your heart's content."

He shook his head slowly back and forth. "The thing of it is,

Henry, I don't actually have the money anymore. But I want to get one thing straight. I did not steal it. I was working with Stan. We're an investment company. I took the money, the million dollars, and I invested it. I can't take the money out now and return it. I have to wait until the investment pays off. That's the way those things work. Think of it as one of those CDs the bank offers. You have to wait until the maturity date."

"What the hell are you talking about?"

"Like I said, I invested the money."

"In what?"

"A film project."

"Are you out of your fucking mind? You took Stan's million bucks and invested in a fucking movie?"

"You make it sound like there's something wrong with that. It's a legitimate investment."

"There is something wrong with it, you moron. You took the money without asking for it—"

"Well, that's not exactly the way things worked."

"What the hell does that mean?"

"Stan knew I was looking for investment vehicles. That was part of our working agreement. He trusted me and I always came through for him. Listen, I couldn't have taken the money out if I weren't authorized."

"But you didn't have the authority to invest without consulting with him, did you?"

"That's not exactly the way it happened, but I think I'll plead the Fifth on that for now."

"There's that phrase again. Not exactly. Not exactly means you took the money without asking Stan and you left town without telling Stan. And then you invested that money, no you *gave* that money to someone to make a goddamn movie so you could be in the goddamn movie business. This was all about *you* and *your* future. It had nothing to do with Stan and his clients. As for taking the Fifth, this ain't no courtroom, pal."

"Now hold on a minute. I didn't steal it. If you want to use another term, a more precise term, I temporarily appropriated it...with permission, mind you. I'm not saying Stan knew exactly how I was going to invest it, and maybe not the exact figure I took, but I've been pretty successful in the past. He'd be the first one to admit that. I have every intention not only of returning the money, but returning it with interest. Sure I wanted to further my career, but there's nothing wrong with that, is there? Everyone wants to better themselves, don't they? You don't want to spend the rest of your life looking for people like me, do you?"

He had me there.

"Leave me the fuck out of it, Rusty. And your idea is that by investing it in a movie, a fucking movie, you're going to return the million dollars with interest? What kind of pie-in-the-sky crapola is that? Even I know that's a fairytale."

"It's not pie-in-the-sky. It happens all the time. Ever hear of a little movie like *Star Wars?* Or *Spiderman?* Or *Frozen?* Or *Ice Age?*"

"So you invested the money in *Spiderman?*"

"Don't be ridiculous."

"Yeah, I didn't think so. How quickly do you think this return of the money is going to happen?"

"I have assurances that within a few months I will not only have my investment returned, but I will have at least ten points on top of it."

"Oh, Jesus, how dumb are you? How the hell is that supposed to happen? The film wouldn't even be made yet."

"Correct. But here's the deal. The script is finished. We're working on attaching a couple of big name actors to the project.

The idea is to shoot several scenes, then put together a trailer. We use the trailer to attract more investors then we get a distributor to buy the film before it's even made. I return the seed money, plus interest, and everybody's happy. There's a built-in market for this stuff. It's a can't-miss proposition. Stan gets his money back, plus interest. I get myself a new career. Everybody's happy. It's what I've always wanted."

"You've always wanted to be in show business?"

"Actually, I was in show business. When I was a kid I was on Broadway. I was one of the Lost Boys in *Peter Pan*. Maybe you saw it."

"No, I did not see it," I said, shaking my head in disbelief.

"You should have. Sandy Duncan was Peter Pan. Man, I had such a crush on her. I was only twelve, but I actually asked her out on a date and can you believe it, she said yes. I hired one of those carriages and took her for a ride in Central Park and—"

"Stick to the point, will you?"

"Yeah, sure. Anyway, I'm not unfamiliar with the business. I know how it works. I know there's a lot of bullshit involved. I know how to cut through that bullshit. I know when something's solid gold and when it's tin."

"Then you know how to get that money back and that's what you're going to do. Now. Because I've got a flight out of here Monday night and I'm not leaving L.A. without that money."

He shook his head. "I'm sorry, Swann, but I don't think that's possible."

"Oh, it's possible, Rusty. It's possible because, as you know, the movies are magic, and when magic is involved, anything is possible. Just click your heels together, man. So what we're going to do is finish dinner and then we're going back to the hotel and you're going to figure out a way to get that money back."

"But you don't understand…"

"You're right. There's a lot I don't understand. I don't understand how planes stay in the sky. I don't understand how they get that toothpaste in the tube. There's even more I don't want to understand. Understanding leads to compassion. Compassion leads to me cutting you some slack. That's not a direction I'm going to take."

"The kind of people I'm involved with, they're not the regular Hollywood kind of people." His voice turned into a whine.

"What's that supposed to mean?"

"It means we're not talking about studio people."

"Are you talking about the mob, Rusty?"

"Not exactly. I'm talking about the kind of people who aren't listed on Wall Street. It's not like I can go up to them and ask for my money back. That's not the way business is done. What I'm saying is we might just have to let this thing play through. But I swear to you, this is a great script. And like I said, the market is there. It's like—"

"Stealing?"

"That's not what I was going to say."

"It's not that vampire thing I read about in *Variety*, is it?"

"Oh, no. I don't know how that even got in the trades. That would be ridiculous. What do I know about vampires? But you know how it is."

"No, actually I don't how it is. What I do know is you're telling me I'm supposed to go back to Stan and tell him he's investing a million bucks in a great script because you tell him it's a great script."

"I know it's a great script because I helped write it. What I mean is, I have a partner who's a writer, but I had plenty of input and it was from an original idea I had."

"Oh, for Christ's sake."

"You don't understand. The kid I'm working with is a genius. He went to Harvard and he just got his graduate degree from the NYU film school. He's the one out there hawking the script. Me, I'm way too old. I couldn't even get in for a meeting, unless maybe I dressed like the pizza guy. But him, are you kidding? He's good looking, like a fucking movie star. I'll get you a meeting with him tomorrow morning and you'll see what I mean. The kid'll charm the pants off you. You'll see what I mean. I'm telling you, you'll want to invest in him and the movie five minutes after you meet him. You won't even have to know what the movie's about. But let me explain, because it's a whole new way of doing business."

"Yeah, why don't you do that?" I didn't mind him rattling on. It was actually kind of amusing watching him squirm. And what better did I have to do with my time?

"See, there's a market out there that most people don't even know about. It's the Christian market. And it's huge. It's centered in the Bible belt. You know where that is, right? Mostly it's the southern states. North Carolina, South Carolina, Georgia, West Virginia, Tennessee, Alabama, Mississippi, and then out here in the west. Utah, Wyoming, Nevada, even parts of California. If you've got the right movie and the right star it's like printing money. It's all about values, Christian values. I'm telling you, we've got a script that goes right to the heart of those values. And we're very close to getting the right actors attached, too. They're probably actors you've never heard of, but you'd probably recognize their faces. Like Kevin Sorbo. You know who he is?"

"Haven't a clue."

"Believe me, he's big. I mean huge. He was Hercules."

"Guess I missed that one."

"The muscle guy."

"I know who Hercules is, Rusty."

"Sure. Sure. The thing is, in this market, guys like him are mucho bankable. And with the million bucks as seed money we've got a couple guys on the hook who can seal the deal. We're this close," Rusty said, squeezing his thumb and forefinger together. "This close. All we need is a little time. Stan'll have his money, with plenty of interest for his investors, plus more than enough to pay your fee, whatever it is, and I'll have my new career. Everyone'll be happy. You want everyone to be happy, don't you, Swann?"

"Actually, I don't care about everyone being happy. All I care about me being happy. All I'm interested in is doing my job and getting the hell out of here. That's what would make me happy."

"All I'm asking is that you come to the meeting tomorrow. You'll meet the kid and you'll meet a couple of the money people we're working on as investors."

"Who are these money people?"

"One's a guy from South Carolina. Lots of dough. All we've got to do is promise him a part for his girlfriend, some former pole dancer or something like that. She's a bimbo. I know that. But there's a part for her. That's the least of our problems. The other's some Arab dude who's got money up the wazoo and wants to be a movie mogul. He doesn't know the difference between Disney and DeLorean, but he's got mucho..." Rusty rubbed his fingers together.

It sounded like a fucking circus and I had a bad feeling about the whole thing, but I also knew the only chance I had at getting Stan's money back was to play along.

"Rusty, tell you what I'm going to do. I'm going to meet the kid and the others, but only because I have to figure out a way to get that money back. I want you to set up that meeting at nine o'clock. At our hotel. Breakfast. And if all of you aren't there, I promise you I'm going to hunt you down and when I find you I'm going I'm going to call the cops and have you arrested and then I'm going to have them send you back to New York, where they're going to throw you into the slammer and you're going to wind up on Riker's Island, where you'll have plenty of time to ponder your next career move. Do you understand?"

"Yes, I do. But—"

"There are no buts, Rusty. You and this kid...what's his name?"

"Josh Ventura."

"You and Josh Ventura and I are going to figure out how to get back Stan's million bucks, because if not, we both know what the rest of your life is going to look like and it's not going to be pretty."

"You'll see, Swann. Everything will turn out fine."

I deposited Rusty at the hotel with yet another warning about skipping out on me. He promised he wouldn't and for some reason I couldn't even begin to articulate I believed him.

9
An Arab, A Jew, A Holy Roller and A Hooker Walk Into a Hotel Suite...

Eight-thirty the next morning, just as I was getting out of the shower, the hotel house phone rang.

It was Jacobs.

"We're waiting for you down in the lobby, man."

"You're early."

"I know. I didn't want you to worry about me skipping out on you."

"I wasn't worried."

"I got us a meeting room where we can have some privacy. It's on the main floor. The Doheny Suite. I've taken care of everything. You like bagels, right? They're not like New York bagels so don't get your hopes up. But we'll have plenty of other stuff. The gang's all assembled. Nine o'clock. Be there or be square."

No one should be that goddamn cheery at eight-thirty in the morning.

When I entered the Doheny room I found a large round table covered with trays of food filled with bagels, English muffins, blueberry muffins, all kinds of cheeses, plates of scrambled eggs, pancakes, bacon, sausages, toast, little boxes of cold cereal, milk, carafes of juices, two coffee urns, one caffeine, one non-caffeinated, plus a tray of various kinds of teas. In all, there was enough food to feed the cast and crew of *Spiderman*. In the room was Rusty, three guys and a busty blonde who was that cheap kind of pretty you see in those cheesy bars along Ninth Avenue in Hell's Kitchen.

The minute he saw me he jumped up and practically sprinted toward me.

"Henry, have a seat," Rusty said. "Grab some food, and I'll make the introductions. Here, sit at the head of the table. Well, actually there is no head of the table 'cause it's round. I specifically asked for a round table. You know why?"

"Not a clue."

"That's the kind of table they used when they negotiated the end of the Vietnam War. It was so nobody could claim to be in charge. You know, at the head of the table. But wherever you sit, that's the head because you're the man of the hour. Without you, we're nada."

"Suddenly, I'm a big shot," I mumbled, as I made my way toward the chair he held out for me. Before I could sit, the blonde, wearing a baby blue sundress cut so low her obviously store-bought boobs were practically spilling out, was filling a plate of food and shoving it in front of me.

"Here we go, honey," she said with an accent so thick I could have used it to sweeten my pancakes, "and you can always come back for seconds. We got plenty. Rusty here saw to that."

"I'm never hungry first thing in the morning," I said

"My mama always said breakfast is the most important meal of the day. So you gotta eat because my mama was never wrong."

"Let me introduce you to everyone, Henry," Rusty broke in. "This is the team. Team, this is Henry Swann. He flew in all the way from New York City yesterday to oversee the project."

"I'm not here to oversee anything," I started, wanting to add, "you pompous ass," but Rusty cut me off.

"Henry, this is Terry Strong. Terry's a businessman from South Carolina, Terry, why don't you introduce yourself to

Henry. You know, tell him a little something about yourself."

"Surely will," said Terry, a middle-aged, balding fellow with a considerable paunch and what looked like a recently dyed comb-over. He wore a bright green blazer, tan chinos and a white button-down shirt, open at the collar. I noticed a small jelly stain on his shirt and couldn't help thinking of my erstwhile "associate."

"Pleased to meet you, Mr. Swann. Well, where should I begin? I know. At the beginning! I used to be in the shoe business but now I'm hankering to get into the show business," he announced in a booming voice that filled the room. "I love the movies, but not the kind of movies they're makin' now. No, siree, Bob. Those movies, they kinda make me sick. You know, with all that sex and violence stuff. I like the old-fashioned movies where there are good guys and bad guys and you can always tell the good guys from the bad guys 'cause the good guys wear white hats and the bad guys wear black hats and the good guys win and the bad guys lose. Those are the movies I wanna see, and those are the movies I want my kids to see and those are the movies I wanna make. Movies you can take the wife and kiddies to and you don't have to blindfold 'em and stick cotton in their ears. And Rusty here, well, he assures me those are the movies we're gonna make. Ain't that right, Rusty?"

"Sure is, Terry. In our movies the white hats kick the butts of those black hats."

Somehow, between the time I left him last night and this morning Rusty had added something of a southern twang.

"That's what I like to hear," Terry said. "And this here's my girlfriend, Jolene. Jolene, say hello to Mr. Swann."

Jolene smiled and curtsied.

"Jolene's a trained dancer, but here's the God's honest truth.

She's the most talented woman I ever met. I think she belongs in the movies, no, she's *made* for the motion pictures, and my friend Rusty here's the man who's gonna make that happen. Ain't that right, Rusty?"

"We're sure as heck gonna do what we can, Terry. And this," Jacobs said, pointing to a smallish man in a black suit sitting quietly in a corner, away from the table, fiddling with his Blackberry, "is Ibrahim Ahmad. Ibrahim is from Qatar. You know where Qatar is, Henry?"

"I don't believe I do, Rusty."

"Well, neither did I 'til I met Ibrahim, but now I sure do. But knowing exactly where it is ain't important. All we need to know is that it's in the Middle East and we know what's in the Middle East, don't we? And it just so happens Ibrahim loves the movies, don't you, Ibrahim?"

Ibrahim, sporting two- or three-day's worth of stubble, nodded almost imperceptibly, without bothering to pick his head up from his Blackberry.

"Ibrahim here's a man of few words, ain't you, Ibrahim?" said Terry.

Ibrahim looked up, stared at Terry a moment then looked back down at his Blackberry.

"And finally, we've got our resident genius. Josh Ventura. Josh, I want you to meet Henry Swann, from New York City. Did I tell you Josh attended Harvard and NYU Film School, Henry?"

"You might have mentioned it."

Josh stood up, looking nothing at all like a great looking movie star unless you consider those nerdy looking kids in those teen movies gorgeous. He was a string bean of a kid who looked like he was in his mid-to-late-twenties, tops. He wore jeans and a vintage *Star Wars* T-shirt. At the moment he was being introduced, he was having his way with a bagel, spread generously with cream cheese and topped with a just as generous pile of smoked salmon. Unlike Ibrahim, Josh did look me in the eye and announced, "Pleased to meet you, man. Rusty says you're a private dick. That true? 'Cause if you are, you must have some truly outrageous stories and I'd sure love to sit down with you some time and talk about them. You know, like maybe we could, like, collaborate on a script or something."

I didn't know what to say so I said like nothing.

"Let's all sit down and get this thing going," Rusty said. "Henry's on the clock. He's got to get back to New York tomorrow."

Everyone pulled up a chair and sat at the table, except for Ibrahim, who remained seated in the corner, head down, still fiddling furiously with his Blackberry.

"Now, you've all read the script, except for Henry, of course, and I think we all agree that it's brilliant," Rusty continued. Terry and Jolene nodded vigorously, Josh smiled, Ibrahim plunked away on his Blackberry. "And the way Josh and I see it, we can bring this baby in for under ten million dollars, which in today's market is bubkes, especially when you consider it can easily bring it ten times that at the B.O. I've started the ball rolling with a million and part of that we're using to put together the trailer. You bring what you say you can, Terry, ditto Ibrahim, and that'll attract the right director and star and that'll guarantee us the rest of the money we need to finish the film."

"What about that part for *Jolene*, Rusty? Because without that, we ain't got no deal."

"I know that, Terry. Josh and I have put our heads together and we think she'd be perfect for the daughter-in-law."

Terry looked over at Jolene, who was now was busily

painting her nails. She looked up, scrunched her face like a three-year-old, shook her head almost imperceptibly then returned to working on her nails.

"Jolene and I have talked it over and we don't think so, Rusty. The daughter-in-law, well, she ain't got but a few lines. I'm afraid that's jes' not gonna cut it."

"That might be true, Terry, but she's absolutely integral to the movie. I mean it's not about the number of lines. It's about the import of those lines and how crucial the character is to the story." He turned to Jolene. "Jolene, as a trained professional, you know that. I mean, she's in what, Josh, how many scenes is she in?"

"Three," Josh managed despite his mouth half full of bagel.

"She's in three scenes," Rusty repeated. "And I'm sure we could do a little rewrite and add her in a couple more."

Josh took yet another bite of his bagel, made a face. "Yeah, I guess I could probably put her in a couple more."

"You see, Terry, we're totally flexible."

"No, Rusty. I'm afraid that ain't gonna do. Not. At. All. Jolene ain't gonna play the daughter-in-law. That just ain't gonna work for us. And no play, no pay. Is that what they say out here?"

Rusty looked at Josh, who by this time had buried his head in his hands. Me, I was getting a kick out of this. But then, it wasn't my million bucks on the line.

"Okay, well, how about Tiffany, the best friend? I think we could work that out, don't you, Josh?"

Terry looked at Jolene again, who didn't even bother looking up from painting her nails as she once more shook her head, this time a little harder.

"I think maybe we're gettin' a little closer, Rusty, but I believe Jolene's even a little better'n that. I mean, you jes' don't wanna waste talent like Jolene's on some itty-bitty part."

"Terry, the fact of the matter is Jolene's never acted before. I don't mean to insult anyone here, but let's face it, she's an amateur, at least when it comes to film. There's a lot of money riding on this. Your money. Our money. You want this thing to work, don't you?"

"Sure I do. But trust me, she's a natural, Rusty. She's been takin' lessons. And she's been performin' since she's been a kid. She's won...how many beauty contests you won, honey?"

"Three," she replied, as she held up three fingers then waved her hand and in the air to help dry the bright red polish.

"She's won three beauty contests. And them beauty contests, they all have what you call talent portions. You don't just get out there on stage and prance around wearin' them skimpy bikinis. Not anymore you don't. That's what you call sexism. That's been outlawed today. That there women's lib did away with all that."

"So you want her to have the lead?"

He shook his head. "Heck no. Not the lead. That'd be ridiculous and unreasonable. I'm not an unreasonable man, Rusty. Neither is Jolene. This is business and I'm a businessman. I know we have to have an experienced name actress in the lead role. People don't know Jolene yet so she ain't gonna put them all-important asses in the seats. Not yet. What I think is that our resident genius here can write another part for Jolene where she's got maybe a bigger role. Not the lead, but maybe a second lead. You know, like there's Butch Cassidy and there's the Sundance Kid. There's Paul Newman and there's Robert Redford. There ain't no reason she can't be the Sundance Kid, if you know what I mean."

This was getting so far out of hand I was having a tough time keeping myself from laughing. I almost felt sorry for Rusty, but that's not why I knew I had to step in. It was more like I could feel Stan's dough slipping further and further away.

"Excuse me, Rusty. Could I speak to you a moment? Outside?"

"Uh, sure. Would you guys, well, you guys just help yourself to more food and I'll be right back."

"This is crazy," I said, as we walked a few feet down the hall.

"I know. But this is the way these things are done out here, Henry. It's all about negotiation. Don't worry. I know what I'm doing."

"It looks to me like you're losing control."

"It might seem that way, but trust me, I'm not. I'll give him what he wants. It's no big deal. He'll get me the money. I'll give Stan back his money. You can go back to New York and I'll take care of everything else. The film'll get made. I'll make money. He'll make money. Jolene will fade into film mediocrity. Que sera, sera."

"I need to walk out of here with a check in your hand and then I'm heading back to New York with the million bucks."

"Well, it might not work exactly like that. But the wheels are turning and that's a good thing. Look, I'm going to be honest. You might have to stall Stan a little, but it's going to happen. I promise you. You just have to be a little patient. Within a week or two, Stan will have his money."

"Not from what I've just seen."

"I know it looks a little like a circus, Henry, but believe me, I've seen worse. There'll be a little more back and forth. Josh'll go back and do a little work on the script. We'll add a part for Jolene. She'll love it. Terry will come up with the dough. We'll sign a couple of actors, get the trailer made, and it'll be great.

Ibrahim will come up with the rest of the dough and Stan will get his money back, with interest."

"A real Hollywood ending."

"Exactly."

"So I'm not leaving here with the money tomorrow, am I?"

"I'm afraid that's not possible. But I'll tell you what. You come back next week and I promise I'll have the money. Not only that, you can watch us shoot part of the trailer. How's that sound?"

"Sounds like the royal run-around. Where's the money, Rusty? I mean, exactly who's got it?"

"You mean like right this minute?"

"Yeah. Like right this minute."

"Well, I couldn't exactly tell you that."

"Okay, let's back up a little. You took the money from Stan. What did you do with it?"

"I brought it out here with me."

"Then what did you do with it?"

"I gave it to someone."

"Who did you give it to?"

"Well, that's kind of confidential information. You know, on a need to know basis."

"That's good, because I need to know. If you don't give me that confidential information, then not so confidentially I'm going to take out my phone and I'm going to not so confidentially call the cops."

"You wouldn't!"

"Sure I would. Then I'll get on my flight back to New York tomorrow. And you know something? I will not feel the least bit bad about it. And you know why? Because I'll just be doing what I'm being paid to do.

His face flushed and his body began to vibrate slowly, like a low jolt of electricity had been shot through him. "But that wouldn't get Stan's money back and his career would be finished and he'd be the one who'd be in as much trouble as I would."

He was right. Maybe he looked and acted stupid but he wasn't stupid. He knew I was bluffing.

"If you don't tell me I'm just going to have to fucking beat it out of you and don't think I won't."

He laughed. "You won't do that, because that's not the kind of guy you are. But if you really want to know, if you really have to know, and this is totally between us, not even Terry or Josh know...Ibrahim has the money. He's the moneyman. He's already put up some of his own dough and he's not about to refund any of mine before the project gets off the ground. So, as soon as Terry comes up with his share, I'll use it to pay back Stan and everyone will be happy. Okay?"

I could see this was as good as it was going to get.

"I'll call Stan and see what he says."

"Tell him I'm sorry. I didn't mean to cause him all this trouble. Really. I didn't. I promise he'll get his money. Really. He will. I'm not a crook. You'll see. By the time this is over, you and me, we'll be friends. That's the God's honest truth."

I wanted to tell him there was no chance of that, but the funny thing was, I wasn't so sure he wasn't right. Stranger things have happened. Consider me and Goldblatt, for instance.

PART 3
NEW YORK

"That depends a good deal on where
you want to get to."
—Lewis Carroll,
Alice's Adventures in Wonderland

"What is ordered must sooner or later arrive."
—James Fenimore Cooper,
The Last of the Mohicans

10
So You Want to Make a Deal

Stan was not pleased when I called and told him I wasn't returning with his million bucks. He cheered up a little when I explained I found Rusty and promised to return the following week to get his money.

"Do you really think he'll have it, Henry?" Stan asked plaintively.

"I do," I lied, not so much to save his feelings but to save me from having to listen to anymore of his whining.

I didn't mention Rusty's claim that he was simply making one more investment for Stan's company. Why bother? Rusty might be one more run-of-the-mill hustler, but it was also possible he was telling the truth and really didn't mean to rip off Stan. Besides, Stan didn't care about Rusty's intentions. All he wanted was his money back.

I told him I'd book a cheap flight back to L.A., stay at a cheap motel, pick up the money from Rusty, then bring back Stan's dough and be done with it. That seemed to calm Stan down a bit.

The red-eye delivered me to Kennedy a little before six a.m. I hopped a cab and was back in my apartment by seven. As soon as I walked in the door, my cell buzzed.

"Welcome home, partner," Goldblatt sang cheerfully. "How'd the trip go?"

"How the hell did you know I was home? Have you got a fucking surveillance camera set up outside my building?"

"Don't need one. Didn't I ever tell you I'm psychic?"

"No. Somehow that never came up in conversation."

"Well, I am. Besides, we've got a special bond between us. You know, like the thing twins have…"

"Give me a fucking break, will ya?"

"So was it a fruitful trip?"

"That's not why you called."

"Mr. Grumpy."

"I'm tired. And I haven't slept in over twenty-four hours."

"Apology accepted. Take a nap. We've got a meeting set up this afternoon."

"What are you talking about?"

"You're meeting with Mary Jones and Tom Seligson, you know, the guy who hired us to take care of that art thing. We're gonna go over some details of the plan. You think I been sitting on my ass playing Candy Crush while you were gone?"

"I have no idea what Candy Crush is and, to be honest, I was kind of hoping you'd forget about this whole harebrained idea."

"Not a chance. I'll see you at Klavan's at noon. And get this, Mary's making us lunch."

No wonder Goldblatt was practically singing; there was a meal involved.

After a short nap I walked uptown and we convened in the Klavan dining room a few minutes after noon. I could see Goldblatt was not totally pleased with the lunch menu, which included plenty of vegetables and no meat. Somehow, he managed to keep his mouth shut about it. The only time he broke protocol was when he asked Mary if she had any bread to accompany the rest of the meal.

Mary disappeared into the kitchen and moments later she reappeared, much to Goldblatt's delight, with a large loaf of warmed up French bread. It wasn't on the table more than a few seconds before Goldblatt grabbed it and proceeded to tear generous hunks. "You wouldn't happen to have any butter?" he asked, as he scooped various salads—chicken, couscous, Mediterranean, shrimp and some mystery concoction she identified as quinoa—onto his plate.

"I think so, but I also have olive oil, if you'd prefer. It's a nice, healthy alternative."

I cringed. Naturally, Goldblatt opted for butter.

Tom Seligson was a good-looking guy in his early-sixties, dark-complexioned, salt and pepper hair cropped short, nattily dressed in dark trousers, a herringboned sport jacket and a powder blue button-down Oxford shirt, open at the collar. After introductions, we got down to business.

"First of all," Seligson said, as Mary passed around plates of food, "I want to thank you, Henry, for getting involved in this. I feel like an idiot. But it's not really about that or the money. I don't think these guys should be allowed to get away with something like this. If they've done it to me I'm sure they've done it to others. I want to stop them."

"I wouldn't normally touch something like this with a ten-foot pole," I said. "It's not what I do and frankly, I'm not sure we can pull it off."

"Sure we can," said Goldblatt, hand-signaling Mary to serve him more salad.

"It might even be illegal," I said.

"I'm a lawyer, I know what's legit and what isn't," said Goldblatt.

"You *were* a lawyer." I shot him a look. He shrugged and began to eat. "And if you really knew what was legit you'd *still* be a lawyer."

"Politics," grunted Goldblatt, as he tore off another hunk of bread. "And since when are you worried about what's legal and what's not?"

"Boys," said Klavan.

"I know it's a bit sketchy," said Seligson, "but Goldblatt assures me bottom-line we're okay."

Klavan laughed. "No offense to Swann, Tom, but that's something he couldn't care less about."

"He's right, Tom. Right and wrong rarely figures into the equation. Best to get this straight from the get-go, I'm no super-hero here to right wrongs. There are no capes hidden in my closet. It's all about the money."

Mary finished serving and sat down next to Klavan.

"I'd like to thank you, Mary, for helping us out," said Tom.

"It sounds like fun," said Mary, a pretty, slim, dark-haired woman who wore a pair of striking black-framed eyeglasses, jeans, and a wild yellow and green print shirt that looked like one of her abstract paintings hanging throughout the apartment.

"So here's the deal," said Goldblatt, who was already well into his second serving. "Mary's agreed to give you a crash course in modern art. You'll spend a few hours this afternoon with her, Swann. You're good with that, right?"

I nodded. I wasn't exactly starting from ground zero. I had taken that course in college—Art in the Machine Age. It wasn't planned. I saw it on the course card of a pretty co-ed I was sitting next to in the auditorium during registration. I took the class but never managed to work up nerve enough to say anything to her during the entire semester.

"And then, when you're up to speed," Goldblatt continued, "we'll set up the meeting with Raucher."

"Where's this meeting supposed to take place?" I asked. "Obviously, it can't be here and it certainly can't be at my shithole and, Goldblatt, I don't even know if you have a place to live."

"Don't worry, smartass. I've got a collector friend who's going to let us use his apartment for the meet," said Goldblatt.

"Suddenly you've got an awful lot of 'friends,'" I said.

"Why shouldn't I? I'm a friendly guy."

"What if they check any of this out?" said Klavan.

"I'm sure they will. But don't worry. All is taken care of," said Goldblatt. "You're gonna use the name of my friend, and his apartment and I've got your backstory all worked out."

"How the hell do you know how to set up a backstory?" I said.

Goldblatt smiled. "I've led a very, shall we say, checkered past. I keep telling you that but you don't believe me. Someday, maybe, I'll write a book."

"Maybe you should read one first," said Klavan.

"Very funny, Klavan" said Goldblatt. "But you don't get through four years of college and three of law school without cracking a book."

"It's not my usual role to play peacemaker," I said, "but in this case, since we're all supposedly on the same side, why don't we try to keep the hostility in check and focus on making sure I don't screw the pooch."

"Good idea," said Seligson. "There's a lot riding on this."

"Speaking of which, Tom," said Goldblatt, "we haven't actually discussed remuneration yet."

"I don't think this is the time or the place," I said.

"Goldblatt is right. I'm not asking all of you to do this for nothing. Since money is not the point as far as I'm concerned, I'd like to make sure you're all well compensated. I'm willing to put twenty-five thousand plus expenses on the table, and you all can figure out how you want to divide it amongst yourselves."

"Sounds fair to me," said Goldblatt.

"So long as I do the dividing," I said.

Goldblatt glared at me.

"What kind of risk are we taking here?" I asked.

"I don't think these people are dangerous, if that's what you mean," said Seligson.

"They're nothing more than low-level con men," added Goldblatt.

"I've been down this road before, folks, and believe me when there's money involved, especially big money like this, there's always the risk of physical violence," I warned.

"Do you think I'm not offering enough considering the possible danger? I don't want anyone to get hurt," said Seligson. "But I don't mind throwing in another ten grand."

"I think that'll be fine, so long as the job remains pretty much what we've been talking about," I said. "But I think we should reserve the right to renegotiate if there are complications."

"If things change, I'll be happy to sweeten the pot," said Seligson.

"So we've got a deal," said Goldblatt, as he cleaned his plate with the last of the French bread. Turned out he'd polished off the whole loaf himself.

"Yes, we've got a deal," said Seligson. "I'll make out a check to you, Goldblatt."

"That'd be me you make it out to," I said.

Goldblatt made a face. He was about to say something but I shot him a look that shut him down. "I guess that makes more sense. I haven't had a chance yet to set up a corporate account, so you might as well make it out to Swann and he'll make sure we all get our cut. Won't you, Swannie?" he said in a tone that left no mistake as to how he really felt about it.

After lunch Klavan excused himself for an appointment to check out a book collection. Before he left Seligson wrote out a check for the retainer while Mary went into the bedroom to collect her things. I walked Goldblatt to the door.

"I really do gotta do something about that business account," he said.

"No rush. I'm fine with the way things are."

"You don't trust me?"

"I trust you as much as I trust everyone else."

He shrugged. "I know what that means. But someday, Swann, you're gonna recognize this partnership is a good thing—for both of us—and that it's not a temporary thing. And then we're gonna actually run it like a real business. In the meantime, you may not trust me but I trust you, so I'm gonna *trust* that you're gonna give me my rightful share. If you need me to be with you when the dude comes over to that apartment, just let me know. For back up, I mean."

"I'll be fine, but thanks for the offer."

"By the way, how did that L.A. thing go?"

I shrugged. "I have to fly back there next week."

"I hope it's not going to interfere with this deal."

"I've juggled two balls before."

"Just don't drop this one. That's a nice chunk of change he's putting on the table. We have to deliver."

I spent almost three hours at Mary Jones's studio in Chelsea. She spent a lot of time on Rothko who, she explained was an American painter of Russian Jewish descent. "He's generally lumped together with the abstract expressionists, but he rejected this label. Along with Pollock, he was one of the most famous post-war abstract painters. He was part of a group that included Ad Gottlieb, Barnett Newman, Louis Schanker and John Graham, all of whom were greatly influenced by Milton Avery," she explained, showing me numerous samples of his work, as well as those of his contemporaries.

Finally, just as my head was starting to explode and the jet lag was beginning to take its toll, she proclaimed, "I think that's pretty much all you'll have to know. Think you'll be okay?"

"I think I know enough to fake my way through."

"You're a quick study. You'll be fine. Tomorrow, you, Ross and I should visit the apartment of Goldblatt's friend and make sure you're acquainted with all the work he's collected. You could blow the whole thing if you mess up on something so basic."

"I'll have Goldblatt set it up. And thanks, Mary."

"Are you kidding? When would I ever get a chance to be part of a scam like this?"

11
How the Other Half Lives

The next morning I got an e-mail from Goldblatt providing me with the name and address of Charlie Schulman, whose apartment and identity I was borrowing. He followed up with a call in which he tried to convince me to let him accompany me.

"You don't want to overwhelm the guy, do you?"

"He's my friend," Goldblatt said. "I don't think he'll be overwhelmed."

"You'll be a distraction."

"Is that how you think of me, as a distraction?"

"One of many ways. How do you know this guy?"

"I know a lot of people. He's one of them."

"I'm not going to get any more out of you, am I?"

"Not unless you let me tag along."

"That's not happening."

"Partners share. You don't want to share with me, I won't share with you."

"I think I could get used to that arrangement."

"You'll change your mind," he said.

I didn't think so.

Schulman's penthouse apartment was in a Tribeca loft building. Schulman, who met us at the door, was in his early-fifties. A handsome man, a little over six feet, he was wearing white cotton trousers and a light blue polo shirt. He had a full head of curly brown hair, and a prominent nose that somehow seemed at ease with the rest of his face.

His apartment was a knockout. Most of the main loft space, which I estimated to be well over fifteen hundred square feet, was completely open, with only a steel grey sectional couch, a few glass tables, and a few contemporary, plush black leather chairs strategically placed throughout. Three separate areas were partitioned off. Bedrooms, I guessed. There was a kitchen area in one corner of the loft with an island separating it from a spacious dining area, which held a dining room table large enough to seat at least a dozen, with as many chairs placed around it. The stark, white walls were covered with art, much of it modern abstract, several of which I recognized stylistically from the artists Mary had drilled me on the day before. Light streamed through the floor to ceiling windows, as well as a skylight over one portion of the loft, heightening the effect of being in a modern museum rather than a New York City apartment.

There was also an expansive outside area, perhaps another thousand square feet, where I spotted several chairs and a few round tables with umbrellas attached, as well as a number of impressive sculptures.

After we introduced ourselves, Klavan couldn't restrain himself. "Man, this is some place you've got here. There's some serious coin here."

"Wise investments," Schulman said in a way that led me to believe we weren't getting any more out of him on that subject.

I tried reading him from his body language and the expression on his face, but didn't find much to work with. There was something suspect about the way he said "wise investments." I didn't have a good feeling about Schulman, but perhaps that was because I couldn't quite figure out his relationship to Goldblatt and what might have brought them together. There was a good reason Goldblatt was reluctant tell me how he knew Schulman. I just didn't know what it was.

"Let's have a seat in the living room and we can get started," Shulman said. "Can I get you anything?"

"We're good," I said, not wanting to drag this out any longer than it had to be.

"Mind if I take a look at your lovely art while you boys chat?" asked Mary.

"Be my guest."

"My wife's an artist," Klavan said with pride.

"I'm always on the lookout for new artists."

"I wouldn't exactly call myself a *new* artist, but it would be my pleasure to have you visit my studio some time. I'll give you my card before we leave," said Mary, as she headed toward the far wall.

"So, gentlemen, I understand you'd like the loan of my loft as well as my name," Schulman said as he settled into one of the chairs then rested his feet on a matching ottoman, leaving the couch to Klavan and me.

"That's right," I said. "How is it you know Goldblatt?"

"We go back a ways. I owe him a favor. I don't like owing anyone anything. This is my chance to even the score."

"Did Goldblatt explain why we need the place?"

"He said I'm better off not knowing, which knowing Goldblatt I'm sure is true."

Mary wandered back. "You've got quite an impressive collection here, Mr. Schulman. Twombly, Rothko, Rivers, Alex Katz, Grace Hartigan, even a small Pollack."

"Thank you." He glanced at his watch. "I'm afraid I've got to be somewhere by noon. Shall we get started?"

"How about a tour of the place, and maybe you can tell us something about each painting, like how and where you obtained it, and how much you paid for each work," I said.

"The tour is fine, but I'm afraid I can't talk price or

provenance. That's not the kind of information any collector wants out there for public consumption."

"I just need a sense of the market and, if asked, at least I'll be able to tap dance my way through the answer and not look like a complete idiot. And a little background on yourself would also be helpful."

"So you're going to be me, are you? There are people out there who think one of me is more than enough." He smiled broadly. His teeth were much too even. A guy like him could buy a new set.

"A much less well-dressed version," I said.

"Maybe you ought to borrow some of his wardrobe, too," cracked Klavan.

Schulman stood up. "Might as well get started."

Although he refused to give exact prices for his collection of artwork, Schulman did give me a ballpark figure of what each piece was worth on today's market. But he refused to say much else, like how he obtained each work. He also refused to let us take photographs, and the only paintings he would show us were the ones in the living and dining room areas. This left me with the uneasy feeling they might not all have been purchased through the usual legitimate channels. After doing some my own research on the art market, I knew that over the years plenty of valuable paintings have been stolen and never re-covered. They had to be somewhere. Did some of them wind up here, with Schulman? Was that why he was so reluctant to talk about his collection and why he wouldn't show us the other rooms?

I kept telling myself I was on the side of the angels, that I was righting a wrong. How different was this from the days I was repoing cars because their owners defaulted on payment? But there was something about this that just didn't seem right.

"Well," said Klavan as we stood outside Schulman's building, "whaddya you think about this whole deal? Think you can pull it off?"

I shrugged. "There's something about this job that doesn't feel right."

"Maybe that's because Goldblatt's involved," said Klavan.

"Not right in what way?" asked Mary, as we headed toward the subway.

"He certainly doesn't mean morally or ethically, Mary."

"Ross!" said Mary, pushing at his shoulder.

"He's right, Mary. I stopped measuring behavior in terms of right and wrong a long time ago. Who decides what's ethical and what's moral?"

"If it's not that, then what is it?" asked Klavan, as we began to stroll toward the Spring Street station.

"I can't put my finger on it, but for one thing, I don't see why Seligson doesn't go to the cops about this."

"What's he gonna say? They didn't really do anything illegal. They're just a couple of hustlers, so I don't see anything wrong in hustling them."

"I don't suppose it matters. Seligson is paying us, so I'm going through with it."

"That's my boy," said Klavan, patting me on the shoulder. "This is America, pal. Anything for a buck. So when's the caper going down?"

"I love it when you use words like caper, Klavan. It gets me hot."

"Me, too, Ross," said Mary as she took her husband's arm and tucked it in hers.

"So when's all this going down?" Klavan asked again.

"I'm meeting Goldblatt tonight for dinner. I'm sure he'll give me the timetable."

"If you need backup, another phrase I've always wanted to use, I can hang around with you when Raucher shows up at *your* loft. I wouldn't mind being a fly on the wall when that happens."

"I think I'll be fine."

"I could play your wife," said Mary. "You know, be there to try to talk you out of buying anything, like any good wife would."

I winced. The word *wife* took me to private places I did not want to go.

"It hasn't exactly worked on me, baby," said Klavan.

"I think having you there would only be a distraction," I said.

"Our friend here likes to work alone, Mary."

I met Goldblatt at John's, in the East Village, a throwback to a '50s restaurant where the large dining room reeked so heavily of garlic it seemed to be embedded in the walls. It was Goldblatt's first time there and he was quite impressed by the menu, especially when he spotted the large portions waiters were delivering to the surrounding tables.

"You shoulda told me about this place before," he said, as he perused the menu while gripping a huge hunk of buttered Italian bread in one hand.

"I figured I'd spare them a visit from you."

"If the food's as good as it looks I might become a regular. Prices don't look bad neither. Not like those fancy uptown joints where they charge an arm and a leg for a lousy salad."

"When was the last time you had a salad?"

"Very funny. How'd it go today?"

"Why don't we order first, then I'll fill you in."

"Okay by me, partner."

I couldn't get used to him using that word. I didn't want a partner. And if I did want one, it certainly wouldn't have been Goldblatt. I like working alone. I need to work alone. It saves me from any illusions that there's someone there I can count on, that anyone gives a damn about me. And yet, I had one now, which was probably why I hated it when he called me "partner."

The thing about Goldblatt is you can never accuse him of having eyes bigger than his stomach. He ordered a large salad— just to spite me, I'm sure—and two appetizers, because he couldn't make up his mind which one he wanted, a plate of chicken parm, which came with a side of spaghetti, as well as an order of garlic bread. He also ordered a glass of red wine, not white, which turned into three by the time the meal had ended. Rules, even culinary rules, mean little to him. I had a small salad, a plate of goat cheese ravioli and a beer.

"So what'd you think of Schulman?"

"He's got plenty of scratch, but I still don't know how he comes by it."

Goldblatt shrugged.

"You going to tell me how you two know each other?"

He waved a hunk of bread in my direction. "Let's just say we done business in the past."

"What kind of business?"

"What does it matter?"

"We're partners, remember, and partners share everything. Isn't that what you keep telling me?"

"I love the way you pull the partner card when it suits you." He shoveled some food into his mouth, chewed and swallowed. "He was in a bit of a jam a while back and I helped him out."

"How's that?"

"I'd rather not say. Confidentiality and all that shit."

"So he was a client of yours?"

"I didn't say that."

"I did. How long ago?"

"What's with the third degree?"

"Just curious."

"You know what they say about curiosity. Let's change the subject. So how're you feeling about all this?"

"Are you asking if I am totally on board?"

"You're on board. We've already taken some dough from Seligso. How do you think we're paying for this meal?"

"It's not the kind of thing I do and there's something a little, I don't know, weird about the whole thing."

"So, let me get this straight, repoing cars is okay but paying back art hustlers, not okay?"

"I do what I do and this is *not* what I do."

"Yeah, yeah, yeah. You're a goddamn fish out of water. It is what you do now, so let's get over it, shall we? You think you're well enough prepared?"

I nodded. "But there is one thing that worries me. Raucher's no fool. I'm sure he's going to do some research on Schulman. There's bound to be a photo of him somewhere, plus information about him, and if Raucher finds anything, the game is over."

"You don't have to worry about that."

"How's that?"

"There are no recent photos of Schulman."

"How could that be?"

"He keeps a low profile."

"What's that supposed to mean?"

"He flies under the radar. He doesn't like to be photographed. He's not the type to get himself on *Page Six*."

"Who the hell is this guy?"

Goldblatt shrugged. "What's the difference? Raucher checks on him he's going to find just what we want him to find. And he won't find any photos. Satisfied?"

"Who the hell are you?"

He puffed up his chest with its assortment of tomato sauce stains on it. "I'm Goldblatt, that's who I am!"

Did Goldblatt really have the power to control the history of someone's life? Did he really have the power to slip me in and out of someone else's skin? I realized I knew very little of my partner's life and what he was capable of.

Even our first meeting was purely serendipitous. I was working for a bail bondsman and one day I got a call from Goldblatt. His client was in jail for armed robbery. The case was ready to go to trial and one of the defense witnesses was missing. Goldblatt hired me to find him. It was an easy job that took less than a day—the guy was a small-time hood and when small-time hoods want to get lost they almost always go back to their old neighborhood, where they think they're safe, where they think no one will think of looking for them. They're wrong. I was just doing what I was being paid to do but Goldblatt treated it as if I'd done him a favor. Doing him a favor meant he owed me the same and over the years I cashed in. Maybe someday I'd find out who and what Goldblatt really was. But that day was not today.

"Seligson's anxious to move ahead. And we can't keep Schulman hanging forever. What say we get it done this weekend?"

"Okay, but I've got to go back out to L.A. Monday. I've already got my ticket."

"I don't like it when *your* business interferes with *our* business."

"That means nothing to me."

"Don't get snippy with me, Swann. You do what you gotta do. But this an important job. We pull it off it means good word of mouth. Good word of mouth means more business. That's what we're after. More business."

"Set up the meeting for this weekend, let's hope the guy takes the bait, then we'll see where it takes us."

Food arrived. Goldblatt called it the second course but I'd lost count. While Goldblatt turned his attention to food—he didn't like to waste time talking while there was a meal to be devoured—I couldn't help thinking about all the mistakes I'd made in my life that had gotten me to where I was now. Goldblatt and others might call it a mid-life crisis, only I was way past mid-life. What the hell *was* I going to do with the rest of my life?

Only when the plates were cleared away and we were waiting for Goldblatt's dessert order, did the conversation resume.

"You still not gonna talk about this L.A. job, are you?"

"Nope."

"I already know it involves Stan, so why not tell me the rest."

"You know what a promise is, don't you?"

"So promises supersede our relationship?"

"You make it sound like we're married, which I'd like to remind you we're not."

Goldblatt pouted, his expression changing only when his tiramisu arrived. "Well," he said, digging into his dessert, "I guess a promise is a promise. But eventually I'll find out."

"Really?"

"No one can keep a secret from Goldblatt forever."

"You think not?"

"I know not. But if you need any help on whatever this secret mission is, you can always come to me."

"I think I can handle it."

"Yeah, well, even though you won't tell me what's going on, I'm still ready to help if you need it. That's what partners do, you know."

"Nice try."

"Whaddya mean?"

"The guilt trip."

"I am mortally offended. I don't need to resort to that. Besides, I know that wouldn't work because I don't I think you're capable of feeling guilty."

"Along with not feeling a lot of other things. So you might as well give it a rest."

Before we parted I agreed to a Saturday morning meeting at Schulman's loft. After that I could focus on Stan's predicament, which was beginning to worry me. I hadn't heard a peep out of Jacobs since I'd left L.A., despite a couple of reminder e-mails I'd sent. I figured he was avoiding me. That wouldn't work for too long.

12
Hook, Line and Sinker

I arrived at Schulman's loft building a little past nine. Schulman had left keys with the doorman who had a knowing look in his eye. Doormen can be a skip tracer's best friend. They know all the secrets of the building. Over the years I've used discontent with their tenants or greed to get information. Most of them, like me, have their price.

There was a note from Schulman on the dining room table, wishing me luck and providing me with his cell number in case I needed him.

Goldblatt, representing himself as Schulman's attorney, and for all I know he was, had been in touch with Raucher. He'd set up our meeting for ten o'clock. Goldblatt warned Raucher I only had an hour, a move that would limit the possibility of my screwing up. Time is the real enemy of most successful crimes. Ask any second-story thief and he'll tell you that.

I did my best to dress the part. Mary had gone shopping for me, providing me with a dark blue, Ralph Lauren Polo shirt, a pair of tan cotton slacks and a pair of slip-on shoes I knew would probably never touch my feet again. "We can't have you looking like *you.*" I would have been offended if she hadn't been right. I'd read somewhere that De Niro wore the same kind of silk underwear Capone wore in order to get him in the right frame of mind to play the notorious gangster in the movie version of *The Untouchables.* I was hoping the same strategy might help me get prepared for the part I was about to play. For a couple of hours, at least, I would be Charlie Schulman.

While I waited for Raucher to arrive I couldn't help nosing

around the loft. I was curious as to what was in those other rooms Schulman had made a point of not showing us. I thought maybe I could find something that would not only shed light on who Schulman really was but, more important, his relationship to Goldblatt. Besides, as Oscar Wilde warned, "I can resist anything but temptation."

Unfortunately, Schulman had wisely locked all the doors. There was a desk in the corner of the living space, but it was simply a slab of glass floating on two white file cabinets, both of which were locked.

A few minutes before ten the house phone rang and the doorman announced that Raucher had arrived and that he was sending him up.

Raucher was younger than I'd imagined, in his early-forties, over six feet tall, with close-cropped brown hair. He was wearing a rep tie, a dark blue sport jacket and grey slacks. His nondescript face reminded me of one of those pug dogs, flattened, a little jowly, the kind of face you forget as soon as the person leaves the room.

"A pleasure to meet you, Mr. Schulman," he said, extending his hand, which was surprisingly dainty, almost feminine.

"Please, call me Charlie," I said with surprising ease.

"Sure thing, Charlie."

"Can I get you some coffee or something else to drink?"

"No thanks. I'm good."

His eyes made a quick pass around the room. I could see he was impressed.

"Why don't we sit over there and get down to business," I said. "I believe my attorney mentioned my time is rather limited."

"You're obviously a busy man. I promise I won't keep you long."

I led him into the living room area, gesturing for him to sit on the couch while I sat catty-corner in the same chair Schulman had used a few days earlier. I even adopted the same pose, arms on the armrest, feet on the ottoman.

"Some place you've got here," Raucher said, as he removed his jacket, folded it in half and carefully laid it beside him on the couch. "You have quite a stunning collection."

"I'd like to take all the credit but I'm a busy man. I don't have the time to do all the proper research, so I've got people who advise me. But I won't buy anything I don't think I can live with, no matter how valuable it might be. I know what I like and what I don't."

"Very wise. Art shouldn't be solely about investment but rather enjoyment. Mind if I look around a bit before I show you what I've got?"

"Be my guest."

He got up and began moving around the loft, with me following a few steps behind him.

"Your curators certainly know what they're doing," he said, as he stopped in front of a small David Hockney painting of a pool. "You've put together a very valuable collection."

"So they say. I understand you have something I might be interested in," I said, as we circled back to our starting point.

"I believe I do. It's a Rothko, and from what I've just seen here I believe it would fit perfectly with your collection."

"Let's take a look."

He pulled out his iPhone, brought up a photo then handed it to me. Bingo! It was the same Rothko Seligson had purchased and then returned.

"Nice," I said, spreading my fingers apart to enlarge the photo.

"It's a beauty, all right."

"How large?"

"About sixty by forty."

"Big."

"He liked to work big. But I'd say you could make room for it here."

"How much are you asking?"

"Far less than its market value."

"How's that possible?"

"I represent a woman whose husband recently passed away, leaving her pretty much high and dry in terms of cash. He had a small collection. This was the jewel. The truth is, she's in a bit of a bind and needs to raise funds quickly. She approached me with her dilemma and I offered to help. It's probably worth close to three quarters of a million, maybe more, but she's willing to let it go for six hundred thousand."

"Why not bring it to an auction house?"

"You know how those work, Charlie. They put it in a catalogue for a sale that might happen four to six months from now. Then you're dependent on how the market it is at that particular time. They also take a hefty commission. My client needs the money immediately. She has estate bills to settle. By the time it's sold at auction, if it sells over the floor she'd set, and the commission is paid, I'm not so sure she'd wind up with much more than she would selling it now at this price. Believe me, it's a steal at six hundred grand."

"I'd have to take a look at it in person, of course. I'm not about to buy something from a photograph."

"Of course."

"What about its authenticity?"

"I can assure you it's authentic."

"So you wouldn't mind if I brought my own expert along?"

"I'd expect that. However, I must warn you that you're not

the only one I'm approaching. My client is anxious to make a deal. If you're interested, I'm afraid you'll have to act quickly."

"I don't like being pressured, Mr. Raucher."

"I completely understand and I don't mean to pressure you. I'm just giving you fair warning."

"How quick?"

"I have another appointment tomorrow morning. And I've already put feelers out to a number of other potential buyers. If any of them meet our price, I'll have to take it."

"If I like what I see, I'm not afraid to pull the trigger. Is the price negotiable?"

He shook his head. "It's already well below market value. If you're not interested, just say so and I'll move on."

He was good. To close a deal you've always got to be ready to walk away.

"When can I see the painting?"

"I can arrange for you to see it tomorrow morning. If you're serious about purchasing the painting I can certainly put off my other appointment."

"I'm not sure I can get my expert on such short notice."

"I'd like to accommodate you, Charlie, but as I said, my client is rather pressed for time."

"Let me see what I can do. Why don't I give you a call this afternoon and if my expert is available, we'll meet tomorrow. Would you mind e-mailing that photo of the painting?"

"I wouldn't mind but the thing of it is, I can't. We don't want it to get around that the painting is on the market. It's a privacy issue. There are other family members involved and my client would prefer they're not made aware of the sale."

"It is hers to sell, isn't it?"

"Yes, but it's a bit of a sticky situation. She's the second wife. The painting was left to her by her husband, but it's a contentious situation and she's afraid if they find out his family might contest the sale, even though I assure you she has every right to sell it."

"I see." I didn't want to seem too anxious and so I added, "Give me a few hours and I'll get back to you with my answer."

He stood up, picked up his jacket, carefully unfolded it, put it on and then scanned the room again. "I have to say, Charlie, the painting would fit in perfectly here. I hope you understand that if you do decide to make the purchase, we'd need a cashier's check."

"Not a problem," I said.

Raucher was good. He knew how to sell himself, which was much more important than selling the painting. I had to believe in him in order to believe his story. And he had to believe I was Charlie Schulman in order to buy mine.

Raucher left me with his card along with a promise from me that I'd get back to him no later than two o'clock. We were moving right along. I had played my part well.

Goldblatt would be very pleased.

13
The Art of the Steal

"How'd it go?" Goldblatt asked anxiously while we stood in line at a SoHo Starbucks not far from Schulman's loft. We were stuck behind several downtown hipsters who would probably describe themselves as "freelancers," instead of what they really were: out of work idlers. I liked it better when people went to work and the streets were left to miscreants like me and the people I spent my life looking for: deadbeats running away from their responsibilities as fast and as far as they could. Now I had to share the day with folks looking for jobs, avoiding jobs, or worse yet, fancying themselves "artists," searching for the meaning of life.

Me, maybe I didn't need meaning. I'm sure I did once, but not now. Now I live day to day, not worrying about the past or the future, just looking to come up with enough dough to pay my bills. Maybe that really was what I was bound to do for the rest of my life.

"Not bad," I said.

"Not bad," echoed Goldblatt. "What's that supposed to mean?"

"It means he took the bait. We have it if we want it."

"Great! It's celebration time. What'll you have, pal? It's on me."

"Iced coffee."

"Tall? Grande?"

"I'm not buying into their ridiculous, meaningless lingo. A good, old-fashioned, well-named medium is fine."

He grunted. "What time is it?"

"What happened to your watch?"

"It's in the shop."

"You didn't hock it, did you?"

"How desperate do you think I am?"

"I don't know. How desperate are you?"

"Just give me the time, will ya?"

I checked my watch. "Eleven-fifteen. Why?"

"Just want to make sure I don't kill my appetite for lunch."

"When did anything ever kill your appetite?"

"I've got a very delicate ecosystem, Swann. I need at least two hours between meals."

"You could have fooled me."

"Yeah, yeah, yeah. Let's just get our order and sit down."

While I sipped my iced coffee and Goldblatt devoured a couple of those scary looking translucent pastries, I gave him the blow by blow of the meeting with Raucher. When I finished, he was smiling, but I couldn't tell if it was because he liked the way things went or he was enjoying his snack.

"What's next?" I asked.

"We take a look at the painting."

"He's going to want the cashier's check for six hundred grand or the deal's off."

"We ain't paying no six hundred grand," said Goldblatt, picking some crumbs from his shirt and popping them in his mouth. "We're going to bargain him down a little. That's how he'll know we're legit. Everything's negotiable. Hell, it's only some paint splattered on canvas. It's only worth what someone's willing to pay for it. We're that someone. We set the price, not them."

"You don't expect me to do the bargaining, do you?"

"I wouldn't trust you with something like that. That takes a pro, so I'm gonna do it."

"Meaning you'll be at the meeting?"

"I'm your expert."

In the past I would have laughed but lately Goldblatt had earned my admiration with his ability to make things happen.

"Okay, say you can bargain him down, can Seligson can come up with dough on such short notice?"

"Not a problem."

"That's an awful lot of money to risk on revenge."

"Seligson's no fool. We're gonna wind up buying that painting for a lot less than it's actually worth because Raucher thinks we're gonna wind up giving it back to him. Seligson's gonna make out like a bandit whether he keeps the painting or resells it. We do our job, collect our dough and we're done with it." He slid his hands together several times and then flicked away air.

"You make it sound easy."

"It is easy."

"In my experience everything 'easy' always turns out hard." I took a sip of my coffee then added more sugar to make it palatable. "'Life is hard and then you die.'"

"What is that, some kind of saying or did you just make it up?"

"John Maynard Keynes."

"What the hell did he know about life?"

"Obviously more than you."

"I don't see what could go wrong. I'll call the dude back, tell him I'm your consultant, and set up an appointment for tomorrow afternoon."

"You really think you can sell that consultant thing?"

"You underestimate me, Swann. I'm a chameleon. Now you see me, now you don't." He feinted his head and shoulders from one side to the other and I couldn't help but smile. "Why should he suspect anything? Since it is the real thing, he won't be surprised when I take a look at it and say it is what he says it is. That's the beauty of his scam. It's foolproof. Only he didn't figure on someone outsmarting him. I'll make the call and set up the meeting and take care of getting the dough. I'll have Seligson give me a check for five hundred grand, not the six Raucher asked for."

"You really think you're going to be able to bargain him down almost twenty percent? What if he doesn't take it?"

"You put half a hero sandwich in front of me, you don't think I'm gonna eat it just because I wanted the whole thing?"

"Point taken."

"But once we're there, you gotta do the selling, Swann. I'm just your art expert. I'm not going to be pushing you to buy it other than telling you it is what he claims it is and it's worth what he's asking for it. It's your money, remember. Sit tight 'til you hear from me," Goldblatt added, as he brushed another mass of crumbs off his shirt.

I had a flight to L.A. Monday morning, so I figured I ought to give Jacobs a call, a reminder I was coming back for the dough. His voicemail picked up. "You've reached Rusty Jacobs's voicemail, leave a message because it makes me feel important." A voicemail message only an exceedingly unimportant man would leave.

"It's Swann. I'll be back there in three days and you'd better have what we agreed on because I'm not coming home empty-handed. Call me back, man. I need to know you got this message."

I figured the chances of him actually calling me back were slim but as Joe Louis said about one of his upcoming opponents, Billy Conn: "He can run, but he can't hide."

A couple hours later, Goldblatt called.

"We're all set. We're meeting him and the painting eleven o'clock tomorrow morning."

He gave me the address, which was the same Chelsea building where Mary Jones had her studio. I promised to meet Goldblatt an hour earlier so we could prep.

The next morning, Goldblatt, clean-shaven, his hair slicked back, dressed in a maroon tie and navy blue sport jacket that actually fit his paunchy frame, met me at ten inside a corner coffee shop.

"Coffee, black," Goldblatt ordered.

"Is that all you're having? If not, order now. We don't have a lot of time."

"I'm good."

"Something wrong with you?"

"What do you mean?"

"I mean I've never sat down with you at a place that offers food where you haven't sampled just about everything on the menu."

"You've never sat with me before an operation."

"Is that what this is?"

"Yeah. I like to have a little edge on me before a caper."

"Now it's a caper?"

"What's your problem, Swann?"

"I don't have a problem. Maybe you ought to relax a little. You look uptight."

"That's the last thing I should do. You either. You snooze you lose. This is not 'uptight,' my friend, this is what focus looks like." He tapped his forehead and trained his eyes on me for several moments to make his point. "These guys are sharp so we gotta be sharper. I hope you got a good night's sleep."

"I hardly ever get a good night's sleep, but that doesn't slow me down."

"I could get you something for that."

"Like what?"

"It's not on the market here yet but it'll put you out like a light, and when you wake up you'll feel better than you ever felt before."

"You're dealing illegal drugs now?"

"Who said anything about illegal? It's used all over Europe."

"That doesn't make it legal here."

"The FDA is way behind the times. If you ask me, this country is over-cautious."

"Really?"

"Too much testing. Too many regulations."

"Interesting."

"What's interesting?"

"I never knew your politics."

"Who said anything about politics? But if you're asking about mine, I'm a Libertarian. Lib and let Lib, is what I say. But I don't want to get into a political discussion now."

"Good."

"Here's the plan. We go up there. You introduce me as your art expert. The name's Herbert Gold."

"Like the writer."

"What writer?"

"Herbert Gold."

"He's a writer?"

"He is."

"Well, he ain't now. Today he's an art expert."

"What if they ask for ID?"

He pulled out his wallet, removed a driver's license with his photo and Herbert Gold's name on it, as well as a business card, also with Gold's name on it and under the name: "Art Consultant."

"Where the hell did you get these?"

"I've got maybe a dozen of these things, all with different names," he said, waving the license in my face. "As for the cards, hell, you can get any kind of card you need made up in less than a day. Cheap, too. The web is a great resource."

"You know this is against the law, don't you?"

"I'm a lawyer. I know what's legal and what isn't."

"You mean you were a lawyer, and," I added, handing him back his phony license and business card, "seeing things like this, it's no wonder it's in the past tense."

"First of all, that's not why I'm not practicing anymore and you know it. Second of all, since when are you the paragon of virtue? Like you've never broken the law. Ha! That's a good one."

"The law is all a matter of interpretation. That's why we have courts. Besides, unlike you, I've never been a sworn officer of the court."

He waved his hand. "Aw, that's just so much bullshit. Lawyers break the law all the time. It's just that some get away with it and some don't."

"And you were one of the latter."

"I told you, I was framed. But I'd rather not get into that now. It's water under the bridge, and as it turns out it might be the best thing ever happened to me. And you. So, here's how it'll go down. You introduce me as your art expert. I take a look at the painting. Then I'm going to pull you aside and whisper in your ear."

"Whisper what?" I asked. I don't know why I got such pleasure out of busting his chops. I just did.

"What the hell does it matter? Anyway, then we go back to

Raucher and you say, 'Yeah, Herb says it's the real thing, all right, but that six hundred grand is a little too steep.' Your money is tied up, you've got other investments in the works. Yada, yada. You tell him five hundred is your final offer. You gotta play the part so you sell the part. You know, sincere. You know how to play sincere, don't you?"

"Is it like whistling?"

"Very funny. Anyway, you do your part, then I'll take it from there and I guarantee we'll get our price. Understand?"

"I think I comprehend the complexities of your ingenious plan."

"Very funny."

We knocked on the door and Raucher, dressed in faded jeans, a button-down white shirt and black V-neck sweater, let us in. The studio was not much bigger than a smallish New York City studio apartment.

"This is Herbert Gold," I said, "my art consultant. I believe you spoke to him yesterday."

"I did. Pleased to meet you, Mr. Gold."

"He's going to take a look at the painting, if you don't mind."

"You're an art expert, Mr. Gold?"

"I am," said Goldblatt, who, for the first time I'd ever seen him, was holding himself with an air of authority. Magically, he appeared slimmer and taller, much less the buffoon. Was it possible that, in fact, Goldblatt was something of a chameleon? Was it possible some of the tall tales he'd regaled me with, and the mysterious past he'd hinted at, were actually true?

"I see that's the painting over there," said Goldblatt, indicating the far wall, which was blank except for the Rothko. Other walls held a number of paintings, none recognizable to me. They looked cheap and tawdry, more like clowns on velvet or dogs playing poker than the kind of art we were purchasing.

"Would you like to take a closer look?" Raucher asked.

"I would, thank you," said Goldblatt as he moved toward the painting, me following a couple steps behind him.

"It's a beauty," said Goldblatt, as he pulled out a pair of eyeglasses I'd never seen him use before. He put them on, adjusted them on his face then let his gaze sweep up and down the canvas, which was two and a half feet wide and probably twice that in height. He took off his glasses, then went into his pocket and removed a magnifying glass, which he held up to the painting while moving it slowly down, then across. He was putting on quite the act.

"Beautiful brush strokes," he muttered. He turned in our direction. "I can say, Mr. Schulman, without hesitation that this painting appears to be a genuine Rothko."

"Of course it is," said Raucher, a hint of irritation in his voice.

"May I ask how you obtained this painting?" said Goldblatt.

"Legally, if that's what you mean," Raucher snapped.

"I didn't mean to insinuate anything, Mr. Raucher. I was just curious as to its provenance." Did I actually hear the hint of an English accent? Goldblatt was masterful. Even I was starting to believe he was the real thing.

"I'm representing an estate."

"Whose estate might that be?" asked Goldblatt

"That's privileged information. I'm sure you can understand the reasons for that."

Raucher copped an attitude. Goldblatt had put him on the defensive. I didn't know if it was purposeful, but whether it was or not it was a smart tactic. Better Raucher dislike and possibly fear Goldblatt, thereby making Raucher less likely to suspect Goldblatt was a phony.

"I'd like to speak to my client…in private, if you don't mind."

"Be my guest."

Goldblatt pulled me aside and whispered, "Go with the flow, Swann. Just follow my lead."

I nodded. I was in awe. Goldblatt seemed to have the situation and Raucher well under control.

"I've advised my client that this painting does have a high probability of being a work of Mark Rothko," Goldblatt said.

"Probability?" Raucher's face reddened. "Look, if you don't believe it's the real thing, we can end this right now."

"Mr. Gold," I said, touching Goldblatt's sleeve. I didn't want to stop him—I figured he knew what he was doing—but at the same time I wanted to stir the pot a little more. "If you have the least doubt about the painting's authenticity—"

"It's authentic," Raucher interrupted. "He just said so, didn't he?"

"Mr. Schulman has retained me to protect his interests and that's what I'm doing," Goldblatt said. "I'm sure, Mr. Raucher, that as a reputable dealer in the world of fine art, at least I presume you are reputable since I have no reason to believe otherwise, you can understand my predilection toward caution. Need I mention the recent Knoedler's fiasco?"

I had only a vague idea of what Goldblatt was referring to, but I did recall reading something about forged paintings being sold by what had been regarded as a very reputable gallery.

"I'm sure we can work this out," I said.

The red began to fade from Raucher's face as I stepped in to take charge. "No, no, I understand," he said. "Totally. You're just doing your job, Mr. Gold."

"Thank you. My client has mentioned your asking price. Under the circumstances, I find it a little on the high side."

"It's quite fair."

"I'm afraid that's a matter of opinion. Right now, the art market is not as hot as it was last year. The most recent auctions at Sotheby's and Swann's—" he looked at me and winked "—would attest to that. There seems to be a softening of the market."

"So you're asking me to lower my price?"

"That's precisely what I'm asking."

"I don't know," said Raucher, squeezing his chin.

"We'll offer half a million dollars. And I'm afraid that's as high as we're prepared to go."

"Are you kidding? That's a hundred thousand dollars less than my asking price, which is already well under market value."

"May I remind you, Mr. Raucher, it's people like my client who set the market price. And today, right here in this room, the market price for this particular Rothko is five hundred thousand dollars. You can take it. You can think about it. Or you can walk away and find another buyer willing to meet your price. Your choice."

Raucher stared down at the floor. We were ready to buy, so he wouldn't let the deal slip away for the difference of a mere hundred grand, especially since he knew he was going to get the painting back with interest. It was a smart play on Goldblatt's part.

"You drive a hard bargain, Mr. Gold," Raucher finally said, his gaze darting back and forth like a snake. "We've got a deal. But only because I'm in a bind and I've been instructed to raise money as quickly as possible...for my client's estate."

"I understand," I said.

"I'll need payment in the form of a cashier's check, of course. Made out to cash, if you don't mind."

"That shouldn't be a problem," I said, reaching into my back pocket for my wallet. I handed him the cashier's check Goldblatt had provided me with.

Raucher smiled and said, "You were pretty confident I would meet your offer."

"We were prepared to walk away if you didn't," I said.

"I assume you'd like to take possession of the painting as soon as possible."

"I would."

"I'll have it delivered after it's packaged properly. We use a bonded service, so there's no risk of it being lost or stolen without you being completely reimbursed for its value, which is now five hundred thousand dollars."

Goldblatt said, "You expect us to leave you with a check for half a million dollars on the promise of delivery? Do we look as if we just fell off the turnip truck?"

"Um...why...of course not," stuttered Raucher. "But you can't take it the way it is now. It must be packaged properly."

"When can you have it ready?" I asked.

"I don't think I can get anyone who can do the job properly before Monday morning. I can have it delivered to you by that afternoon. In the meantime, I assure you it will be safe with me."

"I don't doubt that. But in the meantime," said Goldblatt, "we'll take the check back."

"There's no way I'm delivering the painting without payment."

"How about this? We leave the check with a disinterested third party. When we receive the painting, that party will get a call and you'll receive the check. I noticed there's a Chase bank a few blocks away. That's the bank the check is drawn on. You and I will take a walk over there now and give the check to one of the officers. When we receive the painting, we'll authorize the officer to hand over the check. How does that sound?"

"How do I know you'll make the call?"

"We're all gentlemen here, Mr. Raucher, but if you need some assurance, we'll have the officer make a conference call to both parties at, let's say four o'clock Monday afternoon. Have your service deliver it at that time but instruct them not to release the package until you have the check from the bank officer."

It was a brilliant plan, protecting both sides. I had to wonder if Goldblatt had done something like this before.

Raucher was silent a moment, obviously weighing all the things that could go wrong. Finally, he said, "I guess that works."

"Fine. Mr. Schulman, there's no need for you to waste your time going to the bank with us. Mr. Raucher and I can take care of that part of the deal."

"I'm leaving town early Monday morning, so I'd like to have it delivered to a friend of mine," I said. "His name is Ross Klavan and he's used to taking care of valuable items. He's a rare book dealer."

"I don't see any reason why that can't be arranged," Raucher said. "Write down the name and address and I'll have a bonded messenger service deliver it no later than Monday afternoon at three-thirty. We'll have the bank officer place the conference call at four. I'll need Mr. Klavan's number."

I wrote down the information for him.

He looked at it, folded it, and put it in his wallet. "It was a pleasure doing business with you, Mr. Schulman."

"Likewise," I said. He didn't offer me his hand and I didn't offer him mine.

"I'll walk my client out and wait for you downstairs, Mr.

Raucher, and then we can head over to the bank," said Goldblatt.

"Fine," said Raucher, with a definite edge in his voice.

Outside, I patted Goldblatt on the back. "You were pretty damn good in there."

"You think this is the first time I've been involved in exchanges like this? I'm a pro, Swann, and someday you'll appreciate my talents."

"Nice touch with the magnifying glass. You almost looked like you knew what you were doing."

"You underestimate me, Swann. So do a lot of people. They're usually sorry they did."

"And that was quick thinking about the check and the exchange."

He shrugged.

"But you're not the only one who knows what he's doing," I said.

"What do you mean?"

"While you and he were busy examining the painting I managed to take some photos of Raucher with my phone. I also recorded the entire meeting." I pulled out my phone and showed it to him.

Goldblatt smiled. "You make me proud to call you partner, partner."

"I wish you wouldn't," I said.

"Can't help it, pal. That's what we are."

"I'm going to head over to the bank and stake it out from across the street. When you're finished in there, I'll follow Raucher. I don't want to lose sight of our package and I want to know where he goes next."

14
Follow That Cab

I stood in a doorway across the street and watched as Goldblatt and Raucher emerged from the bank. They shook hands and Goldblatt, after discretely nodding in my direction to let me know he'd spotted me, headed toward the subway. I followed Raucher back to the building. Once he entered, I found a shadowy spot across the street in the doorway of a warehouse, and waited for him to reemerge.

Fifteen minutes later Raucher came out of the building. He carried a large package wrapped in brown paper held together by twine. Why hadn't he wrapped it that way and given it to us? Was he hiding something? Had a switch been made?

Once he hit the sidewalk, he stopped and looked in both directions. I ducked deeper into the doorway. When he seemed satisfied he was on his own, he walked to the corner and hailed a cab headed uptown. He slid the package gingerly into the back seat. I watched the cab pull away then hailed one of my own and instructed the driver to "follow that cab."

The driver twisted around in his seat. "Are you kidding?"

"There's a nice tip in it for you if you don't lose him."

Raucher's cab pulled up in front of a five-story brownstone not far from the neighborhood where I'd had my office back in the day, only a block or two from the old Paradise Bar & Grill. A wave of nostalgia passed over me as I told my driver stop a half-a-block away from where Raucher got out of his cab. I crossed the street and waited a few minutes to make sure he didn't come back out right away. I crossed over and checked the buzzer plate. Raucher's name wasn't there. I pulled out my notebook and wrote down the names that were there. Any one of them might be Raucher's partner.

There was no reason to stick around, so I headed back down to Klavan's apartment.

"How'd it go?" asked Klavan, who was stretched out on his couch, reading a book.

"Good."

"How'd Goldblatt do?"

"Surprisingly well."

"I'll take your word for it, but I still think he's an idiot. Did you get the painting?"

"Raucher's having it delivered."

"You didn't give him the dough, did you?"

"We have a banker holding onto the check until the painting's in our hands. And I took other precautions."

"Like what?"

"I photographed and audio-taped the meeting. I also followed Raucher and I have an address for him."

"Sounds like you've got all your bases covered."

"All but one. I'm going to be out of town Monday and I'd like you to do me a favor.

"What's that and how much will it cost me?"

"Nothing. I gave Raucher your address and asked him to have the painting delivered here."

Klavan sat up. "Listen, Swann, I don't like being involved. In fact, my life's goal is to be involved as little as possible."

"Mary's already involved, which means so are you."

"He doesn't know Mary and he doesn't know me."

"Don't make a big deal out of it."

"Too late for that." He walked over to one of his bookshelves and replaced the book he was reading. "Okay, I'll take the package. But, Swann, in the future, I'd appreciate it if you'd check with me before you make me part of your wacky schemes. I may be a friend, and I may donate space for an office, but unlike Goldblatt, I am not your business partner, and I'm certainly not his."

"Admit it. I add spice to your humdrum life. Once it's delivered, there'll be a phone call. A bank officer will hand over the check as soon as you say the painting has been delivered. The thing is, I'd like Goldblatt to be here to make sure we get the right package. If anything seems off, let him know and he won't release the dough."

"You mean I've got to have that weirdo in my life again?"

"I'll instruct him to be on his best behavior."

Mary walked in. She gave me a hug then asked, "Did it go all right?"

"Very smooth."

"He didn't take the painting with him," said Ross.

"You didn't?"

"These guys aren't into ripping me off by stealing the dough. They're small-time con men. Their game is much more subtle. Besides, you don't think Goldblatt's gonna let us get ripped off, do you?"

"He's a doofus," said Klavan.

"You wouldn't say that if you saw him today. He's a lot more together than he appears to be."

"So he's more than a doofus?"

"Yeah."

"He did get you this far, I'll give him that much. But let's wait and see how this thing plays out before we pin any medals on him. When are they supposed to deliver?"

"Monday afternoon, around four."

"You mean they're delivering the painting here?" said Mary.

"Not my idea," said Klavan

"Oh, goody," said Mary, "I can't wait to get a look at it."

"I'll make sure one of us is here," Klavan said. "Where the hell will you be, Swann?"

"L.A."

"Trying to get back dough for that other doofus. Did you ever think of examining your life to see why you're surrounded by so many doofuses?"

"All the time."

"Any answers yet?"

I shook my head.

"You really think that dude in L.A. is gonna give you back the million bucks?"

"He knows there are consequences if he doesn't."

"I got news for you. Some people don't think about consequences. As for the dough, I know the movie business. It's a black hole. It sucks up money and no one ever sees it again."

"He claims he'll give it to me from the other money he's raised. Frankly, I don't give a damn how or where he gets it. I don't like to lose and I don't give up. It's one of my nastier traits."

It wasn't until later that afternoon that Jacobs finally returned my call.

"It took you long enough," I said in my tough guy voice, the one I honed doing skip trace work up in Spanish Harlem. When you're working without a weapon and you look like I do you'd better come up with other ways to intimidate. The tough guy voice is one of those ways and even I was surprised at how often it worked.

"I'm really sorry, Henry. I got backed up. The good news is, we started shooting the trailer last night. That means we're one step closer to full financing."

"I don't give a shit about that, Rusty. You will have the money, right?"

"Sure, sure, I'll have the money."

"I wouldn't want to come all the way out there and find you were shining me on."

"Why would you say something like that, Henry? We're friends. I wouldn't con a friend."

"Let's get something straight, Rusty. We are not friends. I don't have any friends. And if I did have friends, you wouldn't be one of them. And as far as conning someone is concerned, remember Stan, your boss?"

His voice rose. "I told you, that wasn't a con. It was an honest business misunderstanding. Someday you'll realize I'm telling the truth and then you'll owe me an apology which, because you're now a friend of mine no matter what you say, I'm accepting retroactively."

"Call it what you want. All I'm interested in is getting back the dough. You do have *my* money, don't you, Rusty?"

Silence.

"Would you like me to repeat the question, Rusty?"

"No. I heard you."

"I'll be out there Monday afternoon."

More silence.

"To be honest, Henry, this isn't the best time. I mean we're pretty busy shooting this trailer. I just don't know if I have the time—"

"I show up. You hand me the money. I leave. You get back to shooting your trailer. No time at all."

"Yeah. Well, I wanted you to see us work. You know, so you could go home and tell everyone you were on an honest to

God Hollywood set. Hey, I've got a great idea. How'd you like to be in the film? You know, a little walk on. No lines, so you wouldn't have to be nervous or anything. But who knows what it could lead to."

"That's not happening."

"You want to see how movies are made, don't you?"

"I just want to eat the hot dog, not know what the hell was in it and how it was made."

"It'll be fun. You know, watching how a movie is put together."

"You're not getting this, Rusty. I'm not in this for fun. I'm in it for the money, not to see my face up on the screen. This is not a role I'm playing in a goddamn film. I'll give you a call in the afternoon when I get into town. And you'd damn well better answer."

"Okay, okay. You know, whether you consider us friends or not, I'm looking forward to seeing you again, Henry. You're an interesting guy. And I mean that about you being in the movie. I'll make arrangements for you to come out to the set Tuesday morning. How's that sound?"

"As long as you've got my money, Rusty, I don't care where the hell I meet you."

After I hung up, I e-mailed Goldblatt the audio and photo files of our meeting with Raucher. There was nothing else on my plate so I went online and ordered a couple of Mets' tickets. They were playing Pittsburgh Sunday afternoon. It was early in the season but the Mets were already in mid-season form: losing, which made it easy to get fairly good seats.

I called Klavan to see if he wanted to go. He was busy. I was about to make another call when I realized what I told Jacobs was pretty near the truth. I was pushing fifty and could count the number of friends I had on one hand. I knew a lot of people, but most of them were shysters, con men, miscreants, or worse. I'd spent most of my life on the margins of society so this is who populated my world. As for any meaningful relationship, well, I hadn't had one of those since my wife was killed almost a dozen years ago. After her death, I turned over my son, Noah, to my in-laws, who legally adopted him, and I hadn't seen him since.

I bit the bullet and called the closest thing I had to a friend, other than Klavan. Goldblatt. He was thrilled.

"I'm a Yankees fan myself," he said, "but, man, I love being at the ballpark."

It didn't take long to see why.

By the seventh inning, Goldblatt had consumed three hot dogs, a steak sandwich, an order of fries, a package of peanuts—"You can't go to a ballgame without having peanuts, Swann"—and three beers. He would have eaten more, but the Mets were pretty much out of it by the fourth inning, so I was able to drag him away.

We parted company with me impressing upon him that he had to be at Klavan's no later than three-thirty, Monday. "Try to behave yourself."

"What's that supposed to mean?"

"Mostly keep your mouth shut and wait quietly for the messenger to show up."

"What am I, a child?"

"You don't want me to answer that."

"Maybe this is my chance to show Klavan I'm a stand-up guy. You can attest to the fact that I grow on you after a while."

"Is that what you think?"

Goldblatt gave me that shit-eating grin of his and all I could hope for was that Ross Klavan wasn't there when Goldblatt showed up.

PART 4
HOLLYWOOD

"The way is to be found."
—Confucius, *Book XVIII*

15
The Prodigal Father

I landed at noon, L.A. time, picked up my rental and headed to my cheesy, nondescript motel. I couldn't in good conscience stay at The Beverly Hills Hotel again since this time I knew where Jacobs was. Yes, I do have a conscience, though sometimes you need a magnifying glass to see it

As soon as I got settled, I called Jacobs. He picked up on the second ring.

"Welcome to L.A., Henry," he said cheerfully. "And see, I picked up the call even though I knew it was you."

"You got my money, Rusty?"

"Hey, no hello? No how are you, pal?"

"I'm here for one reason and it's not to make small talk. The money?"

"I'm mortally wounded."

"I couldn't care less. The money?"

"You have nothing to worry about."

"I worry about everything and that doesn't answer my question."

"Why don't you come over to where we're shooting and I'll explain everything?"

I measured each word very carefully so there could be no misunderstanding. "I'll be there, Rusty, but there's nothing to explain. You promised to have the dough and I'm holding you to that promise. If I don't get it, I'm afraid we have a problem. You don't want us to have a problem, do you?"

"Definitely not. But there's not going to be any problem. You'll see. We're in Runyon Canyon. Take down these directions and come on over. And don't worry we'll be shooting well into the night. Have to make every dollar count. Just get here when you get here."

"You do remember the figure, don't you?"

"How could I forget?"

I jotted down directions and told him I'd be there around four, giving myself time to shower and change.

When I got out of the shower there was a message on my cellphone. As soon as I heard the woman's voice I got this terrible feeling in my gut.

"Henry, this is Ellen, Rebecca's mother," a small, thin voice announced. "I hesitated before calling you, but there's something I think you should know. I don't want to worry you...I'm sure there's nothing to worry about...but I thought I should call anyway. It's about Noah. He's...well, we haven't heard from him in several days now. He didn't come home from school Friday. I really don't want to say anything more over the phone. Could you please call me, when you get a chance? I'm sure it's nothing...but please... call when you get a chance, okay?"

I sat in silence, not knowing quite what to think, what to do, not even sure of the significance of what I'd heard. My former mother-in-law was telling me my son was missing. Why hadn't she called me earlier? As soon as I asked myself that, I knew the reason. Why would she think I'd be interested, since I hadn't seen or spoken to Noah in so many years? The guilt I'd bottled up for so long, the guilt that sometimes haunted me in the middle of the night, when I could not sleep, started to bubble up again.

I sat there on the edge of the bed, phone in my hand, not quite sure what I should do, what I should say. I was his father but I hadn't seen him since my wife died and I'd fallen to pieces, unable to take care of myself much less a three-year-old child.

So I did the only smart and fair thing I could do for Noah. I gave him up to my in-laws. They were wonderful people and I knew they'd be able to care for Noah and care about him so much better than I ever could. And when I gave him away, when I abandoned him, even granted them full parental rights, allowing them to legally adopt him, I tried to erase him from my mind. It was the only way I thought I could continue to rebuild my own life and maybe, someday, if I were lucky, if I worked hard enough, I could rebuild a relationship with him. I never forgot him—that would be impossible. I thought about him almost every day, even if only for a second. But I knew the best thing for both of us would be to make believe he did not exist.

But he did exist. And now Ellen was asking for my help. No longer could I believe the fiction I'd created for myself: Henry Swann alone, with no ties, no family, no history. A Henry Swann who only existed in the moment. A selfish conceit created so I could make it from one day to the next. I knew I had to call her back and that making that call might change my life forever, suddenly creating a Henry Swann who *did* have a past.

I took a deep breath and returned the call. It didn't make it to the second ring before she answered. I asked her what was going on

"Noah is missing."

"I got that from your message, Ellen. I can't talk too long. I've got to be somewhere in half an hour." I knew that was insensitive the moment the words escaped from my mouth.

"Where are you?"

"L.A. On a job. Did you call the police?"

"Yes."

"What did they say?"

"That he hasn't been missing long enough, but because he is only fifteen, still a minor, they'd get on it. I think he's run away, Henry."

"Did you check his room to see what's missing, if anything?"

"What do you mean?"

"His backpack, a duffle bag, something he could carry things in. And see if all his clothing is there, especially his favorites. If he kept money someplace check that, too. If he has a laptop, an iPad, see if it's still there. Do it now, Ellen. Then call me right back."

"Do you think everything will be all right, Henry?"

"Yeah," I lied, because how did I know if everything would be all right? Like her, I would think the worst, though I wasn't even sure what the worst could be. "Call me right back."

I hung up and sat on the edge of the bed much longer than I meant to. I wanted to get up and go to where Jacobs was filming, but I couldn't seem to get my body to move. I can't even say what I was thinking as I sat there because my mind moved way too quickly from one thing to another. I pictured my wife. I pictured Noah as an infant, then as a toddler. I pictured us all together. And then I pictured us when we were not. I pictured my wife, in the morgue, almost cut in half by that exploding manhole cover. I pictured myself trying to hold it together at the funeral as a bewildered Noah held tightly to his grandmother's hand.

After what could have been ten minutes or an hour, I finally roused myself and headed out to my rental car. As I started the engine, my phone buzzed. It was Ellen.

"You were right, Henry. His large backpack, the one he uses for camping, is gone. So are a couple pairs of his favorite shirts and jeans. The money he had in his little bank is gone, too. So's his bankbook. And his Game Boy. He never goes anywhere without that. His laptop is here, but I don't see his iPad."

"He's on the run. Do you know how much was in his account?"

"A few hundred dollars, maybe. What he's made from doing odd jobs. We have another account for him, for his college education, but he doesn't have access to that."

"Any idea why he might have taken off?" I asked, as I pulled out of the parking lot. "Did he argue with you? Did he have a fight with Joe?"

"No, no. Nothing like that. He's been a little moody lately, but that's how all teenagers are. It's a stage they go through. Their moods change so quickly. He's been asking about you lately, though, if that means anything. He wanted us to tell him all about you. What you're doing...where you are. How you and his mother met. Things like that."

I felt a pain in my gut. I tried to ignore it, hoping it would just disappear. It didn't.

"Check his computer."

"For what?"

"See what sites he's visited. I suspect you'll find a bus or train schedule site. That should give us an idea where he's headed."

I found the entrance to the freeway and got on.

"Listen, Ellen, I can't talk right now. I'll check in with you later. I assume Noah has a phone. When I hang up, I want you to call me back. I'll let voicemail pick up and I want you to leave Noah's phone number."

"It won't do you any good. He doesn't pick up, Henry. He only responds to texts and he hasn't responded to any of those since he's been missing."

"Just do what I say.... Let me to talk to Joe."

"He's at the police station."

"They're not going to find Noah, Ellen. If he ran away, which I'm sure he did, he's not a priority for them. They'll take down all the information but they won't do much. Besides, he's had too much of a head start and if he's out of the state they have no jurisdiction. Talk to his friends. They'll know more than they're willing to say, but if you keep at them, you might find out something that'll tell us where he's headed. Do you understand what I'm saying?"

"Yes."

"I'll call you in a couple hours, or you can get back to me before that if you learn anything. In the meantime, Ellen, I want you to e-mail me a recent photo of Noah. Don't worry, everything's going to be fine."

"I hope so," she said, her voice trembling. "I'll speak to you soon."

Twice I missed the proper turns to Runyon Canyon. I couldn't think of much other than Noah as I made moved closer to Jacobs and his merry band of filmmakers. I tried to picture what Noah looked like now, but I could not. All I saw was the sad confused face of a three-year-old. I'd asked Ellen and Joe never to send me any photographs, and although they didn't understand my request, they complied. As a three-year-old, he favored his mother, but kids change. Did he look anything like me now? Was he angry? Did he hate me? He should. No matter how you sliced it, I abandoned him. He'd never understand it was for his own good, or that I did it out of love. Why should he? How could he? He was a kid. There are no underlying motives when it comes to children. They are completely literal. They see what is in front of them, in shades of black and white. There is no grey. There are no explanations, there are facts. How could he know my letting go of him was for the best? I could have kept in touch. I could have visited. But I didn't. The why was simple: I wanted to erase him from my life, not because I hated him, not because I didn't want the responsibility of raising him, not because he reminded me of my wife and the life we'd built together. It was because I knew I couldn't take care of him the way he deserved to have been taken care of. Hell, I was hardly able to take care of myself. I've spent the last dozen years of my life looking for things other people have lost in a futile attempt to retrieve what was missing from my life. My gift to Noah was allowing him to have a normal life with normal people who were capable of loving him the way he deserved to be loved.

But how could I expect him to understand that when I wasn't sure I did?

As I drove, I made all kinds of elaborate pie-in-the-sky deals as to how I was going to redeem myself once Noah was safe. I would be the one to find him and when I did, we would build a new relationship, a relationship of father and son. I would get to know him and he would get to know me. I would find Noah and in that moment I would be his father again.

Runyon Canyon is part of a large park at the eastern end of the Santa Monica Mountains. Not the kind of park I am used to: Central Park, Prospect Park, Bryant Park and Washington Square Park. This was a real park, a huge park, a park that included mountains and fields and canyons and streams.

There is a southern entrance, but I headed toward the northern entrance on Mulholland Drive. It was a favorite spot for hikers, many of who took their dogs with them for long walks in the fresh air. The highest point of the park, Indian Rock, was most accessible from the Mulholland entrance.

I parked the car and started hiking up the trail. It was close to four o'clock and it must have been close to ninety degrees with little or no breeze to cool things off. Jacobs said I'd find him halfway up the trail. I had no idea where that would be, so I kept walking until I spotted a number of people clustered around a long, picnic-size table.

I spotted Jacobs, wearing khaki shorts, a green T-shirt, and one of those safari-type hats. He stood next to Josh and they appeared to be going over the script. There was a guy holding a boom mike and another hanging onto a handheld camera, as well as a couple of actor types who were peering down at scripts then lifting their heads long enough to utter a few lines. What was probably the rest of the crew sat around reading newspapers or playing on their cellphones. There was no sign of Ibrahim or Terry, but I spotted Jolene sitting alone in a director's chair under a tree about one hundred feet away from the rest of the group. She was reading a magazine and chewing gum with admirable vigor.

"Hey, boys," I said, as I approached, slightly out of breath.

Rusty looked up. "Henry, you made it. I'm so glad you're here. You remember Josh, don't you?"

"The boy genius."

From the sour look on Josh's face I could tell he didn't find that moniker particularly amusing.

"We're right in the middle of fiddling around a little with this scene," Rusty said. "It's not working the way it's supposed to. But I'm not worried. Josh here can make it better. Can I offer you a bottled water, Henry? It's over there, in the cooler. There's beer and soda there, too." He pointed to a clump of trees to the left. "Help yourself. And when you get back, I'll introduce you to the rest of the gang."

"I'm not interested in meeting the rest of the gang, Rusty. Let's not prolong this any more than we have to."

"Sure, sure, but first get yourself something to drink. Then we'll talk."

I glared at him. He got the point. Talking wasn't what I was there to do.

I helped myself to a bottle of water. The plastic container, wet and cold from the ice, felt good as I held it against my forehead before I opened it and took a couple swigs. When I got back to Rusty and Josh, they were still huddled together.

"Josh, it isn't working, man. All I'm asking is for you to change a couple lines. This isn't fucking *Citizen Kane*, for Chrissakes."

"I'm the writer, Rusty. I know what works and what doesn't work."

"I'm not disputing that, Josh. But it's obvious this isn't working the way it's written. Derek won't say the lines because he says he's not 'feeling it.' And if we want to get Kevin Sorbo in on the action, this has to be perfect. He's not going to sign up for a movie that's got lame dialogue."

"Lame? Are you fucking kidding me?" Josh slapped the script against his thigh. "My fucking dialogue isn't lame. It's real, man."

"I'm not looking for real, Josh. I'm looking for something that'll get us out of here before we lose light. Let's just get through this. All we need is to get something Derek can fucking 'feel.'"

"Derek's feelings are of absolutely no importance to me. Just let him say the fucking line the way I wrote it and then we can get the hell out of here. I'm sweating my ass off."

No wonder. The boy genius was wearing a pair of heavy jeans and a ratty crimson sweatshirt that had Harvard printed across the front. I've never met anyone who's attended Harvard, even for a short time, who doesn't let you know within the first two or three sentences they attended that Ivy League bastion of education. Josh didn't even wait that long. He had it emblazoned all across his scrawny little chest. But anyone can buy a sweatshirt, so I couldn't be sure Josh had ever come anywhere near Cambridge.

Rusty lowered his voice as he put his arm around Josh. "We all want to get out of here, Josh. That's why I want you to make a few changes. And if you don't make them, honest to God I will."

"It's my script, Rusty."

"It's *our* script. I came up with the idea. You just executed it."

"Just?"

"It's my money, Josh, therefore what I say goes."

"I hate to interrupt," I said, "but technically it's *my* money. Or at least it will be very soon. Isn't that right, Rusty?"

"What's he talking about?" said Josh.

Rusty swiveled to face me. "Henry, why don't you let me finish with Josh and then we can discuss our business." His tone had turned dark. His face was alarmingly red. The heat or the argument? I couldn't be sure. "Why don't you go over there and keep Jolene company. Maybe run lines with her or something. We won't be long. Ten minutes, tops. I promise."

"What the fuck's he talking about, Rusty?" Josh persisted.

"Nothing."

I looked over to where Jolene sat. In the shade. It's where I wanted to be. "Okay. But I haven't got all day, or what's left of it."

Rusty gestured to a young girl, holding a clipboard, who was standing with the actors. She rushed over, as if the sultan had beckoned.

"Melissa, would you mind getting Mr. Swann a chair and

bringing it over to where Jolene is sitting." Rusty turned to me. "Josh and I will sort this out, get the shot, then I'll be all yours."

I grunted my best tough-guy grunt then headed toward the shade of the old apple tree. Melissa dragged over a chair and set it up next to Jolene, who looked up from her magazine, smiled flashing me a perfect set of white teeth, and said, "Hey, how ya doin'?"

"I'm doing just fine, Jolene."

"Henry, right?"

"Right."

"You're the private eye guy."

"Yeah. That's me."

"Darn, it's hot out here, isn't it?" She closed the magazine and began fanning herself.

"You're from the south, shouldn't you be used to the heat?"

"What I'm used to, honey, is air-conditioning."

"Where's your boyfriend?"

"Back at the hotel. He was here for a while this morning but he couldn't take it no more. To quote him, 'It's too damn hot and this is too damn boring.' So he left. He don't understand the movies, is all."

"He's right. Looks pretty boring to me."

"Oh, no, honey. Nothing could be further from the truth. There's something happening all the time. Look at those two." She stopped fanning and aimed the magazine at Josh and Rusty, who were still going at it. "They're real creative geniuses, trying to make this film even better than it already is."

"You think that's possible?"

She looked at me straight in the eye and said in a surprisingly serious tone, "Of course it's possible, honey. The trailer's got to be perfect so Terry can go out and raise more money, else we don't have us a movie and all them acting lessons Terry paid for was for nothing."

"So how's your part coming along, Jolene?"

"It's coming along fine, honey. Thanks for asking. 'Course it was a lot smaller but Rusty and Josh have put their big ol' genius heads together and I tell you, it's just getting better and better."

"Yeah, they really are geniuses, aren't they?"

"You know, I been thinkin' 'bout your name and all. It's so pretty and all. I know it ain't none of my business, but I was just wondering, is Swann your real name?"

"As opposed to borrowing it from someone else?"

She laughed. "No, honey. I meant did you change it from something else, 'cause everyone out here seems to have changed their name from something to something else."

"How about you?"

"Oh, no. Terry says I have the perfect name for the movies. Jolene Campbell, like the soup. Or like that *Wichita Lineman* fellow."

"I'm sure Terry knows what he's talking about."

"So is Swann your real name?"

"Afraid it is and believe me, there isn't a joke you can tell or a reference you can make that hasn't been done before. So, Jolene, why don't you tell me about the movie?"

"Well, I don't know if I'm allowed to. It's, like, supposed to be hush-hush, top secret."

"We're in this together, so I don't see why we should keep secrets from each other. Like Rusty said, we're all on the same team."

She looked me in the eyes. Mine are blue, but not as blue as hers. But it was not the Caribbean blue of her eyes that surprised me. It was what was behind that. If I were involved with her, she would break my heart, not because she was beautiful and sexy, but because she was a whole lot smarter than she let on and because she was completely in control. And when she didn't need me anymore, or Terry anymore, or Rusty anymore, she would kick us into the street and move on to the next guy who could give her what she wanted. That's what I saw in those stone-cold blue eyes of her. And that's when I started to feel sorry for Terry.

"That's quite a ring you have there," gesturing toward the enormous rock on her left hand.

She looked down. "It sure is somethin' special, all right. It's a gift from Terry. Not an engagement ring or nothin', 'cause Terry ain't even divorced yet."

I couldn't help wondering about this Christian values stuff they were trying to peddle. But then what could I expect? A Jew, an Arab, a pole dancer, a soon to be divorced philander and a kid who probably didn't believe in God at all get together to make a movie based on good old-fashioned Christian values. Pursuing this conversation was going to get me nowhere, so I almost dropped it. But I couldn't help myself. "I didn't realize he was married," I said.

"Oh, it ain't really a marriage when two people aren't in love with each other. As soon as we get back Terry's goin' right back to North Carolina to file the papers."

"He's promised to marry you?"

"It ain't come up in so many words, but I'm in no rush to be married. I was once, you know, back when I was still a teenager. It was a big mistake. Only lasted but four months. I hardly remember his name. Just between you and me, Henry, I'm not so sure the married life is for me."

"I think you're onto something, Jolene. That's when all the trouble starts. So tell me about the movie."

"It's about this young girl who leaves home to come out to Hollywood to become a star."

"That would be you?"

She laughed. "Well, aren't you the sweet-talking gentleman. No, honey, that couldn't possibly be me. Least not yet. But we're working on it." She winked. "Anyways, this girl comes out to Hollywood and she falls in with the wrong kind of people, which you know could easily happen because there are an awful lot of bad people out here."

"I've got news for you, Jolene, there are bad people everywhere."

"Yeah, but nothing like out here. Terry says it's like Sodom and Gomorrah. You know, from the Bible. Anyway, this young girl gets involved with this cult-like thing and then her daddy comes out to find her and bring her back."

"That would be played by Kevin Sorbo?"

"We sure as heck hope so."

"What's your part?"

"I play this woman the runaway girl befriends when she first gets here, like an older sister, you know? And when her daddy gets out here, he meets up with me and we start looking for his daughter together. In the original script, Bethany, that's her name, had a small part, but Rusty and Josh have really been beefing it up so that now I'm the sidekick for the father. That would be the B line. It's kind of a nice dramatic adventure story with lots of action, but it also has meaning, you know, talking about the difference between right and wrong, about strong family ties. I'm not in any of the action part, that's put in there for the kids, to get them to come. The other stuff is for their parents. Between you, me and the lamppost, I hope there's a little romance brewin' 'tween me and Mr. Sorbo. That would be nice, don't you think?"

"I'm no movie expert, Jolene, but the plot sounds a little familiar."

"You don't understand the film industry very well, do you, Mr. Swann?"

"I'm afraid I don't. Since we've got nothing but time maybe you ought to explain it to me."

"First of all, there are only like eleven basic stories in the world."

"I think that's seven, Jolene."

"No, I'm pretty sure it's eleven. Anyways, no matter what you write you're bound to hit on one of them. And the other thing is, people don't want to see something different. They want to see something they've seen before, something they recognize, only a tiny, little, itty bit different. You know, somethin' that takes them outta their comfort zone, but not too far out. People don't like that. It makes 'em feel stupid and nobody wants to feel stupid, right?"

She didn't wait for my answer, not that I had one. I just wanted her to keep talking because for some reason, maybe it was the accent, the sound of her voice was drowning out the voice in my head that kept asking if Noah was safe.

"...but that only happens when you've got a great screenwriter like Josh and a great producer and director like Mr. Jacobs."

"Rusty's the director?"

"Just for the trailer part. After that, we're gonna get ourselves an honest-to-goodness real big-time director, one with a big name and what they call a track record. So, what we're doin' is to make it the same, only a little different, if you understand what I mean."

"An oxymoron. You know what that is, don't you?"

"I'm afraid I don't. But you could certainly enlighten me. I love learnin' new things."

"It's a figure of speech that juxtaposes elements that appear to be contradictory. You know, like cruel kindness, or business ethics, or act naturally."

"That's very interesting and I really appreciate your putting it into a sentence for me. I'm going to use that with Terry tonight and see if he knows what it means. But I don't understand how the word 'act naturally' fits into that, 'cause it's what we actors are supposed to do, isn't it? Act naturally?"

"You know something, Jolene?"

"What's that, honey?"

"I've got a sneaking suspicion about you."

"Really? Now, what would that be, honey?"

"I think you're a damn good actress."

She laughed and started fanning herself again. "Now how would you know that about me? You haven't even seen me act yet."

"Sure I have."

She looked me in the eye, her sweet, innocent hick from the country look disappearing for a moment. "Now, where would that be?"

"Right here. Right now."

"What could you possibly mean by that?"

"I'm talking about this dumb country girl, gee-whiz act."

"I surely don't quite understand what you're getting at, Mr. Swann," she said, her eyes actually twinkling. Don't ask me how she did it but she did.

"You'd like me and everyone else to believe you've got sawdust for brains, but I think you're smart as a whip. I think you knew exactly what an oxymoron is."

"How's that, honey?"

"Because you didn't have that faraway look in your eyes when I used the word 'juxtapose.' You know that word, there's a damn good chance you know what an oxymoron is, and a lot more."

"Aren't you the smart one?"

"Not necessarily. But I know people. I know when they're lying, which is most of the time, and when they're telling the truth, which is not so often. And I know when they're putting on an act, even if they're very good, like you. I'm willing to bet money you graduated college."

She stopped fanning, leaned back and smiled.

"Rambling wreck from Georgia Tech?" I guessed.

"Bryn Mawr, actually."

"Never would have guessed that one. So, what's with the dumb act?"

She shrugged. "It gets me where I want to go."

"Like with Terry."

"Like with Terry. I usually wind up getting what I want by playing what people expect me to be. Sometimes it's better to be the person people think you are rather than the person you really are. But congratulations, honey, you've cracked the code."

"How about telling me straight, Jolene? Where's the money coming for all this?"

She leaned close enough for me to smell a combination of jasmine and honeysuckle. "Rusty and Terry would kill me if they knew I was talking about this," she whispered.

"I can keep a secret."

"You know something, Mr. Swann, I believe you can. The way I understand it, Rusty himself has put up a good bit of the money. Mr. Ahmad also put up some money, or at least he's promised to. I'm not sure if they've actually got his yet. And

Terry, well he'll be putting up some money now that he knows my part's going to be substantial enough. But I hear they're still looking for more investors. You wouldn't be interested, would you?" she asked, her eyes blinking wildly.

"Not unless they need change for a buck. How much do they need to make the movie?"

"Oh, I don't know. Terry was throwing around numbers like five or six million."

"Sounds cheap in terms of today's budgets."

"Rusty's supposed to be a whiz at milking a budget, massaging the numbers. At least that's what Terry says about him."

"That doesn't leave much for the actors."

"I'm not worried about that. I'll get all kinds of exposure...and I don't have to take my clothes off to get it."

I tried hard to keep from imagining her without clothes. Turned out that was a losing proposition.

"Terry thinks we'll make our money on the backend," she continued.

"What do you think?"

"It's not something I think much about. I've got my own agenda, in case you haven't figured that out yet."

"I have."

"Besides, if they ever get this thing made, they'll make money. These kinds of movies do really well at the box office without opening up in New York or Hollywood. I'll bet you didn't even know they existed."

"You'd be right. But I don't know if you're making the right decision here, Jolene."

"What decision is that?"

"Hitching your wagon to Terry and Rusty's star."

"You're worried about me?"

"I guess I am."

"Well, ain't that sweet," she said, suddenly recovering her lost accent. She leaned over, put one arm over my shoulder and kissed me lightly, briefly on the mouth. It felt good. I wanted more. But I knew she wasn't going to give it to me. Not then. Not there. She was an actress. The kiss wasn't meant for me. It was meant for her.

She leaned back and smiled. "You liked that, didn't you?"

"I won't lie."

"Are you still worried about me?"

"Not in the least."

I wanted her to do it again, but I knew she wouldn't. It was what it was and that's all that it was.

I looked over to Josh and Rusty. It appeared they'd finished their discussion. Rusty gave Josh a pat on his shoulder, then headed for us, looking a little grim. "Okay, Jolene, we've got it all worked out. We're ready for your shot. You good on your lines?"

"Yessir, got 'em down perfect," she said, her voice melting back into that sugary obsequiousness that was part of the character she was playing, both off and on-screen.

"Great. Why don't you stand over by Tex so he can make sure the lighting is perfect, too. I'll be right there."

"Sure thing." She got up and positioned herself so that she was standing between me and Rusty. "I'm sure I'll be seeing you again, Mr. Swann," she said, extending her hand. I didn't know if she wanted me to kiss it or shake it. I did the latter. She winked, dropped the magazine on her chair, then headed off toward the cameraman, who leaned against a tree smoking a pencil-thin, brown cigar.

"She's a real piece of work," I said, as Rusty plopped into Jolene's chair.

"She's trouble."

"I know. Can she act?"

"She's working on it. I'd say she's got potential."

"More than you know."

"Huh?"

"Nothing. How about my money?"

"Oh, yeah. We're very close on that."

"Close is not a word I want to hear. All close means is you don't have my money yet."

"I'm very close. This close." He squeezed his thumb and forefinger together. "Another day of shooting with Jolene and I'll have all I need to prove to Terry we're on the up and up."

"What about the money you started with, Rusty? The money you stole from Stan."

"I hate that word 'stole,' Henry. Invested is the right word."

"Not according to Stan. He doesn't think it was an investment. He thinks you stole it."

Rusty shook his head back and forth slowly. "That's the way Stan represented it to you, but it's not the truth."

"It's my truth, Rusty. It's Stan's money, or his investors' money, or the Tooth Fairy's money, or the fucking man-in-the-moon's money. It's anyone's money but yours. Stan wants it back, he's paying me to get it back, so I'm here to get it back for him."

"He will get it back, with interest. I swear. He just has to be a little patient."

"It's not his patience you should be concerned with, Rusty. It's mine. I'm having a particularly shitty day. It's hot. It's sticky. I hate L.A. I hate the people. I hate the air. I hate that it's fucking sunny every fucking day. I want to get the hell out of here as soon as possible, but I'm not leaving without Stan's dough. And I don't mean a personal check that bounces as high as the moon. I want a cashier's check or I want it in cash, but I want it. I don't plan to spend the rest of my life hanging out with you and Jolene and Terry and Ibrahim, and that little pissant cum laude, Josh."

"I hear you, Henry, and I sympathize with your position."

"Go fuck yourself, Rusty."

"Whoa! I thought we were friends."

"I'm afraid you've been misinformed. I am not here as your friend. I am here in a business capacity, a business I'd like to conclude as soon as possible. Friends hang out. Friends have a beer, go to dinner, catch a movie. You and I do not do that and we will not do that. Ever."

"But if you'd be patient I can make it worth your while."

"How's that?"

"You're the kind of man who could be very useful to this production. How does the title 'Executive Producer' sound to you, plus points, of course?"

"Why do I have the feeling that executive producer is to movies as bank teller is to banking?"

He laughed. "I like you, Henry. You've got a great sense of humor. That's a very winning personality trait in a person. It goes a long way out here, by the way."

"Cut the bullshit, Rusty. Right now I am the most serious person you're ever going to meet. I don't want anything to do with your goddamn movie project. I just want what I came for."

"You're absolutely, one hundred and ten percent right. Give me one more day, okay? And in the meantime, stick around and maybe I can use you in one of the shots. You'd like to be in a movie, wouldn't you?"

I sighed. No matter what I said I could see it wasn't registering with him. There was nothing I could do but wait and hope that he'd really come up with the dough. I would give him one more day.

"Yes, Rusty, it's been my lifelong dream."

16
No Direction Home

I wanted out of there as quickly as possible, but Rusty insisted I stick around and even convinced me to do a "cameo" in the trailer or, as he put it, a "walk by." I was to walk down the Runyon Canyon trail as the "principals," Jolene and some well-muscled dude in a tight T-shirt, a stand-in for Kevin Sorbo they assured me, passed me going the other direction. When I jokingly asked Josh what my "motivation" was, he gave me a blank stare.

After I performed my walk by, Rusty yelled "Cut!" like he was a professional director. He asked for another take, but I told him that once I got started in a direction I wasn't about to turn around.

When I got back to my car, I sat down in the passenger's seat, flipped on the air-conditioning, called Ellen, and asked her if she'd spoken to any of Noah's friends.

"They all said they didn't know anything," she replied, "except his best friend, Chris, who gave me the name of Noah's girlfriend. I didn't even know he had a girlfriend, Henry. I should have known that, right?"

I ignored her question because I didn't know the answer to it.

"He's with her," I said.

"You think?"

"What did you find out about her?" I asked, as I pulled out my notebook and pen.

"Her name is Delilah Baker. Chris said they met in acting class."

"Noah's interested in acting?"

"Oh, yes. I'm sure I wrote you about that. He's been in a couple of school plays. Nothing big, of course. He's a little shy so I never would have thought he'd do something like that, but evidently it's good for him to be someone else, even if it's only for a few hours."

Just like his delinquent dad who wanted to be anyone other than who he was. Suddenly, I felt closer to my son than I ever had. It was an uncomfortable feeling, one I wanted to shake. The only way to shake it was to turn back into who I was: Henry Swann, finder of lost souls.

As for knowing about the acting, it was probable Ellen did write about it, but those letters mostly remained unopened, collecting dust in a desk drawer. I didn't have the stomach or the heart to read any of them. The less I knew about Noah, the better. And yet I didn't throw them out. Maybe because I thought someday I'd have the strength to read them, the strength to face myself. But the way I was going that would probably be a long time in coming, if ever.

"Did you find anything on the computer that might help?"

"I asked Chris to come over and he checked what he said was the history, and found Noah had checked out the bus schedules from Minneapolis to Los Angeles."

My heart started pumping loud enough to hear over the low steady hum of the air-conditioning. My son, the boy I hadn't seen in almost twelve years, might be only miles from where I was now. I could hardly get out the next words. "Is there anything else, Ellen?"

"Chris told me Delilah moved out of town not long ago and he thought Noah went to visit her. I asked him where Delilah was, but all he could tell me was somewhere in Los Angeles."

"If she's here, I'll find her. And if he's with her, I'll find him, too. Please remember to send me the most recent photo you have of Noah. And see if you can get a photo of Delilah. Ask Chris if he can find one. If he can't, try the school. They'll have something. As soon as you get it, send that to me, too."

"Of course. I'll do that right away. And thank you, Henry."

I wanted to tell her not to thank me. That he's my son. But the words stuck in my throat, or someplace far deeper than that. Instead, all I could manage was a pathetic, "Don't worry about anything, Ellen. I'm sure I'll be able to find him. Send me that information as soon as you can."

I couldn't do anything about finding Noah until I heard back from Ellen, so I slid over into the driver's seat, started up the engine, and headed back to my motel. Part of me wanted to drive straight back to New York, back to the people I knew: Klavan, Goldblatt, and the other denizens of the deep. Here, in L.A., with its overwhelming feeling of isolation and alienation, I felt as if I were melting away into nothingness. All I wanted was to clear up the matter with Rusty, find Noah, go home, and burrow my way back into the deep, dark, uncomfortable hole I'd dug for myself.

As soon as I got back to my room, my phone rang. It was Klavan.

"Your package arrived," he said.

"Did you open it?"

"We did."

"Is it the real thing?"

"Goldblatt said it was the one you saw at the studio, so he had the check released. When will you be back?"

"Not sure. There've been some complications."

"About getting the dough back?"

"That and something else."

"What else?"

I wasn't sure I wanted to talk about it but the urge to share—oh how I hate that word—with someone was too strong because, without thinking, I blurted, "My son is missing."

"I didn't even know you had a kid. Come to think of it, I don't know shit about your life."

Of course he didn't. No one does. That's the way I want it. The minute someone thinks they know you, they begin to have assumptions about you. They try to give meaning to everything you do. Why would I want someone thinking they know me when I'm not even sure I know myself?

"I don't like talking about myself," I said, hoping that would kill any further conversation.

Instead, Klavan pressed on. "What's this about you having a kid and about him being missing?"

"He's fifteen, almost sixteen. He lives with his grandparents in Hibbings, Minnesota, wherever the hell that is. I haven't seen him since he was almost four, since my wife died."

"Well, I'll be damned. I didn't even know you had a wife. What happened?"

"She died."

"How?"

"Accident."

"You don't like talking about this, do you?"

"You can tell?"

"And the kid's missing?"

"He ran away. There's a good chance he's here in L.A. Followed a girlfriend. I need to find him before I come back."

"I get it. Listen, if there's anything I can do to help, let me know. Okay?"

"Thanks."

I didn't want to talk anymore. I'd already said too much. I pressed the disconnect button.

I was going to shut the phone down altogether but before I could it rang again. It was Goldblatt.

"Hey, pal, how's it going?"

"Fine."

"That mean you'll be back soon?"

"Not necessarily."

"Whaddya mean. You're not going all Hollywood on me, are you?"

"Not yet."

"Then what's keeping you out there?"

I'd said enough about Noah. I certainly didn't want to tell Goldblatt. It was none of his business and besides, I didn't want to get into a whole discussion which, with Goldblatt, is exactly what it would have been, including some kind of bullshit advice that would somehow end in doing what was best for him, not me.

"Business."

"You disappoint me, Swann."

"How's that?"

"I always thought of you as an efficient man. Whatever it is, it's taking you much too long. I hope not too much longer. The painting arrived at Klavan's and I released the check."

"I know. Klavan called."

"I figure we got about a week before Raucher's partner contacts you, talks his way into Schulman's, apartment, and plants doubt that the thing is legit."

"Seligson's got the painting, which is supposedly valued at way over what he paid for it, and he's not going to give it back, so why not just let it go at that?"

"Because he wants revenge."

"I can't be bothered with that petty bullshit. We've already pulled off the most important part of the operation. We got him the painting for way under market value."

"Not to him. The most important part for him is revenge."

"Screw him."

"Jeez, what bug crawled up your ass? You're even crankier than usual."

He was right. I don't apologize much, but this time I figured I should. After all, it wasn't Goldblatt's fault my life was falling apart at the very moment I was trying to figure out how to put it back together.

"Sorry. Bad day."

"Apology accepted. Like I said, I hope you don't have to be out there much longer. We don't get the other half of our dough until the job is completed."

"Mark Twain was once asked, after it rained for a few days straight, 'Do you ever think it'll stop?' His answer was simple and to the point. He said, 'It always has.'"

"Which means you'll be back when you'll be back."

"Precisely."

"Okay, but I hope it's sooner rather than later. I got bills to pay and my cut ain't that big to begin with. Which is something we have to discuss when you get back."

"Maybe you can cut down on your expenses, starting with your food consumption."

"Don't be ridiculous. I need all those calories for all the walking around I do."

"That's funny because I don't think I've ever seen you walk."

"I can't wait 'til you get back, Swann. Your insults are so much more entertaining when they're dished out in person."

17
One Thing Leads to Another and Then Another

My meeting with Rusty wasn't until tomorrow so I had some time to look for Delilah Baker. I typed her name into a search engine and found a fit. Delilah Baker had a public Facebook page. And according to her status it appeared as if she'd recently moved to West Hollywood.

I clicked on her timeline and found plenty of pictures of her and her friends. Her last post was from a few days ago, a selfie of her standing in front of Grauman's Chinese Theatre, with the caption: "Looking for my star. Haven't found it yet, but it won't be long. LOL." I went through her profile pictures, close to three dozen of them, and found a couple that looked recent. I downloaded them to my phone, alongside a couple photos of Noah Ellen had e-mailed earlier. I hadn't yet had the nerve to even look at them yet.

The Bakers were too new to Los Angeles to be listed in the telephone directory, but I figured since the kid was only sixteen she'd have to be enrolled in a school. I got a list of high schools in the West Hollywood area then made a few calls. West Hollywood Opportunity School, on Fairfax, had Delilah Baker listed as a new student.

With less than three hours sleep I planted myself in front of the high school, a few minutes before eight. By eight-thirty no one who looked like Delilah had made it to the front entrance. Time was running out so I cornered a couple of girls who looked to be the right age. One recognized Delilah from the Facebook photo.

"Yeah, she's the new girl, right?" the girl said, squinting over a pair of oversized sunglasses.

"You know her?"

"Not really."

"But you know who she is?"

"Yeah. Maybe I might have a class with her. Like English, maybe? She's kinda stuck up, I think."

"Her name's Delilah Baker."

She shrugged.

"Then you don't actually know her?"

"Not really. Like know her, I mean."

"What's your name?"

"Jessica."

"Well, Jessica, do you know someone who does know her?"

"Like I said, she's kinda snobby, but I think maybe she hangs out with Cat."

"How do I find Cat?"

"I could, like, text her, I guess."

"Could you do that for me, honey?"

She shrugged.

"It's important."

"How important?"

"Very."

"You're not some kind of perv, are you?"

It was too complicated to give her the long answer so instead I said, "No. I'm looking for my son, Noah." I showed her the photo of Noah, without looking at it myself. "Does he look familiar?"

"Nah."

"How about texting Cat and seeing if she knows where Delilah is or where she lives?"

"Okay, but you know she might already be, like, in class and we're not allowed to, like, use our phones while we're in class."

"She can text you back later. I'll give you my number and then you can text me."

Jessica pulled out her phone and got to work, her fingers flying across the small keyboard with amazing speed.

"I have to get to class now," she said.

I gave her my card. "Don't forget about me, Jessica. I'm afraid my son might be in trouble and Delilah can help me find him."

"Okay," she said, "but it's probably, like, better if you text your number to me because I might lose this card."

She gave me her number and I texted mine. Then she disappeared into the building, and I suddenly realized I'd left Noah's fate in the hands of a ditzy teenager.

I drove around West Hollywood aimlessly, killing time. Maybe in the back of my mind I was hoping I might catch sight of Noah or Delilah wandering the streets. By noon I was hungry and sick of driving, so I parked the car at the first available spot and grabbed lunch at one of the numerous outdoor cafes on Hollywood Boulevard.

When I finished, I called Rusty to find out where he was.

"I was just going to call you," he said.

"I'm sure."

"Really. I was. You know what you are, Swann?"

"Yeah, but neither of us has the time or the stomach to hear the list."

"You're a cynic, that's what you are."

"And you're an excellent judge of character. So what? Where are you?"

"In Venice, on the boardwalk."

"It's a big place. I'll need directions."

"If it's inconvenient, we can meet tonight."

"We'll meet as soon as I get over there."

They weren't far from what's known as Muscle Beach off the Venice boardwalk. Rusty instructed me to walk past that playground for muscle heads until I saw a skateboarding area. That, he said, was where they were shooting for the afternoon.

A trip that should have taken no more than half an hour took close to an hour. But that's L.A. for you. Nothing is close to anything else. It's all just a bunch of nothing.

I found a parking spot a few blocks from the boardwalk. I walked past shops that hawked T-shirts and caps and all kinds of other crap, plus small cubby-holes that boldly advertised medical marijuana, until I spotted the area Rusty had described. There were two deep concrete pits, where ten to fifteen skateboarders were doing their thing, diving down into the pit, then coasting back up, defying gravity.

Rusty and Josh were standing together at a railing, in deep conversation, not unlike the way I'd left them the day before. Jolene was nowhere in sight, nor did I see Terry or Ibrahim.

I came up behind Rusty and tapped him on the shoulder. His body twitched.

"Nervous, Rusty?"

"Henry. I wasn't expecting anyone."

"You were expecting me."

"Oh, yeah. I was expecting you and now you're here. You've come at the right time. We were about to make an important shot here. It's gonna blow your mind. These kids do some fantastic things on their boards. It's really gonna add a great cinema reality feel to the scene. It wasn't in the original script, but Josh figured a way to work it in."

"That's because he's a fucking boy genius."

"Yeah. Right. He's a genius."

"I'm not here to watch you make a movie, Rusty."

"Yeah, sure, sure. I understand, but…"

His head was bobbing in all directions. I wanted to grab it and hold it still. So I did.

"That's a word I don't want to hear, Rusty. The word 'but' means there are complications. I don't like complications because in this instance that only means you don't have my money."

"I have it. I just don't have it here. On me."

"That is the very definition of not having it. And you've wasted a good two hours of my time. I don't think you want to do that," I growled in my best tough-guy voice. He wasn't taking me seriously and I don't like it when people don't take me seriously. I'm a serious guy. At least that's what I like to think. "When there's a but, there are also consequences." I started to walk away.

He grabbed my arm. "Wait a minute. Wait."

I turned. "Why should I wait, Rusty? You don't have the money. There's nothing for me to wait for."

"But I need your help."

"You need *my* help?"

"Yes. I want you to help me."

"Help you what?"

"Help me get the money back…and some other money, too. *Our* money."

"You've got to be kidding!"

"No. Really. I'm not kidding. Let's go over there, to that café. We can sit down and have a civilized conversation. I can explain everything."

"We're way past civilized conversation, Rusty. You've been giving me the runaround for a week now and I'm losing what little patience I had."

"I understand your position, Henry. I really do. I don't

181

blame you for being pissed off. If I were in your position I'd be pissed off, too. But you have to understand, I'm as much the victim here as anyone else."

"Are you kidding me?"

"No. And if you just give me fifteen minutes of your time, you'll see what I mean."

I looked at my phone. No word from Cat or Jessica. There was nothing else I could do, so why not give this clown fifteen minutes?

"Okay. Fifteen minutes. That's it."

"Thank you, Henry. Believe me, after you hear what I've got to say, you'll totally understand my predicament and I even think you'll wind up sympathizing with me."

I'd ask myself how do I attract these kinds of people, but I know the answer. I was and always have been a magnet for losers, poseurs, imposters and the impossibly lost. We do not choose our professions randomly. They choose us. I shudder to think I choose these people to be in my life, but it is probably true. I know the true nature of man. Working in the element in which I work my opinion of our species only lessens. I have learned we are capable of anything and everything. I have seen the depths to which people can fall and the more I see the more I wonder if I am any better than the lowest of the low. Have I been corrupted by those around me or am I just naturally one of them? What am I not capable of doing? And most important, is this the way I was going to spend the rest of my life?

Once we were seated amidst bare-chested pseudo-surfers, bikinied chicks and assorted weirdoes, I got right down to it.

"What's your story? And you'd better make it a good one."

"It's not a story," he said though I could barely hear him over the din of a bongo player beating his instrument no more than ten feet from us. I wanted to strangle the poor guy.

"Hold on a second," I said. I got up, climbed over the waist high barrier, approached the drummer, waved a twenty in front of him and said. "Look, pal, take a break for fifteen minutes and this is yours."

He grabbed it and sat himself down on a bench on the boardwalk. He pulled out a joint, lit up, and I returned to my seat in the café.

"Nice work," said Rusty.

"I'm not the type to sit around and let things happen to me, Rusty. I make them happen. You might want to keep that in mind."

"I shall remember that," he said, taking a swig of his iced coffee.

"I don't have all day. Let's hear it."

"You mean my story?"

"No, not your story. I don't have time for stories. I want a story I'll watch some crummy Hollywood movie. I want the truth. Why you don't have my money. The short, *true* version."

"Okay. Here it is. The truth. First of all, like I said before, I didn't steal the money. Stan knew exactly what I was doing. I had his blessing."

"Then why does he say you stole it and why does he want it back?"

"Maybe he got cold feet. Maybe he thought better of it. You'd have to ask him."

"I don't want to ask him. I don't need to ask him. As far as I'm concerned, it's his money because he says it is. You have it and now he wants it back."

"That's where you're wrong."

"How's that?"

"Well, I don't actually have it. Anymore."

"Then where the hell is it?"

"Okay, so here's what happened. God's honest truth." He raised his left hand.

"You might want to try the right hand, Rusty."

"Oh, yeah. Sorry." He put down his left and raised his right. "Ibrahim is our moneyman, right? I got him involved because he was going to be the executive producer. I was in charge of raising the money, that's how I got Stan involved and that's why I found Terry. Anyway, whatever money I raised went straight to Ibrahim, who promised to double whatever I gave him. He was going to be the one to pay all the bills. And he has. Up 'til now. That's how I have enough money to make this trailer. He gave me fifty thousand dollars."

"You gave him a million and he gave you fifty thousand? That doesn't sound like very sound business practice, Rusty."

"Maybe not where you're from, but that's the way things are done out here. And that's all I needed for this part of the project. He was going to hold onto the rest. Then when you showed up wanting the million back, I went to him and asked him for what was left. That, plus the money Terry was going to give me would have been enough to give you the million and get you and Stan off my back."

I held my head in my hands.

"Let me guess. Ibrahim has disappeared into the night."

"How did you know?"

I shook my head, then rested it in my left hand because if I didn't I thought it would fall off my neck. "I know people, Rusty. That's my job. I didn't like him from the moment I saw him."

"Why?"

"Because he just fucking sat there in the goddamn corner playing with his fucking Blackberry. He didn't say a goddamn word. He didn't even look up. He didn't engage. He didn't seem the slightest bit interested in what was going on. Because all he fucking cared about was you handing him the dough. And when you asked for it back, he disappeared. Am I right?"

"Yeah. That's exactly what happened. I really thought he was off somewhere and wasn't getting my messages. That's why I told you to come back Monday. I was sure I could find him by then and get the money. Or, at the very least, I could get Terry to come up with enough to cover what I owe Stan."

"But that didn't happen."

"Not yet. I'm sure Terry will come up with something, but I don't think it'll be enough. And I was hoping you might be able to help."

"How's that?"

"By finding Ibrahim."

"That's not going to happen."

"Why not?"

"Because I'm not being paid to find Ibrahim. I'm being paid to find you and bring back the dough."

"But that's part of bringing back to the dough. If you find Ibrahim you'll find the money and then you can bring it back to Stan."

"Who's going to pay me for that, Rusty?"

"I figured it was part of your job. You know, bringing back the money."

"You figured wrong. I work for pay. I don't do jobs for nothing. This is the way I make my living. You may think it's just another form of stealing, but it's not. It's honest work. Something you might not be familiar with."

"That's a low blow, Henry. I thought you were better than that."

"Obviously you were wrong."

"Then I'll pay you if I have to."

I laughed.

"What's so funny?"

"How much money do you have in your pocket right now, Rusty?"

"Oh, I don't know, a couple hundred. Maybe a little more. Petty cash, in case we need it."

"And that's pretty much all you have, right?"

"I've got a little more. But I owe on some bills. And I always pay my debts."

"Not always."

"But this wasn't my fault."

"Whose fault was it, Rusty? Mine? Stan's? Jolene's? Obama's?"

"What I mean is that I fully intended to repay the money, with interest, but then I trusted someone who turned out to be a thief."

"Trust is a bitch, Rusty."

"You're a cynic."

"Maybe. But I don't owe someone a million bucks I can't pay."

"I can pay it. Just not right now. And I will be able to pay it if I can find Ibrahim. That's why I need your help."

"What makes you think even if I could find him, which I'm not going to, that I could get the million bucks from him?"

"Because I'm not stupid. I've got proof I gave him the money. Signed receipts. If you find him and he doesn't pay up, I could go to the cops and have him arrested. And then deported. I don't think he wants to risk that. So you've got to help me find him. Then everything will be fixed."

"I've got other things to do, Rusty. More important things."

"Sure, sure, but this is important. To me. To you. To Stan. And remember, you're working for Stan—you owe him—and if you find Ibrahim, you'll have your money and you can keep your promise to Stan and everyone comes up smelling like roses."

"I don't like roses. When I smell them I'm forced to think of something nice and sweet and comforting. I don't want to think of something nice and sweet and comforting, because it would be a damn lie. I want to wallow in the truth, Rusty. I hear enough lies in my life. I even tell them to myself. I don't need to hear them from roses or you or anyone else."

"I'm beginning to feel sorry for you, Henry."

"Don't feel sorry for me, Rusty. Feel sorry for yourself. You don't have the dough and you're the one going to jail. When I tell Stan you don't have it, that's exactly what he's going to do. Go to the cops and you'll wind up doing time in the Greybar Hotel."

"He hasn't done it yet."

"Only because he hired me to get it for him. When I don't come through for him he simply pays me what he owes me, then he looks around for other options. His only other option is the cops."

"Even if you don't help me, I'll have the money eventually. When we finish this trailer, Terry can use it to raise all the money we'll need. And more. This Christian movie thing is a sure bet. We're playing with the house's money. Listen, how about this? If you do this for me, find Ibrahim and get my money back, then I'll cut you in on the film. I'll give you a piece of the action. Plus, I'll pay you your daily fee. I've got enough for that. I'll even pay that in advance. What do you say?"

I thought a moment. I didn't give a shit about having a piece of a film I wasn't sure would ever get made. But the extra money Rusty would pay me—and I'd get it up front—would certainly help. Especially since I was probably going to have to spend some dough to find Noah. And the truth is, I didn't think finding Ibrahim would be all that tough.

"I don't give a shit about your movie, a movie which, by the way, is a fucking lie because you don't believe in those so-called Christian values. You're only doing it for the money."

"That's what Hollywood is all about, Henry."

"I'm not judging you, Rusty. Do whatever the hell it takes to make a living, to make it through the day…"

I stopped myself. I realized I was no better than him or anyone else in this town. He was offering me extra dough and I was going to take it, like anyone else here would.

"Okay, Rusty. I'll do it. But I have conditions. I get a grand a day. I want two grand up front. I'll work three days, tops. If I can't find him by then, it's over. We're done. You're done."

"Yes! Thank you so much, Henry. It's a deal. I'll write you a check right now."

"No checks. Cash. We'll go to your bank and you'll take out the money."

"Okay. I can do that. But it'll have to be in the morning. I've got to finish today's shooting, and it might run into evening. We have to keep on schedule. We're almost done. Tomorrow morning, bright and early. Nine o'clock. I'll meet you at the bank and you'll have your money. In cash. Then you can start looking for Ibrahim. How does that sound?"

We made a time to meet. He gave me the address of his bank. I needed to ask him a few questions about Ibrahim.

"Where did you meet him?"

"It was more like he met me. He found out I was trying to make this film and he contacted me."

"How'd he find out?"

"The trades, probably. That's why you plant items like that.

To drum up interest. People think if you're in the trades, there's something really happening."

"You're making a Christian film and he's an Arab or a Muslim."

He shrugged. "The color of money is green no matter what you are. Besides, he said he was a Christian, not that I care one way or the other."

"From where?"

"He said his parents were Egyptian but he grew up in Lebanon."

"Did you check that out?"

"I didn't think I had to."

"You get in bed with a guy and you put him in charge of the money, then you hand him a million bucks, and you don't check him out?"

"I'm not stupid. I ran a credit check on him and I checked his references."

"Credit checks are meaningless and references can be forged, asshole."

"Hey, there's no need for name-calling here. I did what I was supposed to do. How would I know he was a crook? What does a crook look like?"

"You might try looking in the mirror."

"I told you, I'm not a crook!"

"You and Nixon. All I know is you made a million bucks of money that wasn't yours disappear. That pretty much fits the definition of crook as far as I'm concerned. Where does he live?"

"He was staying at the Mondrian, but he's not there anymore. I checked."

"I suppose you asked for a forwarding address."

"Um, I didn't think of that. I just figured he'd moved and he'd let me know where he was."

After Rusty and I had finished, and I began heading toward my car, my phone buzzed. A text was coming in from Jessica's friend, Cat. She left a phone number. Maybe I was one step closer to finding Noah.

18
A Complete Unknown

I didn't get much from Cat, but it was enough. Yes, she was friends with Delilah. Delilah hadn't been in school the last couple of days. She lived in West Hollywood. She didn't know the exact address but she gave me the street and described the building. Delilah's mother's name was Louise. Cat knew that because Delilah never called her mother "mom" or "mother." Always Louise.

It wasn't difficult to locate the three-story apartment complex Cat described. A check of the mailboxes turned up L. Baker in a ground floor apartment in the back. I pushed the buzzer but heard nothing, so I knocked on the door. A dog barked from one of the adjacent apartments. I knocked again. More barking. I could make out a rustling sound from inside the apartment, like someone was shuffling toward the door. A moment later, a woman wearing a rumpled flowered dress answered the door. She looked to be in her mid- to late-forties. She had frizzy red hair, the kind that comes out of a bottle, and looked as if it hasn't seen a comb in days. She wore no makeup and smelled vaguely of alcohol, like it was seeping out of her pores or clinging to what she wore.

"I guess you're here about Delilah."

"I am." I guessed she was used to being asked about her daughter, the source of some trouble in her life. This did not bode well for Noah. A woman who's trouble inevitably leads a man to even worse trouble.

"I can't help you," she said.

"Where is Delilah?"

"She's not here."

"She's not in school, either."

"You don't look like any truant officer I ever seen."

"What does a truant officer look like?"

"Not like you."

"Invite me in and you'll find out why I'm here."

"Why should I care? I don't know you."

"I think you know my son, Noah."

Her eyes widened then quickly collapsed into slits, focusing on me hard, as if examining me under a microscope.

"You're not his father. His father's dead, least that's what Delilah told me."

"To him, maybe, but I was there when he was born."

She opened the door enough so I could peak in to see chaos.

"Okay, but I'm warning you, I've got my cellphone in my pocket and nine-one-one on speed dial."

"You won't need it."

She opened the door wide enough for me to slip through then shut it quickly behind her.

"Place is a mess."

"I'm not from the Board of Health, either."

She was right. The place was a mess. She led me through the small hallway into the living room. Old newspapers were strewn all over the floor, and a mound of clean or dirty clothes were in a pile in one corner of the room. The room was dark. The shades were drawn and she might as well have been living underground.

"Sit down," she ordered, pointing to a ratty, old couch covered with cat hairs.

"That's okay, this won't take long," I said.

"Suit yourself. So what's your story, Mr. I'm-Not-a-Truant-Officer or from the Board of Health?"

"I'm looking for Noah and I understand he's friends with your daughter, Delilah. I thought she could tell me where he is."

"She might be able to, if you could find her. Sweet kid from what I saw of him, but he's like a little puppy dog. Followed her all the way from bum-fuck Minnesota. I'd say it was cute if I didn't feel sorry for the poor kid."

"Why's that?"

"Because Delilah's a class-A bitch, that's why. The little narcissist only thinks about her own damn self. You think she helps out around the house? Look at the place! I work nights and even some days, trying to put food on the table for us. And when I'm not working I'm trying to catch up on my sleep. I don't have no time to straighten out the place. But all *she* does is read movie magazines. And half the time she's skipping school, like now."

"Where'd Noah and Delilah go?"

"I don't know."

"I don't buy that."

"What I mean is, I don't know exactly where. She was talking about some cult thing. I'd guess that's probably where she's headed, with him tagging along behind her. Or maybe they went to Vegas to get married by an Elvis impersonator. How do I know? Delilah wants to be an actress, that's why we come out here, so she can get in the movies. We're on our own. My husband went out for cigarettes one day, never came back. Can't say as I blame him. We weren't exactly Ozzie and Harriet. And Delilah, well, she's a handful. Anyway, your son, well, I guess he's been writing her or texting her ever since we come out here, and the other day, just like that, he shows up at the door. If Delilah knew he was coming, she sure as hell didn't tell me."

"When did they take off?"

"I don't remember exactly. They were out most of the day. Used this place like a motel at night. He slept on the couch. I wouldn't allow any funny business under my roof. Then yesterday they both disappeared."

"What's this cult thing you're talking about?"

"I'm not sure it's a cult exactly, but it's this big thing out in the mountains somewhere. I overheard them talking about it. Some big deal actor-shmactor, hippie loser kinda thing, if you ask me. But Delilah was always talking about the guy who was running it. 'He's so great. He knows everything about acting. He knows everybody in the business.' Stuff like that. She said there were a lot of actor types who'd be there. It's my guess that's where they're at now."

"You don't seem very worried about your daughter."

"She can take care of herself. Always has, always will. I don't know about your son, but she'll watch out for him until she gets tired of having him around. She's like that. Protective. For a while. But when she's done with you, she's done with you."

"Is there a name for the thing they went to?"

She scratched her head. "Something like that Johnny Cash song. What's the song? Oh, yeah." She started singing. "I got caught in a...Ring of Fire. That's it. That's the name of the thing they went to. She got involved with those people when she took some high-falutin' acting classes. They're the ones told her about it. Like I said it's run by some guru guy. It's supposed to be about being free and taking charge of your life, or some bullshit like that. I don't listen to her much when she goes on about stuff like that. It was Delilah's idea, so Noah, the poor kid, well, he's in love with her, or at least he thinks he is. At that age they fall in love at the drop of a hat, right? What do they know? Try living in the real world for a while and see how far that takes you. My guess is he tagged along for the ride."

"Do you know where it is?"

She shook her head. "I guess you could look it up on the Internet or whatever."

"And they left yesterday?"

"Yeah. Or maybe it was the day before. They all seem the same out here. You get up every morning, you look out the window, and it's the same goddamn day. The sun is shining and you know it's gonna be seventy, eighty degrees. Another fuckin' day in paradise. I don't know how they stand it. I don't know how much longer I can make it out here."

She didn't look as if she were making it at all.

"How did they get where they were going? Does Delilah drive? Does she have a car?"

"She's got her license, but no, she ain't got no car. Maybe they hitched, or got a ride from someone they knew."

"Didn't you think about calling Noah's parents and telling them he was here?"

"Thought you said you was his dad."

"He lives with his grandparents. He thinks of them as his parents."

"Why should I? He ain't my kid, he ain't my responsibility. I got one kid to take care of, you think I want to worry about two? Besides, how did I know he ran away? I didn't even know where Delilah knew him from. School, I guess. But she's older than him, so they weren't in the same grade. It's not like they sat around and chatted with me about their hopes and dreams. They came in, they went out. Didn't even leave a note."

She reached for a can of beer that was on the counter that separated the kitchen from the living room. "I guess I should keep more tabs on her, but she's seventeen, almost eighteen, and in a few months she's going to be out on her own anyway.

Besides, she don't listen to anything I say. But I'll tell you this, she's not a bad kid. Not one of those bad seeds, I mean. A little wild maybe. She never really got into much trouble and she really is serious about this acting thing. I even seen her a couple times in school things, you know, like high school plays, and she's good. Sings, too. I don't know where she got her talent from, but I do know where she got her stubborn streak from. That would be me. I wouldn't worry too much if I was you. They'll be all right. She'll look out for him and he seems like a good kid so he'll probably look out for her. I don't see him wandering off on his own and getting into any trouble."

"He's just a kid."

"He don't act like no kid. Now that I look at you I guess he favors you a little bit."

"That's too bad."

"Listen, you find Delilah, you tell her to get her ass back here. I don't like her hanging out with those kinda people. I miss her and I'm worried about her, but don't tell her that."

Back in my car I Googled "Ring of Fire." The next thing after the Johnny Cash song was some kind of big gathering out in Santa Susana Pass State Historic Park. I looked it up. That part of the park had been home to the Spahn Ranch, where the notorious Manson group holed up for a while. The gathering was organized by a group called Saraswati. It was run by a bearded dude named Benjamin Auster. I found his website. He was a former actor who appeared in a few small roles in even smaller films. He'd held a number of jobs, among them car salesman, motivational speaker, and advertising copywriter. He'd founded Saraswati three years ago. It grew out of his time as a motivational speaker and from what I could gather was the usual crap about taking responsibility for your own life and, as result, reaching your full potential then attaining your dreams.

As if you can re-invent yourself at the drop of a hat. As if you can suddenly make a success out of a life of failure. But somehow, no matter how ridiculous it sounds, this kind of crap seems to strike a chord with lost souls who need to look outside themselves for the answers. When I was skip tracing, most of the people I looked for thought they could find quick success. And where did that get them?

This "Ring of Fire" event was supposed to "cleanse the soul" and lead to a rebirth and a regeneration. What a load of bullshit. It lasted four days. Yesterday had been the first day.

I came up with a plan. I'd do some preliminary work on finding Ibrahim in what was left of the afternoon, then in the morning I'd meet Rusty and get my dough for the job. After that, I'd take off for the State Park, find this "Ring of Fire"-thing and yank the kid the hell out of there and send him home.

My starting point would be the Mondrian, which was one of those cute, semi-precious "boutique" hotels located on Hollywood Boulevard. Walking into the lobby was like entering a hipster's paradise.

"I'm sorry, sir," the clerk said, after checking his computer screen. "Mr. Ahmad checked out two days ago."

"That's odd. I was supposed to meet him but my trip got all screwed up and I wound up getting here a day late. I thought he'd still be here. You wouldn't happen to have any forwarding information for him, would you?"

"I'm sorry, sir, but I'm afraid he left no forwarding address."

"Oh, man, I really screwed this one up. Look, I'm in a bit of a pickle here. I was sent here by my boss and I'm gonna catch hell if I can't find him. When he checked in he had to show you I.D., probably his driver's license, which had his home address, so perhaps you could bend the rules a little and share that information with me."

"I'm afraid I couldn't do that, sir."

I pulled out my wallet and, although it broke my heart, removed a Benjie, which I discretely folded in half, so he could see it, then placed it on the counter between us. "Listen, the last thing I'd want to do is get you in trouble, but I know you've got that information on the screen in front of you and all you have to do is tilt it slightly in my direction, turn your head for a minute, and no one will know the difference."

I could see that wasn't going to do the trick so I took out another Benjie, folded it in half, and placed it on top of its twin.

He looked down at the two bills then gave a slight push to the screen so I could see it. While I took a look, he slid the bills toward him until they dropped under the counter.

The driver's license information gave a Santa Monica address. Now I knew where he lived, but I had no intention of going any further until I actually saw the color of Rusty's money.

Back in my room by eight o'clock, I was beat. All I wanted to do was sleep—the only safe place for my mind. I was just about to crawl into the sack when my phone rang. It was Stan.

"Any progress to report? Have you got the money yet?"

"Not yet."

"Oh," he said, and I could hear the disappointment heavy in his voice. "I figured by now you'd have my money and be on your way back home."

"It's not that simple, Stan."

"I realize that. It's just that...well, you seemed so close and I thought it would be a matter of you going out there and bringing back the money. Once you found him, I mean."

"If it were that easy you could have done it yourself. By the way, I'm hearing an interesting story from Rusty Jacobs that conflicts with yours."

"What's that?"

I could hear the change in the tenor of his squeaky voice that suddenly got even higher and squeakier.

"He claims he didn't steal the money."

"Why would I say he did if he didn't? Do you think I'd just hand him a million dollars? And if I did, why would I hire you to find him and bring the money back?"

"He says you gave it to him to invest."

"And you believe him?"

"I don't know what to believe, Stan. Truth is, I know him about as well as I know you, maybe even better now that I've spent some time with him, and frankly his story could be just as true as yours."

"Why would I hire you to bring it back if I gave it to him?" I could hear the agitation in his voice. "That's ridiculous."

"He says you gave it to him to invest."

"Invest in what?"

"In movies."

"Me, invest in a movie? I don't know anything about movies."

"You're doing a Fred Astaire, Stan."

"What do you mean?"

"You're dancing around my question."

"I'm offended by your accusation, Henry." His voice had turned hard, tone stern, the squeak oiled out of it. "It's my money, or to be more precise my investor's money, and I want it back. I need it back. That's what I hired you to do. So if you don't mind doing your job, which is what I'm paying you for, I'd appreciate it if you would you'd bring the money back."

"Relax, Stan."

"I can't relax. You wouldn't be relaxed if you were in my shoes."

"No, I wouldn't."

"I want that money back, Henry. I need that money back."

The connection went dead. He'd hung up on me. I didn't like that. I was beginning to not like Stan very much. Maybe Rusty was telling the truth. And maybe there was more to it than the two sides I was hearing.

19
Truth or Dare

Before meeting Rusty at the bank I needed to work some things out, so I phoned Klavan, hoping he could help.

"This whole business with Stan and the missing million bucks is beginning to stink and I need to talk it out with someone."

"Sure."

"Jacobs says the dough was given to him as a legitimate investment and Stan claims that's a lie, that Jacobs took it without his knowledge. I'm not sure who to believe."

"Does it matter?"

"Maybe not, but I hate it when I feel like I'm being played."

"You can't go wrong assuming everyone lies. Especially out there. You wake up in the morning and someone tells you it's raining when there isn't a cloud in the sky. The scary thing is, they actually believe it themselves. That's when you start doubting your sanity. And that's the time to get the hell out of there. Remember, that's the business they're in, selling lies to the public. And now that they've discovered CGI, all semblance of truth is lost. The line between reality and fantasy is completely blurred. If I see another one of those comic book movies being released, I'll shoot myself."

"Funny thing is, Jacobs got hustled out of the dough by someone else."

"The player gets played. I love it."

"Now he's paying me find that guy and get the money back. By the time I get to the guy who has the money, I'll probably find out there wasn't any money at all."

"If you want my advice, and who wouldn't, just do the job and you can worry about who's telling the truth later. You said there was something else."

"I did."

"Is it about your kid?"

"Yeah."

"You still haven't found him, have you?"

"Not yet. He followed a girl out here. I think they're at some kind of New Age cult gathering. But I'm not sure I should interfere by going up there and dragging him back."

"He's a kid. He shouldn't be out on his own. Go the hell out there, grab him by the scruff of his scrawny little neck if you have to, and bring him the hell home."

Klavan was right, of course. I didn't have a choice. He was my kid and that's the kind of thing a parent does for his kid.

When I arrived at the bank in West Hollywood, Rusty was already standing out front, texting on his phone.

"Bet you thought I'd blow you off," he said when he looked up and saw me approaching. "Come on. Let's get your money and get started."

While we stood in line waiting for an open teller, Jacobs asked me the one question I hate. "You think you'll be able to find him?"

"I've got a couple leads."

"You mean you started working on it already?"

"The idea of being out here any longer than I have to rattles what little soul I might have left, so yes, I did a little preliminary digging yesterday."

Jacobs grinned. "That means you're starting to trust me. That's one step closer to us being friends. Be honest. I'm growing on you, aren't I?"

For a split second I had to consider Jacobs's question. The truth was, I was beginning to like the asshole. But I wasn't going to let him know that because if he did it would be bad for business.

"Don't count on it," I said, hoping he'd drop the subject.

I was saved not by the bell but by a new teller opening up. I made a quick move and we were first in line. I stood a few feet back as Rusty withdrew two grand in hundreds then handed them to me, dramatically snapping each bill and holding it up to the light to make sure it was the genuine article.

"What the hell are you doing? You got them from the damn bank. Don't you think they'd know if they were passing phony dough."

"You can never be too careful, Henry."

He counted out the last bill and then handed it to me. "So we're all square, right?"

"Not really. Remember there's still that little matter of a million bucks. Whether I find Ibrahim or not, you're the one I'm holding responsible."

"But when you find him, you'll get the money back, right?"

"Listen, Rusty, I don't do strong-arm work. You're paying me to find him and if I can convince him to give back the dough, fine. But if not, he's all yours, and at the end of the day you're the one who still owes Stan. By the way, I had little chat with him last night and I have a sneaking suspicion there's more to this than meets the eye."

"You mean you're starting to believe me?"

"I wouldn't go that far, but your story about him giving you the money might have a grain of truth to it."

If I had looked down at his feet I would have seen them floating six inches off the floor.

"It has more than a grain," he gushed. "It has the whole, damn wheat field. Like I told you, I didn't steal that money. He gave it to me to invest. Now he's got cold feet so he sent you out to get it back, making like I stole it from him. You know what? I might sue him for defamation of character."

"In this town I doubt they give much concern to character. And don't jump the gun. He's paying me to bring back that dough and that's what I have to do. And if it means you paying me to find Ibrahim, all the better. Did you know he lives here in L.A.?"

"You're kidding. I thought he was from out there in the Middle East somewhere. At least that's what he told me."

"Only if by the Middle East you mean Santa Monica."

"That lying sonuvabitch. So you found him?"

"I know where he lives. I'll head over later today to see if he's actually there."

"That bastard planned to rip me off from the get-go" said Jacobs, his face turning red.

"It appears so."

"He's a crook!"

"Well, you could blow me over with a feather. I mean, a lying crook in L.A. What are the chances of that?"

"I've got this movie to make."

"With Ibrahim and your money gone, I don't think you've got anything more than what you can pay for yourself. And it doesn't look like that'll get you very far."

"Hey, don't be so negative. I'm Rusty Jacobs. I can make it happen. All my life I've made things happen. You'll see."

"I hope you pull it off, pal. But if you do, it's going to be without that chunk of dough I'm bringing back to Stan."

I left Jacobs standing on the sidewalk, looking forlorn or maybe it was angry. Sometimes you can't tell the difference. I probably should have felt bad for sticking the pin to his bubble, but the truth is, guys like that always manage to bounce back. They're like that old Joe Palooka blow-up figure I had as a kid. You knocked it down, it came right back up at you. The harder you slugged it, the faster it came back up. Rusty would probably find a way to get that money. And I had to admit there was something inexplicably likeable about the guy.

With mid-morning traffic, it took almost an hour to reach the edge of Santa Susana Pass State Park, a trip that according to Google maps should have taken no more than half an hour.

The site of the gathering was supposed to be secret. I assumed that was to keep the authorities from swooping in and closing it down, or to keep strangers from crashing the party. But a quick search of the web found enough loose lips enabling me to pretty much pinpoint the location.

The area was dotted with numerous hiking trails that afforded access to what purported to be beautiful panoramic views of the San Fernando Valley. I don't mind walking, I do it all the time back in the city, but to me the word hiking connotes walking up as opposed to forward or down. The latter requires effort, something I try to avoid at all costs.

After talking to a number of picnickers, I found a couple of tourists from Norway who pointed me in the right direction.

"I don't know if these are the people you are looking for," said a blond, bearded fellow. "But we wandered off one of the trails about an hour ago and noticed a group of thirty or forty people who were camped in a fairly large field, surrounded by a rocky, wooded area."

"Can you tell me exactly how to get there?"

"Of course," replied his companion, a pretty redhead. She pointed in the direction of a couple of oak trees. "You take that trail and go straight up. If you go too far south, you'll see a line of electrical towers. And if you drift too far to the north, you'll come to the railroad tracks."

"Eventually," the bearded guy continued, "you will get to a paved road and if you follow that, you will wind up at a small electrical plant. You will see a break in a chain link fence by two telephone poles. If you follow that straight...Greta, do you remember if the camp is on the left or right?"

"No. I'm sorry. I cannot even remember if we noticed it going up or going down. But I think if you listen closely, you will be able to hear noise coming from the camp. I hope they are who you are looking for."

"Me, too," I said, not looking forward to the climb in this heat.

"I would bring water with you, sir," said Greta.

"Yes, that would be a good idea," said her companion. "I believe you can purchase some at the recreation center. And don't worry, you will not get lost. There are too many hikers around and the trails are too well-marked."

"But I would not stay out once it starts to get dark," warned Greta.

"I'll find them before that," I assured them, having no intention of staying in the woods any longer than I had to. The whole area gave me the willies.

I rolled up my sleeves, pulled my shirttail out of my jeans and with the bottled water I'd purchased, I headed toward the path. As I plunged in, it brought back not so pleasant memories of the time I found myself deep in the Mexican jungle—a case that broke my spirit so bad, I ended up quitting my so-called career as a skip tracer and found work as a cable TV installer. Back then, I promised myself I'd never get myself into another position where I ventured into territory more dense in foliage than Central Park. But promises are so easily broken or forgotten.

By the time I reached the paved road and spotted the break in the link fence, the combination of the heat and the climb had taken its toll. I needed to rest, so stopped and leaned up against a tree, took a few slugs of water from my now half empty bottled, and cursed myself for not buying two. I checked my watch. It was close to two and I hadn't had anything to eat but a day old Danish and an exceedingly lousy cup of coffee since I'd left my motel earlier that morning. After a few minutes I forced myself to move on, heading toward the break in the chain fence.

I'd been walking nearly half an hour when I heard sounds coming from off to my left. It sounded like music. I stepped off the main trail and found that there was a smaller trail that led off toward the direction of the music. I pulled out my keys and scratched marks on a tree every ten or fifteen feet, a trick I'd learned back in Mexico years ago.

The music stopped. It was replaced by an amplified voice.

I walked several hundred yards along the path until I spotted an open field. In the middle there were a maybe a dozen brightly colored tents pitched in a large semi-circle. In the middle of the semi-circle there were several dozen people, legs folded Indian-style, listening to a bearded man wearing loose-fitting white trousers and a flowery shirt open at the neck. He wore one of those over the head microphones and his amplified voice echoed off the tree line. I figured this was Auster. Behind him was a weird looking, monstrous figure, maybe twenty feet high, made of sticks and leaves. It reminded me of a Golem, the anthropomorphic creature made from inanimate matter, usually stone and clay, written about in Psalms and other medieval writing.

I crouched behind a tree several yards beyond the perimeter and watched as Auster spoke, pacing back and forth in front of his audience who seemed mesmerized. If he moved left, their heads moved to the left. If he moved right, their heads moved to the right. If he stood still, their heads remained still, their gaze riveted to him. I got this scary feeling that what I was witnessing was a cut-rate Charlie Manson.

There were half a dozen men scattered throughout, all dressed like Auster, and from the way they held a hand to their ears, I assumed they were wearing earpieces. Every so often they moved in a clockwise direction, as if on the lookout for intruders. When one got a little too close to where I was hidden, I melted further back behind the tree-line.

It was after three p.m. I'd been there nearly half an hour and Auster was still talking.

My legs were cramping. I got up and began to quietly circle the encampment so I'd be able to spot Noah or Delilah. I checked my cell. No bars. Useless. I stuck it in my pocket and kept moving, careful to be a quiet as possible.

Just short of four o'clock, Auster finally ended his sermon. He raised his hands high above his head then thrust them out toward the crowd, as if saluting his followers. He brought both hands to his lips, kissed them, then thrust them back out to the crowd, as if throwing them a giant kiss. They stood and cheered. Auster bowed several times then began moving through his followers, high-fiving them, as if he were some kind of heroic figure.

Slowly he moved away from them, toward a bright red tent pitched twenty yards away from the others, at one end of the horseshoe-shaped area. The audience, still silent, began to rise and move toward their tents. I figured this was as good as any time to make myself known, but before I could, I felt a hand on my shoulder. I turned to find one of the burly men who had been standing guard around the perimeter.

"You lost, friend?" he asked.

"And now I'm found."

"This is a private meeting, my friend. I suggest you find your way back to the trail and leave us alone."

"I believe we're on public property."

"This is a private meeting, sir," he repeated, "so I think it best you move along."

"If I don't?"

"I'm afraid we'll have to take steps to remove you."

"Maybe you ought to speak to your leader before you make a decision you might regret."

"We're all equals here."

"Looks to me like some might be more equal than others. Listen, why don't I speak to Auster?"

"Mr. Auster is busy at the moment."

"Then I guess I'll just hike back down the mountain and speak to the authorities to see if you have a proper permit for a gathering this size."

I guessed he didn't know any more than I did if they had a permit or if they even needed one, but he didn't want to risk making the wrong decision.

"I'll speak to Benjamin."

"I'll wait here."

"No, sir, please come with me."

When we reached the red tent, he went inside. A moment later he was back.

"Benjamin has agreed to see you."

He lifted the flap of the tent and motioned me inside.

The only light was cast from lanterns scattered throughout an area the size of a small New York City studio apartment, with a cot, a couple of those nylon fold-up beach chairs, and a fold up card table behind which Auster sat.

"Please, have a seat," he said in a soft voice, gesturing to one of the chairs set up in front of the table. As soon as I sat, Auster moved his chair so that it was facing me, only inches away.

"My name is Benjamin Auster."

"I know."

"I'm flattered. I'm afraid I can't return the compliment."

"I'm Henry Swann."

"I love swans. They're beautiful creatures but if you get too close they can be dangerous. Are you dangerous?"

"I don't know."

"I understand you were observing us. Is there any particular reason?"

"I was lost. I heard you. I got curious. I thought I'd see what was going on."

He smiled. "I don't think so."

"What *do* you think?"

"I think you're here for a reason. And if you're honest with me, my brother, then I'll be honest with you."

"You mean we should trust each other."

"Trust is a beginning, brother."

"Maybe we can start by cutting out that 'brother' shit."

"That bothers you? Being called brother?"

"I have a brother and I don't particularly like him. One brother to dislike is more than enough."

"You assume we'd dislike each other?"

"I doubt we have much in common."

He shrugged. "Perhaps that's true. Would friend suit you better?"

"I don't have many friends and I suspect there's probably a good reason for that."

He smiled. "You're not going to make this easy, are you?"

"I get what I came here for and I leave. How's that for easy?"

"What did you come here for?"

It was getting dark. I was tired of sparring. I needed to get to the point so I could find Noah and drag him the hell out of there. Would he come with me? Did he hate me as much as I hated myself?

"I have reason to believe my son is here."

"What is your son's name?"

"Noah..." I suddenly realized I had forgotten for a moment the last name he was using, his mother's maiden name. "Ellis. Noah Ellis."

"I'm certainly not aware of everyone here, but to my knowledge we do not have a Noah Ellis. There are so many people and though I know most of them, I can't say I know them all. But I will by the end of the weekend."

"How about a girl named Delilah, seventeen, maybe eighteen. I have photo of both of them." I pulled out my phone and showed him.

"Yes. I do know Delilah Baker. She's a very talented young woman. Once she starts believing in her talent, I think she has a bright future ahead of her."

"And you'll help her start believing that?"

"I do my best to help people realize their full potential."

"Maybe you can do that for me someday, but right now I need to find Noah and bring him home."

"If he's here with us, I can assure you I'm unaware of it."

I stared into his eyes. They were a deep shade of blue. He caught my stare, matched it and wouldn't let go.

"He's only fifteen. A minor. I need to bring him home."

"No one is held prisoner here. We're not some kind of dark, murderous cult, no matter what you might think."

"You have guards."

"I assure you they're not guards. They're unarmed. They're aides. They're here to make sure no one wanders off and gets lost, as well as to make sure people like you don't interrupt our meeting. Everyone is here voluntarily. To find themselves. To better themselves. To reach his or her full potential. They're here to bond with others and themselves. If Noah is here, and I don't believe he is, and he wishes to leave with you, I won't stop him. We don't keep prisoners and we don't keep tabs on anyone. People are allowed and encouraged to come and go as they please. This is meant be a joyous learning opportunity, not a prison camp."

"Fine. Let's see if we can find her. If he's here, I want to leave before it gets dark."

"I'd be happy to accompany you and visit each tent."

"Let's go."

As we moved past the enormous stick figure I asked Auster, "What's with the Golem?"

"It represents all the things that hold us back in life, things we have created to block ourselves from success. At the end of our meeting we burn it, as a representation of how we must destroy those parts of us that hold us back from success."

"I've heard about the wildfires here."

"I can assure you, we have taken every possible precaution."

As we made our way from one tent to another, Auster couldn't help telling me a little about his organization that he claimed had been established for the sole purpose of helping people reach their full potential. He said he hated the word "followers," which connoted blind obedience. Most of "*his* people" were in the entertainment business.

"These are some of the most insecure people in the world," he said. "They need to ground themselves, to know they are capable of doing great things, to know they can and will survive rejection, which is an integral part of the life they've chosen. It is the life of all artists, and only the strong will survive. I'm simply a facilitator. Obviously, not all of them will succeed, but those who do must believe they can. These three days are to help them shut out the outside world by eliminating all outside distractions. This allows them the opportunity to look deep into themselves and reach that conclusion on their own. I'm no swami or guru. I know it's easy to dismiss me as a dangerous kook, like Jim Jones or like David Koresh. Many of these people have been told all their lives that they're not good enough, that they won't ever succeed. I'm here to turn that around. We're all here to learn and have some fun in the process."

"I'm here to find my son, not myself."

"I hope you do both."

Inside each tent there were half a dozen men and women, most of them in their twenties and thirties, though there were a few older. We had no luck with the first four tents. Finally, half way through the encampment, we hit pay dirt. Delilah Baker was lying on a cot and reading a book about acting. Noah was nowhere in sight.

"That's her," I said, gesturing toward Delilah.

"Delilah," Auster said softly. "Delilah Baker."

She looked up. She was prettier than her photo. Her round face still reflecting remnants of "baby fat." Her eyes were enormous, reminiscent of those Keane paintings.

"There's someone here who'd like to speak to you," Auster said.

She squinted at me through the dim light.

"It's all right, Delilah," Auster assured her.

She put the book down and got up slowly. She was tall, perhaps five-seven, with strawberry blonde hair tied back in a ponytail. Her eyes were an almost unnatural cobalt blue. She wore faded blue jeans and a halter-top. I could see how Noah would be attracted to her with her Lolita-like quality.

"Let's talk outside, Delilah," I said, as I backed out of the tent, Auster beside me.

"I'll let you two talk alone," said Auster. "If you need me, Delilah, I'll be right over there." He gestured toward a large stick figure.

"Did my mother send you?" she asked, arms akimbo, her hips thrust forward.

"No."

"I didn't think so. She doesn't really care what I do and where I am, so long as I don't cause her any trouble."

"Are you the trouble-making kind?"

Her mouth morphed into a pout and she thrust a hip forward. "What do you think?"

She wasn't looking for an answer and I didn't give her one. "Where's Noah?"

She squinted, her head cocked to the side. "Who?"

"You know who I'm talking about. I want to know where he is."

"Why should I tell you?"

"Because I'm his father and I want to know."

"You're not his father."

"I'm not going to argue with you, Delilah, because in so many ways you're right. But I still want to know where he is."

"He's not here."

"But he came here with you, didn't he?"

"Maybe."

"Where is he now?"

She shrugged and looked down. So did I. She was wearing Chuck high-tops. The same as me. Only hers were pink and mine were green.

"When was the last time you saw him?"

"Maybe yesterday."

"Here?"

"Maybe."

I knew that meant yes. "Why isn't he here with you anymore?"

"I told him to go home."

"Why?"

"Because he didn't belong here, that's why." Her tone had turned petulant, annoyed, dismissive.

"Why's that?"

"Because he's a kid. He was following me around, getting in the way. I have to concentrate on my career. That's why I came here. This is very important to me. I have to focus. I can't have some kid hanging around, a kid I have to look out for." Her eyes collapsed into slits. She was wearing pink eye shadow that matched her Chucks. "I have enough trouble taking care of myself."

"You're his girlfriend, aren't you?"

"I am *not* his girlfriend."

"Does he know that?"

"He should. I told him enough times. He just didn't get it."

"Get what?"

"That I didn't want him around. I don't know why he followed me out here."

"Because he likes you. And maybe you led him on."

"I did *not* lead him on. I did *not* ask him to come out here. I told him a hundred times to go home. At least a hundred times."

"You hung out with him. A guy can get the wrong idea when you do that. We're stupid like that sometimes."

"That doesn't make him my boyfriend. He likes me, okay? And he's a cute kid. A nice kid. A smart kid. But I didn't tell him to come to L.A. What am I going to do with a kid hanging around me? I'm an actress. I'm here to find work. And to work on my..." She searched for the word. Finally it came. "Craft."

"Your craft," I repeated.

"Yes! You have to be in the right frame of mind to get work and to do the best you can when you get it. Mr. Auster says it's all about attitude. You have to imagine success. If you do, it will come. Mr. Auster helps us with that. He helps us reach our true..." Again, she searched for the right word. "Potential. He teaches us to believe in ourselves."

"And all that's supposed to get you a movie contract?"

She looked at me like I was some kind of alien. "Duh!"

"So you think you're going to walk down this mountain tomorrow and there's going to be an agent standing there with a movie contract with your name on it?"

"Mr. Auster tells us all about people like you. You're the 'disbelievers.' The negative people who are always telling you what you can't do, what can't happen. The nay-sayers. Those are the real losers in life. I think maybe you're one of them. One of the losers, I mean."

"I won't argue with you there, Delilah. But right now all I'm interested in is finding Noah."

"I don't know where he is."

"What happened the last time you saw him?"

"We had a fight."

"What kind of fight?"

216

"For about the hundredth time I told him I didn't want him hanging around anymore and he got mad. So he left."

"That was yesterday?"

"Yup."

"What time?"

"I don't know. No one's supposed to have watches here. Or cellphones. Or anything that will break our concentration."

"Was it night or day?"

"Day."

"Was it before breakfast or after?"

"After."

"Before lunch or after lunch?"

"I know what you're getting at. I'm not a moron, you know. He left in the afternoon, okay? Right after lunch. I told him he was getting in the way of my aura, so he split."

"Did he say where he was going?"

She shrugged. "I guess he was going home."

"Did he have any money?"

"Not so much. He spent most of it getting out here, I think. And then we did some things. Like, he wanted to go to Disneyland. I told you, he's just a kid."

"Do you think he'd go back to your mother's place?"

"He didn't like being there. Neither do I. The only thing she imagines is failure. She's...toxic."

"Do you have any idea where Noah might have gone?"

She shook her head.

"Do you think he's headed back home?"

"Maybe. I guess. That's what I told him to do."

"All right, Delilah. Thanks."

She walked to her tent, her ponytail swinging back and forth like a shampoo commercial. I walked over to where Auster was standing.

"I presume she told you he's not here," he said.

"She did."

"I hope you find him, and more important, I hope you find what *you're* really looking for."

I didn't ask him what he thought that was. Maybe that's because I didn't have to.

20
Beware Doll, You're Bound to Fall

By the time I reached the recreation area, the sun was setting. I was tired. I was thirsty. I was hungry. I was pissed off. Nothing was finished. No Noah. No million bucks. And Goldblatt's ridiculous art caper was still hanging over my head. I couldn't help thinking back to those halcyon days in Spanish Harlem, when I was working for food stamps and chump change. At least those cases were relatively simple. A runaway spouse. A repo. A bail jumper, who usually jumped no further from home than a couple of subway stops. None of them took more than a few days to clear up. My life seemed to be getting more complicated rather than less complicated.

Since I'd hooked up with Goldblatt, life was more trouble and troubling. He would argue the payoff was bigger, and he'd probably be right. But at what cost? Is this who I was? Is this the way I wanted to spend the rest of my life? Maybe those guys back at the poker game had the answer because I sure didn't.

But now was not the time for naval gazing. I had to find Noah. Bitten by chiggers and scratched by branches, I was no closer to accomplishing that than I'd been earlier, when I was sure he was with Delilah.

I purchased another bottle of water and a bag of chips. I sat on a bench facing the trail and pondered my next move. Should I call Ellen and see if she'd heard from Noah? No. I wouldn't call her until I had something solid. This is what I did for a living. To own up to not being able to find my own son would be to admit that I was even less than who I pretended to be.

But I called her anyway, not out of compulsion or guilt, but because I finally began thinking about someone other than myself. If I were her I would be anxiously awaiting a call from me. She needed a connection to me, and through me to Noah, and this was the least I could do for a woman who took on a burden I was not willing to bear.

"Henry. Have you found him?"

"Not yet. But I know he was with Delilah until yesterday."

"What happened?"

"They had a parting of the ways. She told him to go home. That he was too young for her."

"She's right. He is."

"Unfortunately, she didn't get around to telling him that for a couple days."

"Where do you think he is he now? Do you think he's all right?"'

The panic rose in her voice. Why wasn't I as panicked as she was? The answer to why was simple. She was a better parent to Noah than I could ever have been. It was hard to swallow but it was true. Could I change that? Would I change that?

"I'm sure he's fine, Ellen. If something happened to him, you would have heard. He'll call you when he gets over his embarrassment. Or he'll show up at your door."

"Embarrassment?"

"He knows he did something foolish and it's going to take him time to suck up his pride and admit it."

"What are you going to do, Henry? He's only fifteen. He's all alone—"

"I'm going to do my best to find him. Meanwhile, if he calls, I want you to let me know right away. And if he asks for money, make sure he gets it. He has no reason to hang around L.A. He's resourceful. He'll find some way to get back home. But if he's still here, I'll find him."

I hung up the phone emotionally drained. Every second Noah was missing only accentuated what a failure as a human being I was. I had to find him before he got into trouble. And if there was trouble to be had a teenager alone and loose in L.A. would find it. But to be able to focus solely on finding Noah, I needed to find Ibrahim. And quick.

Late the next morning I set out to look for Ibrahim. The address I had for him was not far from the beach, a quiet, tree-lined street in Santa Monica that bespoke wealth. The two-storied house, painted a pastel shade of pink, was large, protected by a six-foot high hedge.

I parked my car across the street, passed through a wooden gate then walked the stone path to a front porch. Besides a divan and a few rattan chairs, there were also few toys scattered on the floor.

I rang the bell. A moment passed. I rang again. The door was opened by a Hispanic woman dressed in a light blue and white maid's uniform.

"May I help you?" she asked in a heavy Hispanic accent.

"I'm looking for Ibrahim Ahmad."

"He's not home now."

"Do you know where he is?"

"Work?" she said, as if it were a question.

"Do you know where that is?"

She shook her head.

"Do you know when he'll be back?"

"Maybe tonight. Maybe not tonight. Maybe he's away..." She paused. "On business."

"Is there anyone else here I can talk to?" I knew there was someone else home. I could hear the sound of kids coming from the back. I guessed they were playing in a swimming pool. I asked her if Ahmad's wife was there.

She said yes and closed the door. Instead of waiting for her to return, I circled round back. There was a large swimming pool with a couple kids splashing around in it. Set maybe a hundred feet behind the pool was a single, empty tennis court. Spread out on a chaise longue by the pool, her face to the sun, a magazine covering her stomach, was a blonde in a bikini. Beside her, on a small, round table, was a half-empty glass and a bowl of fruit.

As I started toward the woman the maid burst through the back door. "*Senora,*" she said, "*hay un hombre afuera para Senor Ahmad.*"

I stepped forward.

"That would be me."

The blonde sat up, swinging her shapely, tanned legs over the side of the longue chair, then tipped her sunglasses toward the edge of her nose with one finger. She was a knockout, mid- to late-thirties, her breasts spilling out of her tiny bikini top. She reminded me of one of those *Playboy* centerfolds I used to drool over as a kid.

"May I help you?" she purred in a sexy, smoky, gravelly voice, kind of like Demi Moore.

"I hope so—"

"Boys! Hold it down, will you? Mommy's talking to someone." She turned back to me.

"I'm looking for Ibrahim Ahmad," I said. "Your husband, I presume?"

"You presume correctly. Pull up a chair, why don't you?" She pointed to one of the chairs scattered around the edge of the pool. "Just toss the towels on the lawn. The boys don't use them anyway."

I sat down and she readjusted her lounge chair upwards so she was in a seated position.

"May I ask why you want to see him?"

"We're business associates."

"You don't look like any business associate of his I've ever met. What kind of business might that be?"

"He's in the film business, isn't he?"

She shrugged, a gesture I didn't know quite how to interpret. "Oh, how rude of me. Perhaps you would like something to drink?"

"I'm good."

"I don't think so. It's hot. You look thirsty."

"Then maybe you're right. I should drink something."

"Sonya," she called out to the maid who was behind the glass door, staring at us.

"*Si, senora,*" she said, sliding it open and stepping outside.

"Please bring this gentleman a margarita."

Sonya nodded and disappeared into the house.

"You'd think since she's Mexican she'd know how to make one, but no, she didn't have the foggiest idea. I had to teach her. But now she's gotten quite good at it."

"I'm sure she thanks you for it every day."

"Are you mocking me?"

"I didn't mean to, Mrs. Ahmad."

"Please call me Yvonne. Evi, if you prefer. And if you think I don't treat her and her family well, you'd be wrong. She's part of our family."

"I have no idea how you treat your family."

"You've got an attitude. Did anyone ever tell you that?"

"About every day of my life."

She laughed. Throaty and deep.

"There's something about you I like, but I can't quite put my finger on it."

"I'll try to make this quick so you keep that feeling before the phrase 'familiarity often breeds contempt' comes into play."

Sonya arrived with two margaritas on a tray and set them down on the table beside us. Evi downed what was left in her half-empty glass then picked up the new one.

"Cheers," she said, clinking her glass with mine.

"Cheers."

"So, you're in the movie business."

"Did I say that?"

"You said you had business with my husband, something about the film business."

"I said that's why I want to see him." I looked around. It was like one of those places you see in magazine spreads. It reeked of money and ostentation. I was jealous.

"It appears the movie business has been good to you and your husband," I said.

"I don't ask my husband how he makes his money. I just make sure he keeps making it." She smiled, tipped her glass toward me and took another sip.

"So you don't know anything about his business?"

"Not a thing."

"Do you know where he is now?"

"I have absolutely no idea."

"When was the last time you saw him?"

She licked the salt off the rim of her glass, took another sip of her drink, put it down on the table, tipped her sunglasses back toward her eyes with one finger, readjusted the chair, leaned back, and aimed her face toward the sun. It was quite a performance. I couldn't take my eyes off her and she knew it. I didn't think it was polite for her to drink alone, so I took another sip of mine. She was right. It was very good. She must have been a good teacher.

"A couple days ago."

"Is that normal? That you don't see him for a few days?"

"Nothing about Ibrahim is normal."

"Where was he?"

"I never ask where he goes. If I did, I probably wouldn't get an honest answer. Ibrahim tells me what he wants me to know. I'd say it was cultural, but I think he's probably just a prick."

"Sounds like you don't like him very much."

"Define very much."

"They say one out of every two marriages ends in divorce."

"What? And give up all this?"

"I was under the impression California was a community property state."

She laughed.

"What's so funny?"

"My husband's a prick but he's also a very smart man. He knows how to hide his assets. Besides, I would guess most of his money is out of the country, somewhere in Qatar or Abu Dhabi or wherever the hell he's from."

"You don't know?"

"I probably don't pay as much attention as I should."

"I'm sure you could find a good attorney to help you out."

"That would cost money and I'm on a very short leash. There's no way I'm going to use up what I've managed to squirrel away on a lawyer. Besides, I'm afraid he'd take the boys. They can be a pain in the ass but I love them. Don't I, boys?" she said in the direction of the two kids in the pool who weren't paying the slightest bit of attention to us.

"If he's so well off why would he steal a million bucks?"

Her head popped up. The glasses went down. "Who said he did?"

"That's what I've been told."

"I suppose that answers the question of why you're here."

"The margarita is good, you're easy on the eyes, but that's not what I came for. You didn't answer my question."

"You mean why would he steal money? Ibrahim is a complicated man. He gets pleasure in many different ways. Like I said, he doesn't speak to me about his business. But if I were to venture a guess, I'd say he might just do it for the sport of it. Or he might do it because he's tired of dipping into his own money, or rather his family's money. Or for some other totally insane reason. I'm not sure he's ever worked for a dime of what he has. He has a strong sense of entitlement. What's his is his and what's yours is his. I think that comes from the way he was raised. If he screwed someone out of money, it's possible he did it for the hell of it. Or because he could." She turned her head slightly so she could look me in the eye, or at least I thought that's where she was looking. "Or even because he really needed it. If you want the real answer, you'll have to ask him."

"I would if I could find him."

"I wish I could help you."

"You can. You might not know it."

"I'm willing to learn."

"Does he have an office somewhere?"

"Probably, but I don't know where it is. He does what he does out of the house most of the time. When he's not 'on the road.'" She gave me the air-quote thing.

"Would you mind letting me poke around in his office?"

"I wouldn't mind, except he locks it when he's not here, which as you've probably guessed is often."

I noted more than a hint of annoyance in her voice. She

wasn't going to work too hard to protect him. "Friends?"

"Mine or his?"

"Either, if they might know something about him."

"Maybe you should tell me what this is all about before I start showing you around the house."

"Maybe you don't want to know."

She took another hit of her margarita. So did I. I wanted her to trust me, at least for the moment. Mimicking her actions was a way of subconsciously bonding with her. Besides, the drink really was good. Just sweet enough. Just tart enough.

"Maybe I do want to know."

"He's had some business dealings with someone and I don't think he's been completely straight with him."

She laughed. "Ibrahim not on the up and up? Alert CNN."

"Obviously you do know something about his business dealings."

She shook her head. "Like I said, he doesn't tell me anything. It's a character thing."

"That doesn't mean you don't know. You strike me as a smart woman."

"Really? What makes you say that?"

"I'm a good judge of character. It's a job requirement."

"What is your job exactly?"

"It's hard to explain."

"I have a college education. I might be able to handle it. And if you want to know any more about Ibrahim, you'd better give it a try."

I could have lied, but I didn't see the point. "I'm a skip tracer."

"What's that?"

"I find people who are lost."

"Well, you're in the right place, honey, because I'm the one who's lost in this family. Ibrahim always knows exactly where he is."

"Where's that?"

"Like I said, at this moment, I couldn't tell you. And frankly, I couldn't care less."

"So how about that tour of the house?"

"Sure. I'll be happy to show you around. Boys," she yelled out to her sons. "I want you both out of there. Right now! Come over, dry off, and get ready for dinner."

The boys stopped splashing about and headed toward the stairway out of the pool.

"I'm going inside with this gentleman," she continued. "By the time I get back, you'd both better be dry and sitting at that table. Do you understand?"

"Yes, Momma," the boys said in unison.

"Sonya will bring out your lunch. You can eat out here."

She headed into the house with me following close behind. She didn't bother to put on anything over her bikini. Her tanned, toned body was perfect—not a hint of cellulite—and she moved with the grace of a cat.

Once inside she turned to me and said, "Where would you like to start?"

"Surprise me."

She led me around the spacious, expensively-furnished house. The den was first. Big screen TV, pool table, a bar set up against one wall, and a large cabinet that had a lock on it.

"What's in there?" I asked.

"I'm not sure."

"You're a woman. You're not going to have something in your own house you don't know about."

"That's sexist."

"Yeah, well, shoot me."

"Funny you should say that, because I believe that's what my husband has in there."

"Guns?"

"Yes. But it's not like he actually shoots them."

"What's that supposed to mean?"

"I believe," she whispered, getting so close to me I could smell the not unpleasant mixture of suntan lotion and perfume, "one of his sidelines is selling weapons."

"What do you mean, you believe?"

She backed away a step. "I might have heard things."

"What kind of things?"

She paused, weighing what she should tell me against loyalty to her husband. I could tell she was pissed at him. I didn't know why. I didn't care. All I cared was that I'd presented her with a way of getting back at him. In the end, she'd tell me everything she knew.

"I've heard conversations. When he thought I wasn't listening."

"And?"

"He was talking to someone about a shipment of arms. But I don't know the details. He calls himself an importer/exporter, so I guess that's one of things he imports and exports. But it's all legal, right? I mean, people buy weapons all the time."

"They do. As to whether or not it's legal, it depends on what he's selling and who he's selling to. But I'm not interested in that."

This is what I said but what I was thinking was this douche bag is probably heavily into some highly illegal stuff. And I wouldn't have been surprised if it were more than weapons. Selling contraband is contagious. One thing leads to another, which leads to another. It shouldn't be surprising. It's the American entrepreneurial system.

"You won't say anything about this, honey, will you?"

"My lips are sealed."

She smiled. "Not all the time, I hope."

"On the right occasions they do open up."

She smiled and moved closer to me. I knew what she wanted. She knew what she wanted me to do. I don't know why I did it because usually I do the opposite of what people want me to do. But I felt like it, so I kissed her. And it was good, like fulfilling a childhood fantasy. Kissing a *Playboy* centerfold. And what better place to do that than Hollywood? I wanted to kiss her again, but I knew if I did it would lead to other things, things that aren't necessarily bad but things that would take away the most precious thing I had right now. Time. I had to find Ibrahim. I had to find Noah. I had to get back that million bucks. I had to get back to New York where Goldblatt was waiting for me. Goldblatt. The thought of him was more than enough to ice anyone's libido.

I savored the kiss a moment longer then slowly pulled away.

"What's the matter?" she said.

"Nothing."

"Didn't you like it?"

"I did."

"The boys are with Sonya. You're not afraid of Ibrahim finding out, are you?"

I laughed. Not at the question but at the concept. "Not much frightens me anymore," I lied.

"So what is it?"

"I've got things to do. The first thing on the list is to find your husband."

She frowned. "I thought we had something."

"We did. It was a moment and now it's gone. And under

other circumstances we might find other things, but not today, not now."

She shrugged. "Your loss."

"I know. Maybe you'll give me another chance."

"Maybe." She flashed a mischievous grin.

I leaned forward and kissed her again. This one was shorter than the first, even though I wanted it to be longer.

"Ibrahim is a creature of habit and he's a fanatic about keeping in shape," she said. "If he's in L.A., you'll find him in the gym every morning. If he's here that's where you'll find him. But you have to promise me won't let on you spoke to me. He'll kill me if he knows I was talking to a stranger about his business."

"I hope you don't mean that literally."

She didn't answer.

"Don't worry. I'm not interested in what he does to make money. I just need him to give back what isn't his. Anything else is none of my business."

"He's not always a nice man."

"You'd be surprised how many people fit that description."

"He's especially not nice to me."

"You want me to get him in trouble, don't you?"

"If I do anything to hurt him, he'll take the boys out of the country and I'll never see them again."

"Where's the gym?"

She told me. It was in West Hollywood, not far from where I was staying. I never work out. I think it would kill me if I did. But the next morning I'd have to take that risk.

21

Everything He Can Steal

"I'm looking for one of your members, Ibrahim Ahmad," I asked the girl at the reception desk of Ibrahim's gym. She was a perfect ad for keeping in shape. Like most everyone else I'd seen in L.A., she was blonde and perky and young and had a well-toned body.

"Has he been in yet today?"

"Should I be telling you something like that?"

"I don't look dangerous, do I?" I lifted my arm. "Could these biceps cause anyone trouble?"

She giggled then said, "Yes. He was in early this morning."

"Does he ever come back after he's already been in?"

"Not usually. But he'll be back today because Dolph, his trainer, wasn't in this morning. He loves Dolph. Everyone does because he's such a good trainer. It's not easy to find the right one, you know. It's a very personal choice. So he made an afternoon appointment."

"What time?"

She scrunched up her face. "Should I be telling you this?"

"Why not?"

"What if you're some kind of a process server or something? I've only been here eight months and I've already seen three people served. I could get in big trouble."

"I'm not going to serve him with anything."

"You don't look like a process server."

She was wrong. I'd served more than my share. It wasn't my favorite pastime but it was an easy way to pick up a few bucks.

"So, I guess it's okay. Eleven-thirty."

I looked up at the clock on the wall. It was almost eleven.

I sat in the car, listening to talk radio no more than fifteen minutes before I spotted Ibrahim, dressed in fancy workout clothes, coming from behind the gym, where he'd parked his car in the lot. Nothing had changed since I'd last seen him. He was still playing with his Blackberry. I jumped out of the car and stood in front of him before he could enter the building.

"Remember me?" I asked.

He looked confused. "Not really," he said, holding his Blackberry up between us, as if it would afford him some protection.

"I'm not surprised."

"I have no idea who you are and I've got an appointment inside," he said as he tried to push past me. I pushed back.

"We've got some unfinished business," I said.

"I don't know what you're talking about."

"Yeah, you do. And you'd probably prefer we talk about it out here rather make a scene inside. You don't know me well enough to know this, Ibrahim, but I'd have no problem making a scene. I can probably make an Academy Award-winning scene, given the opportunity and the audience. You don't want that, do you? I don't think it would make a good impression on Dolph or any of your gym-rat friends."

He stared at me, his face hardening into a glare meant to intimidate me. I could see how living with him would be no picnic.

"All right. We can talk over there," he said, nodding his head toward an outdoor café down the block. "But I have an appointment at eleven-thirty."

"So you'll be a little late."

We sat at a table away from the entrance to the café. We ordered a couple of coffees.

"To state the obvious, I'm here to get Rusty's money back. And please don't waste my time by asking what I'm talking about."

"It's not Rusty's money. It's the production's money."

"You're half right. It's not Rusty's money, but it's not the production's money either. That million bucks is someone else's money, someone who hired me to get it back. And you have no idea the lengths I'll go to," I said in the toughest voice I could manage. Sometimes, if you talk the talk you don't have to walk the walk. But by this point it wasn't all an act. I was fed up with L.A. I was fed up getting the run-around. I was fed up with people like Rusty Jacobs and Ibrahim Ahmad, who took money that wasn't theirs and refused to give it back. In short, I was fed up with just about everything going on in my life. This was not the time to fuck with me.

"What if I told you I don't have it?" he said.

"I've been to your house. I've seen how you live."

"You think I've got a million dollars lying around?"

"I don't have to think about you at all. I have a job to do. You took the million, so you're the one who can give it back."

"I had it, but I don't have it anymore."

"What's that supposed to mean?"

"I'm a businessman. I move money around."

"This was not your money to move around. This was money meant for Rusty's movie."

"I will have it when the time comes."

"The time has come, Ibrahim. Hand it over."

"You think I can just write you a check for that kind of money?"

"Listen, pal, it's not my problem how you get it. I just need you to get it. And if it's in the form of a check, it damn well better be a bank check because personal checks don't cut it with me."

"The money is tied up right now."

"Untie it."

"Let me try to make you understand. That kind of money should not just be left sitting around doing nothing. That kind of money must be used to make more money."

"So you're telling me you used it for something else?"

"Precisely."

"What?"

"I cannot say."

"Let me guess. Either you used it for weapons or for drugs."

"Drugs? Never!"

I had mortally offended him. I didn't give a damn.

"I guess that answers the question."

"Are you wearing a wire?" he asked in a half-whisper.

"I'm wearing fucking jeans and a T-shirt. Where the fuck do you think I'd have a recorder hidden? In my crotch?"

"You have not answered me."

"No, I'm not wired. I'm no more a fed than you are."

He blinked. There was something else going down here, something I wasn't getting. My mind raced from one thing I'd learned about him to another. A picture was beginning to emerge. I didn't know if it was the right picture, but it was a picture. It wouldn't hurt to give it a shot.

"You used that money to buy weapons, didn't you?"

I detected a slight twitch under his left eye. His tell.

"But there's more to it than that. You're a snitch, aren't you?"

No twitch this time. Instead, his whole body tensed. "I...I don't know what you're talking about."

"Yeah, you know what I'm talking about. The feds have

something on you and the only way you can get out from under is to make a deal to get you off the hook."

His body slumped. He looked down. I'd taken a shot and I'd hit the bullseye.

"Does Rusty know anything about this?" I asked.

He shook his head.

"I couldn't give a fuck about what you do and what happens to you. All I want is that money back."

"It's gone. I used it."

"I'm not going to be the one left holding the bag. Mortgage your fucking house. Sell your fucking kids. Ask your fucking family for the money. I don't care how the hell you get it, just get it."

"I need time. I can pay it back in time. But first I have to save myself and my family."

I didn't have the heart to tell him his family didn't want to be saved by him. Maybe he already knew that. Maybe he was using his family to play me. It wasn't going to work.

I leaned back in my chair. What could I do? The money was gone. Disappeared down a black hole. Ibrahim would make his deal for the weapons, then probably trade the information to the government, but the chances of me or Rusty or Stan seeing that dough again were practically nil. What was I left with? What was Rusty left with? What was Stan left with? What was anybody left with?

I got up. "You pay the fucking check," I said. "I'm sure you can come up with that much."

"You won't say anything?"

"What am I going to say and who am I going to say it to?"

The only way Stan was going to get his money back was if Rusty somehow pulled off a miracle and made that film and the movie actually made money. Of course, that didn't do me any good.

When I called Rusty, he was on location again, this time not far from the La Brea tar pits. I didn't tell him the bad news over the phone. I figured this was the kind of thing you ought to tell someone in person.

As I made a turn onto Wilshire, I glanced into my rearview mirror and noticed a black Lexus creeping up my ass. I've been accused of being paranoid and perhaps, after all these years in a business where I'm following people for a living, maybe I have good reason to be. But there was something about that car that didn't sit right. I decided to see if it was tailing me. I made a right at the light ahead of me then slowed down. The black Lexus mirrored my turn. I made a left at the next intersection. The black Lexus did the same. I slowed down a little and checked my rearview mirror again. I could see two men in the car, neither of whom I recognized.

I made another left, then pulled slightly to the side and stopped in the middle of the street. The black Lexus stopped about six feet behind me. We all sat in our respective cars for at least a minute. Finally, I got out my car, pulled out my phone and walked slowly toward the passenger's side of the Lexus. I stopped in front of the car and snapped a photo of the license plate, then photographed the two men sitting in the front seat, both dressed in the same dark jackets and striped green and white ties. They weren't cops and they weren't feds. I knew that from the license plate number, which was a rental. I texted both photos to Goldblatt, then I moved to the driver's side of the car and made a motion for him to roll down the window. He did.

"How's it going?" I asked.

The two men, both dark-complexioned, looked straight ahead and said nothing.

"Can I help you?"

The driver, who spoke with a slight accent, said. "Yes. You can move your car. You're blocking the street."

"There's plenty of room for you to go around me."

"Why did you photograph my car and us?"

"Why are you following me?"

"We are not following you."

"Sure you are. I do this for a living. I know when I'm being tailed."

The guy on the passenger's side got out and moved toward me. He was big. Bigger than me. Bigger than almost anyone I knew. He also had a bulge on his left side, under his jacket. It wasn't a pack of cigarettes. I quickly snapped his picture and texted that one to Goldblatt, too.

"What are you doing?" the driver asked.

"Buying myself a little insurance. Anything happens to me, a friend of mine will have everything he needs to track you guys down."

The second man backed up.

"I'll ask you again. Why are you following me?"

"We're here to deliver a message."

"What is it?"

"That you should stop meddling in affairs that don't concern you."

"Ibrahim sent you, right?"

"I do not know any Ibrahim."

"You're full of shit."

A car pulled up behind the Lexus. The driver, a middle-aged woman, honked her horn. I waved her to go around us. She did, driving slowly while peering out the window.

"It's okay," I said. "Just a little accident. We're exchanging information."

I looked back to the driver who was tapping nervously on the steering wheel.

"If we don't move along, someone's gonna call the cops. I'm guessing you don't want that to happen."

"No."

"Then finish delivering the damn message and let me get the hell out of here. What affairs are you referring to?"

The driver said nothing. Instead, he motioned for the other man to get back into the car. As soon as he did, the driver's side window started to go up.

"Hold on. If you're here for Ibrahim, you can tell him something for me. I don't give a fuck what kind of business he's in. I came here to get something and he doesn't have it, so I'm moving on. Tell him he doesn't have anything to worry about. And tell him if he ever sends anyone else to deliver a *message*, I'm going to make sure he doesn't have any secrets left. He'll know what I mean. Oh, and you might mention the photos I have of you and your vehicle."

The driver turned on the engine, backed up slowly, and made a right turn onto another street. When the black Lexus was out of sight, I got back into my car, pulled it over to the curb and texted Goldblatt. *Hold onto those photos I sent you. I'll explain when I see you.*

They were in the middle of a shot when Rusty spotted me walking toward him. He handed his clipboard to his young assistant and practically ran toward me, his arms open, like one of those silly hair product commercials.

"You found him?"

I nodded.

"You got the money?"

I nodded in the opposite direction.

"You didn't get it?"

"He says he doesn't have it."

"And you believe him?"

"As much as I believe anyone. What does it matter? I'm not going to turn him upside down and shake it out of him."

"Why not?"

"I've told you before, Rusty, that's not the way I work."

"If he doesn't have it, who does?"

I shrugged. "The Tooth Fairy."

"What's that supposed to mean?"

"It means it might as well be with the Tooth Fairy because we're not going to get it."

"I need to sit down."

"Get your assistant to bring over that director's chair, the one with your name on it."

"I need a drink."

"There's probably beer in that cooler over there."

"I need to go somewhere with you, and have a drink."

We found a little place not far from the location where we could sit outside. That's what you do when you're in L.A. You sit outside. That's one of the few things L.A. is good for. Otherwise, what's the point?

Rusty looked like he'd been hit by a truck. I didn't feel a lot better.

"You *have* to explain what happened, Henry."

"It's complicated, Rusty. All that matters is the bottom line. The money is gone."

"I needed that money," he said, sinking his head into his hands.

"You seem to forget that it wasn't yours in the first place."

"It was. It really was. Well, not really mine, but mine to

invest. How am I going to pay Stan back? And those investors. What's going to happen to them?"

"I guess they're shit out of luck. Unless..."

"Unless what?"

"You've got enough money to finish the trailer, right?"

"Barely." He thought for a moment. "I guess I could convince Terry to throw in a few more bucks, enough to finish it up. I just hope he doesn't keep pushing to get Jolene more screen time. I don't know how much further I can push Josh."

"As far as you have to. And when you finish the trailer, you have to convince people to invest enough money so you can make the film. Then you have to make one that's good enough to clean up on the Christian circuit. The way I see it, that's the only way you're going to make the money back."

"Oh, my God."

"What are you whining about? That's what you planned on doing in the first place, isn't it? And that's what you're good at, right? Talking people out of money."

His head was still down, buried in his hands. "I guess so," he muttered.

"Then nothing's changed."

His lifted his head. "But what about Ibrahim and the money. Do you think he is going to pay it back?"

"He says so, but I wouldn't count on it. This is Hollywood. What is the worth of a promise here? If you're part of the system, you have to believe in the system."

His head sunk again, along with his shoulders. He was not a happy man. But then what is happiness but an illusion that things are going well when we all know that any moment that fantasy, because that's what it is, can evaporate into the atmosphere, rising as high as the farthest star. Poor guy. I almost felt sorry for him.

"If you build it, they will come, Rusty." I don't know why I said that. I didn't care if he built it or if they came. At that moment all I cared about was finding Noah and then trying to put my life back together, though the chances of that were pretty slim.

"What are you going to do?" he asked.

"I'm going to finish the other business I have here, then go back where I belong, where life is what it appears to be. Sloppy, unmanageable and futile."

"What will you tell Stan?"

"The truth. That is a concept you're familiar with, isn't it?"

"He'll freak."

"I'm sure he will."

"I didn't steal the money. You believe me, don't you?"

"What does it matter if I believe you or not? The money's gone. You'll have to replace it with new money, money that's built on yet another illusion. Let the Christians pay back Stan."

"The film will make money. It's guaranteed."

"That's what you have to believe, so I'll believe it, too."

"Tell Stan he'll get his money."

"Why don't you tell him?"

"I can't. I'd be too embarrassed."

"Congratulations on having a conscience. It seems to be a rare commodity out here. I could tell him, and I will because I'll have to tell him something, but it would be better if it came from you. I'm sure you guys will work it out. I suspect he'll stall his investors, move some figures around, and eventually you'll pay it back. It's all about numbers anyway, isn't it?"

He grinned. "Yes. Yes. It is. I'll figure out a way to pay him back a little at a time. Enough to stave off the investors for a bit. We can fudge the paperwork. Buy time. That's all I need.

Time. I'll work on Terry and with Sorbo signed—I told you we signed him, didn't I?"

I shook my head.

"Well, we did. He'll attract some big bucks. I won't use all of the money we raise on the film. I'll use a chunk of it to pay back Stan. And then, when the film is bought and the money starts rolling in, not only will he get his money back, but with interest on it. Like I said, Henry, it was always just another investment."

"I never said I didn't believe you, Rusty." And the funny thing is, by this point he practically had me convinced.

22
You Used to Be So Amused

Stan's case was finished. He'd hired me to find Rusty Jacobs and I had. He hired me to find the money and I had. I knew exactly where it was and where it wasn't. Technically, he didn't hire me to get it back, though eventually there was a chance that he would. Oddly enough, I believed in Rusty. I believed he would, at some point, return the money, even if it was in bits and pieces. I don't know why I believed this, I just did. I don't know why I thought he'd get enough funding to make his damn movie, but I did. And if it was made, I had little doubt he'd be able tap that Christian market and the money would flow. That's what I would tell Stan, and then it would be up to him whether or not he blew the whistle on Rusty.

That wasn't my problem. Not anymore. My problem was finding Noah.

Trying to think like a kid is tough. Especially a kid with raging hormones. I hadn't heard from Ellen, so I assumed Noah hadn't made it home yet. He was either in the midst of getting home or he was still hanging around L.A., hoping to get another shot at Delilah. But I didn't believe he was stupid enough to do that. At least I hoped he wasn't. My money was on him trying to get back home. The cheapest way to get back to Minnesota was by bus, so that's where I started the search.

Once I spotted the station, I found a place to park the car then walked to the one-story building with its brightly painted mural over the front entrance.

If you ask me, it doesn't get much more depressing than bus stations. It's the cheapest form of travel, and so those are the

244

kinds of people you see there. People at the end of their rope. People trying to get away from something or someone but don't have the dough to do it quickly. People on the edge. In short, people like me.

Inside the station there were several rows of perforated metal chairs, a few occupied.

I checked the schedule for buses to Minneapolis, then the price, which was close to two hundred bucks. I doubted Noah had that kind of money left, so I had to imagine how he might go about getting it. If it were me, I'd try my hand at asking folks for it, using the runaway teenager trying to get home story.

It was a long shot, but maybe someone who'd sold him a ticket might recognize him. I showed the picture of Noah on my phone to ticket sellers at the three open windows. No one remembered seeing him. The stock answer: "I sell dozens of tickets a day, you think I even look at these people?"

I looked for the security guard on duty, figuring if Noah had been panhandling, he might have crossed paths with security. I found the security office, knocked on the door, opened it, and walked into the small, cramped room. Sitting behind the desk was a guard, middle-aged, bald, paunchy. His jacket was off, his shirt sleeves rolled up. He had a cup of coffee in one hand, a donut in the other.

"What can I do you for?" he asked.

"You in charge here?"

"Right now I am. You got some kind of problem?"

"I'm looking for a runaway."

He snorted. "We get plenty of those."

I pulled out my phone and showed him Noah's photo.

"Looks kinda familiar. It might be the kid I saw."

"When?"

"Yesterday. Maybe the day before."

"More likely yesterday?"

"If you say so."

"Tell me about him."

"If he's the kid I think he is, he was hanging around here, begging for money. We get a lot of that. My job is to get 'em out. This ain't no homeless shelter."

"Did you talk to him?"

"Yeah."

"What did he say?"

"Said he was tryin' to get dough to get back home. I told him not around here, he wasn't. He was an okay kid. Not one of those wiseass gangbanger types. I almost felt sorry for him. He stopped as soon as I spoke to him, and then when I looked around a little later, he wasn't here no more."

"You didn't see him again?"

"Didn't say that." He took a bite of his donut, then a slug of coffee. "I guess it was yesterday, now that I think about it. Late afternoon, maybe, he was back. Only this time he was sittin' on one of them seats, with his knapsack, lookin' like everyone else waiting for a bus."

"He had a ticket?"

"I guess. I was gonna go over and say something to him, but there was no use hasslin' the kid. He wasn't doin' nobody no harm. After my break I kinda looked for him again, just to make sure he was okay, but he wasn't nowhere. Ain't seen him since."

Somehow Noah had managed to raise the money and was now on a bus home. Good for him. I shed a small layer of worry and guilt. Not enough to make me feel good, but enough to give me momentary relief. I was proud of the kid. He'd figured out a way to get out of a bad situation. Then I realized I didn't have the right to be proud of him. I'd done nothing to raise him, so why should I feel proud? Other than half his genes, my only contribution was dumping him on someone else to be raised.

I was certain he was on that bus headed home, but part of me wished he wasn't. Part of me wished he were still hanging around L.A., lost and confused, and that it was me who found him, rescued him from the streets, saved him from who knows what kind of danger. In Rusty's movie that's the way it would have happened. Father searches for long-lost son, finds him, brings him back to the family then becomes a part of his life.

That's how it happens in the movies. Life, not so much. In life, salvation isn't always so easy to come by.

Now that I was sure Noah was safely on his way home, what about me? Would having Noah thrust back into my life change anything for me? Would I use this opportunity to reconnect with my son, to make myself part of his life? Probably not. I wasn't ready to face that yet. I was afraid. Afraid of what? It was a question I wasn't ready to answer. Maybe I never would be ready to answer it. Maybe this was an opportunity for reconciliation. An opportunity to restore part of myself that had been missing for so long. Wouldn't it be pretty to think so?

I sat there in the bus station, on one of those hard metal seats, the kind that leave striated impressions in your ass, thinking about what I should do next. I stared at the people on line to buy tickets to somewhere, or seated on the same kind of chair as me. Some were hugged goodbye. Others, alone, read newspapers, magazines or books, drank coffee or ate sandwiches, doing whatever it took to pass the time.

Finally, after what could have been ten minutes or an hour, I took out my phone and called Ellen. I told her Noah was on his way home. I think, before we hung up, she asked if I was going to visit and I think I probably lied and said yes. Or maybe I was telling the truth. Sometimes it's so difficult to tell which is which.

PART 5
NEW YORK

"There is a reason that all things are as they are."
—Bram Stoker, *Dracula*

"Stop at the start."
—Ovid, *Remedia amoris*

23
Que Sera Sera

At least somebody was happy I was home.

Too bad it was Goldblatt.

It was as if he had some kind of invisible GPS device implanted under my skin. I hadn't been back in my dingy little apartment an hour before he nailed me.

"I don't hear those highway noises so I'm guessing you're back in the city," he said.

"Yeah, I'm back."

"Good. Now we can wrap up this Seligson thing."

"As far as I'm concerned, it is wound up. I don't see where there's much more for us to do."

"Raucher's man contacted us. It's go time."

"What's that supposed to mean?" I said, as I held the phone with one hand and pulled dirty laundry out of my bag with the other.

"It means phase two of the operation has begun."

I laughed. It felt good. This was reason enough to keep Goldblatt around.

"Phase two? Operation? What are we, operatives for the CIA?" I tossed a pair of jeans, covered with dirt stains from my trip in the woods, onto the floor.

"Do not mock me, Swann. I know whereof I speak. And until phase two is complete, we don't get the rest of our dough. Am I speaking your language now?"

"Suddenly, you're coming in perfectly clear. What's next?"

"You're going to call this dude back, the art dealer who was in touch with Schulman, and see what he wants. Play it cool.

The object is to get him over to Schulman's apartment so he can see the painting. Then we'll let him cast doubt on its authenticity. He'll supply the hook, but we'll reel him in. I'd love to see his face when you refuse to sell it back to him."

"Okay."

I was exhausted, mentally and physically, but the idea of getting paid the second half of our dough invigorated me. Besides, it would take my mind off calling Stan and telling him his money was now dependent on some independent Christian film project. "What about Schulman? Is he still willing to play along?"

"Don't worry about Schulman. I got him in my back pocket."

"Someday you'll have to explain that to me."

"The painting's still at Klavan's, right?"

"As far as I know."

"Okay. I'll give Schulman a call, see when it's convenient for us to come over with the painting then you'll give this art dealer dude a call and invite him over. But don't be too eager. We gotta reel him in slowly."

A short nap turned into three hours. By the time I'd awakened, it was late afternoon. I made myself a cup of coffee then called Stan.

He did not like my news. If I'd been there in person, I might have seen a grown man cry. It was more than unpleasant. It was pathetically sad. If I'd had a heart, it might have bent a little.

He kept repeating over and over again, "What am I going to do?"

"I'm sure there's something, Stan."

"Like what? I'm ruined. He's ruined me. You were supposed to help me."

"First of all, he didn't ruin you. You had some part in this."

"What do you mean? He took the money. He entrusted it to some thief. Now it's gone. How am I responsible?"

"He didn't take the money. You gave it to him."

"What are you talking about?"

"You know the truth as well as I do. Rusty worked with you. He came to you with a plan to invest the million. You approved that plan. Then you had second thoughts. You didn't know how else to get the money back and save face, so you hired me. Now the money's gone. If you hadn't given it to him—"

"I told you. He stole it."

"No. He didn't. He'd done pretty well with his investment advice and when he came to you with this plan, you okayed it. Maybe you even liked the idea of becoming a Hollywood player. How do I know? You took a risk, rolled the dice, and it came up snake eyes. All you can do now is hope he's successful and you get your money back."

"He's a thief!"

"He's a fool and a dreamer, but I don't think he's a thief, at least that wasn't his intent. Sometimes fools and dreamers hit the jackpot. Rusty might be one of those people. Maybe you'll get lucky. I sure hope so, for both your sakes."

"I should call the cops."

"You could do that, but I don't think it would be wise. Who'd win? Certainly not you. You'd have to prove you didn't give Rusty the money, and that would be difficult. Either you'd be guilty of shoddy business practices, letting him have access to your accounts, or you'd be a co-conspirator. Either way, everyone loses. I'm afraid the only chance you have for redemption is if Rusty really does pull this off. But if it makes you feel any better you're not the only loser. I'm out a recovery fee."

I could have sat there and listened to more whining,

commiserated with him, talked him through it. But that would have made me a better man than I am, so I didn't.

That evening, while I took myself out to dinner at a local pub, the call came in from someone calling himself Gray Basnight, a phony name if I ever heard one. He gave me some cock-and-bull story about being an art dealer. He learned I was a collector and hoped I might be interested in some of the artists he represented. He'd heard about my "fine collection" and wondered if he could stop by some time to discuss business. Without appearing to be too eager, I let myself be talked into inviting him over to my place. I told him I'd check my calendar and get back to him.

Goldblatt, of course, was thrilled.

"Just as we planned," he said, when I got him on the phone. "Like shooting fish in a barrel."

"When was the last time you did that?"

"Did what?"

"Shoot fish in a barrel."

"Someday, Swann, you're going to take me seriously."

"I eagerly await that day, Goldblatt."

"I'm gonna give Schulman a buzz now. Hopefully, he'll let us use the place tomorrow afternoon. I'll call you back ASAP."

"Then I'll speak to you ASAP."

Less than ten minutes later, as I was paying for my meal, my phone rang again.

"All systems go," Goldblatt said.

"When?"

"Tomorrow afternoon, around three. That'll give us enough time to retrieve the painting from Klavan and have it delivered to Schulman's place. I got a guy who can do it for us. Let's meet there around two. That'll give us time to go over how we're going to play this."

"No need to get someone else involved. I've got some work to do in my office in the morning, so I'll pick up the painting and bring it over."

"Be careful," warned Goldblatt.

"My middle name," I replied. "Or is it careless?"

The next morning I got to my office in Klavan's apartment a little after ten. Klavan was on the phone in his office.

"Hey, there," I said, sticking my head into the kitchen where Mary was putting away groceries.

"Hey, there. How was your trip?"

"I'm glad I'm back."

"Was it profitable?"

"Not for me."

"Too bad. When Ross gets off the phone, we wanted to talk to you about something."

"Hope I'm not being evicted."

"Nothing that dramatic. Oh wait, on second thought maybe it is."

"I'm intrigued. And a little worried. I'll be in my office. Just come get me when you're ready."

I was logging in my expenses when Mary knocked gently on the door. "Ross is off the phone. Let's go into his office."

"Okay," I said, as I finished clipping my receipts together.

Klavan was sitting at his desk, the painting, unwrapped, leaning up against a bookshelf to the right. Mary sat down in one chair. I sat in the other.

"Happy to be back?" Klavan asked.

"You bet."

"We've got something of a surprise for you."

"I don't like surprises."

"This might amuse you. Tell him, Mary."

"Well," she began slowly, the hint of a smile creeping across her face, "it's about the painting."

"What about it?"

"Naturally I was curious, so I took another look. There was something about it that didn't sit right, so I decided to do a little research. I went online to check out Rothko's work, and then I went out and got a comprehensive catalogue of all his paintings. Funny thing is, I couldn't find any mention of this painting. I couldn't match it against anything he'd done and that was more than a little strange. But I figured, well, a painting might have been missed. So I took a photograph of this one and brought it to an expert in the field and he recognized it immediately."

"That's a good thing, right?"

"Yes and no. It's good because it means it's probably legit, but it's bad because he said it had been stolen in a museum robbery years ago."

"You mean the damn painting's hot?"

"That's right."

"You mean these guys have been peddling then buying back a hot painting?"

She nodded.

"That's fucking brilliant! I always wondered what someone would do with stolen art. You can't advertise it for sale and whoever does finally buy it can never show it to anyone. So how much can you possibly get for it? Probably pennies on the dollar. But these doofuses came up with the perfect plan. They rent it out, make money on it by buying it back at a lower price, then rent it out again. Each time they rent it out, they make a hefty profit. And since it doesn't stick in the buyer's hands very long, there's no way it can be identified as stolen goods. It's just about perfect."

"Not now it isn't," said Klavan.

"Sure it is. What are we going to do? Tell Seligson he's bought a hot painting? Do you think he wants to be a receiver of stolen goods?"

"How would anyone know unless he showed it publicly?"

"He wouldn't have to. If they don't get it back, they could threaten to turn him in. And does he or any other collector want to be known as someone who's received stolen property? I don't think so."

"So what are you going to do?" asked Klavan.

I thought for a moment. I was in awe. These guys, who we thought were just small-time con artists, had come up with an ingenious scheme to make money from stolen art.

"I guess I have to tell Goldblatt. I'll leave it up to him how he breaks it to Seligson. After all, he's been taken once and now, when he thought he was getting back at them, he's on the hook again. The best thing he can do is sell it back to them, getting the best deal possible, maybe even letting them know he's on to their little scheme, and hope they think he'll report them. Of course, if he does, there's no way he's going to recoup the dough he's already laid out. Besides, he runs the risk of being charged with receiving stolen goods."

"Pretty fuckin' brilliant, isn't it?" said Klavan.

"Better than forging paintings, that's for sure."

"You could report them to the cops and the rightful owner of the painting could get it back," said Mary.

We both looked at her like she was crazy.

"It was a museum, Mary," said Klavan. "They're insured. The only one out the dough is the insurance company, and I'm sure they've made it back in spades by raising their rates."

"Besides, that would mean I'd be doing the right thing and that's not something I'm used to doing," I added.

"And if we did that, poor Seligson would wind up with nada."

"I guess you guys are right," said Mary.

"I'll let Goldblatt handle it. Seligson's his friend."

"I'd love to be there when you tell him," said Klavan.

I met with Goldblatt later that afternoon. I thought he'd hit the ceiling when I told him the story, but I was wrong. He laughed. Harder than I'd ever seen him laugh.

"I didn't think you'd take it this well," I said.

"It's a pretty damn clever scam, don't you think?"

"It is. But your friend's probably out another fifty grand. Unless he wants to blow the whistle and wind up with nothing."

"He'll take the loss. He won't take it well, but he'll take it."

He started laughing again.

"I'm glad you're enjoying yourself."

"I am. I really am."

"This is a friend of yours, isn't it?"

"More of an acquaintance, really. But between you and me, his hands haven't always been so clean. Maybe he was due to get his bell rung. Anyway, we made some dough out of it, that's all I care about."

"What are you going to tell him?"

"The truth. And you got it figured right. He's gotta sell it back. He can't sit there with a hot painting. There's nothing else he can do. Good thing he can afford to take the loss. In the meantime, I've been working on another case for us. Wanna hear about it?"

"Not now, Goldblatt. I'm a little jetlagged."

"But you've gotta eat, right?"

"Yeah, I guess I've gotta eat."

We wound up back at E.J.'s and it was Goldblatt's lucky day. They had the special pulled pork sandwich and a special banana split.

"I think we're really starting to roll," said Goldblatt. "I've got a line on a couple more cases."

"Not so fast."

"Whaddya mean, not so fast?"

"I'm not so sure I want to do this anymore."

"What are you talking about? What the hell else are you going to do?"

"I don't know."

"Oh, jeez, not this mid-life crisis bullshit again."

"Call it what you like. I don't know if this is the way I want to spend the rest of my life."

The waiter arrived with Goldblatt's banana split. "Hey, how about a little extra chocolate sauce?" Goldblatt said to the waiter.

"You're a little burned out, Swann. Maybe you should take a vacation. You could use some of the dough we just picked up from Seligson."

"That's not gonna help."

Goldblatt dipped his spoon into the mound of chocolate ice cream, twirled it around a bit, making sure it was covered with chocolate sauce, then stuffed it into his mouth, swallowed and said, "I don't have time for this, Swann. You're a little depressed, though God knows why. They got pills for that. I know this doctor who can prescribe anything you need."

I shook my head. "I don't know what I want to do with the rest of my life, but I don't think this is it."

"Sugar. That's what you need."

Just then the waiter arrived with a small metal pitcher filled with chocolate sauce. Goldblatt grabbed it out of his hand, and smiled as he poured the entire contents over the ice cream and slices of banana.

Goldblatt was in heaven. Me, I was pretty much back where I started from. Wondering what the hell I was going to do with the rest of my life.

ACKNOWLEDGMENTS

I'd like to thank those people who graciously allowed me to use their names in this work of fiction. Their characters are fictional but they are not. At least I don't think so. First, Mark Goldblatt and Ross Klavan, who have become mainstays in the Swann series. They seem to have become so popular that someday they may threaten to push Swann into the background. Others include Rusty Jacobs, Jessica Hall, Gray Basnight, Tom Seligson, Glenn Raucher, Tim O'Mara, Stan Katz, and Charlie Schulman. And a special thanks to Sarah Byrne, who won the dubious distinction of having her name used as one of the characters in the book by outbidding dozens (or at least I'd like to think it was dozens) at the Bouchercon 2015 raffle. I'd also like to thank Catherine Ventura, who attempted to teach me how to be media savvy, my publicist and her team, Julie Schoerke, my editor, Lance Wright, who tediously went through this manuscript and I hope caught all my mistakes before I was publicly embarrassed, and, of course, Eric Campbell who swooped in and brought Swann back to life.

And finally, to all my students and friends and colleagues in the crime writing community who have been so supportive to me over the years. Believe me, I couldn't have done it without you all.

Charles Salzberg is the author of the Shamus Award nominated *Swann's Last Song* as well as the sequels *Swann Dives In* and *Swann's Lake of Despair*. He is also author of *Devil in the Hole*, which was chosen as one of the Best Crime Novels of 2013 by *Suspense* magazine. He lives in New York City and teaches writing at the Writer's Voice and the New York Writers Workshop, where he is proud to be a Founding Member.

www.charlessalzberg.com.

OTHER TITLES FROM DOWN & OUT BOOKS

See DownAndOutBooks.com for complete list

By J.L. Abramo
Catching Water in a Net
Clutching at Straws
Counting to Infinity
Gravesend
Chasing Charlie Chan
Circling the Runway
Brooklyn Justice
Coney Island Avenue (*)

By Trey R. Barker
2,000 Miles to Open Road
Road Gig: A Novella
Exit Blood
Death is Not Forever
No Harder Prison

By Richard Barre
The Innocents
Bearing Secrets
Christmas Stories
The Ghosts of Morning
Blackheart Highway
Burning Moon
Echo Bay
Lost

By Eric Beetner (editor)
Unloaded

By Eric Beetner and
JB Kohl
Over Their Heads

By Eric Beetner and
Frank Zafiro
The Backlist
The Shortlist

By G.J. Brown
Falling

By Rob Brunet
Stinking Rich

By Angel Luis Colón
No Happy Endings

By Tom Crowley
Vipers Tail
Murder in the Slaughterhouse

By Frank De Blase
Pine Box for a Pin-Up
Busted Valentines
and Other Dark Delights
A Cougar's Kiss

By Les Edgerton
The Genuine, Imitation,
Plastic Kidnapping

By Jack Getze
Big Numbers
Big Money
Big Mojo
Big Shoes

By Richard Godwin
Wrong Crowd
Buffalo and Sour Mash
Crystal on Electric Acetate (*)

By Jeffery Hess
Beachhead

(*)—*Coming Soon*

OTHER TITLES FROM DOWN & OUT BOOKS

See DownAndOutBooks.com for complete list

By Matt Hilton
No Going Back
Rules of Honor
The Lawless Kind
The Devil's Anvil
No Safe Place

By Lawrence Kelter
and Frank Zafiro
The Last Collar

By Jerry Kennealy
Screen Test
Polo's Long Shot (*)

By Dana King
Worst Enemies
Grind Joint
Resurrection Mall (*)

By Ross Klavan, Tim O'Mara
and Charles Salzberg
Triple Shot

By S.W. Lauden
Crosswise
Crossed Bones (*)

By Paul D. Marks and
Andrew McAleer (editors)
Coast to Coast vol. 1
Coast to Coast vol. 2

By Bill Moody
Czechmate
The Man in Red Square
Solo Hand
The Death of a Tenor Man

The Sound of the Trumpet
Bird Lives!

By Gary Phillips
The Perpetrators
Scoundrels (Editor)
Treacherous
3 the Hard Way

By Tom Pitts
Hustle

By Robert J. Randisi
Upon My Soul
Souls of the Dead
Envy the Dead (*)

By Ryan Sayles
The Subtle Art of Brutality
Warpath

By John Shepphird
The Shill
Kill the Shill
Beware the Shill

James R. Tuck (editor)
Mama Tried vol. 1
Mama Tried vol. 2 (*)

By Lono Waiwaiole
Wiley's Lament
Wiley's Shuffle
Wiley's Refrain
Dark Paradise
Leon's Legacy (*)

(*)—*Coming Soon*